THE UNSPEAKABLE UNKNOWN

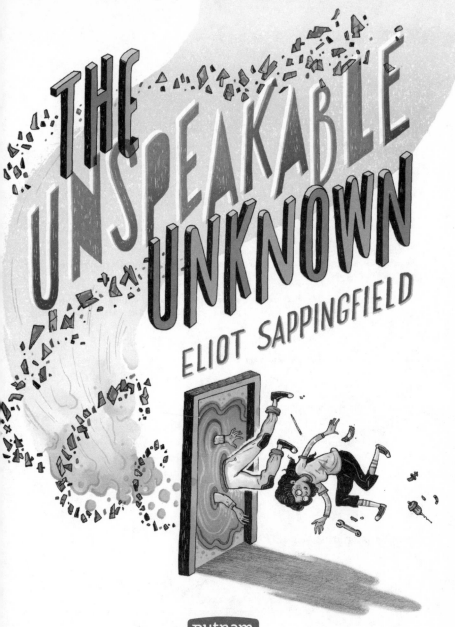

THE UNSPEAKABLE UNKNOWN

ELIOT SAPPINGFIELD

putnam

G. P. PUTNAM'S SONS

G. P. Putnam's Sons
an imprint of Penguin Random House LLC
375 Hudson Street
New York, NY 10014

G. P. Putnam's Sons is a registered trademark of Penguin Random House LLC.

Library of Congress Cataloging-in-Publication Data
Names: Sappingfield, Eliot, author.
Title: The unspeakable unknown / Eliot Sappingfield.
Description: New York, NY : G. P. Putnam's Sons, [2019]
Summary: Nikola Kross's father, who was kidnapped by extraterrestrials, is still missing and it is up to Nikola, thirteen, and her new friends at the secret boarding school for scientific geniuses to rescue him.
Identifiers: LCCN 2018012358 | ISBN 9781524738488 (hardcover) | ISBN 9781524738495 (ebook)
Subjects: | CYAC: Genius—Fiction. | Boarding schools—Fiction. | Schools—Fiction. | Friendship—Fiction. | Extraterrestrial beings—Fiction. | Science fiction.
Classification: LCC PZ7.1.S2643 Uns 2019 | DDC [Fic]—dc23
LC record available at https://lccn.loc.gov/2018012358

Theoretical edition available via personal self-conceptualization.

Printed in the United States of America.
ISBN 9781524738488
10 9 8 7 6 5 4 3 2 1

Design by Eileen Savage. Text set in Leitura News.

For my daughters, Marilee and Zoë
May your futures be as bright, challenging,
wonderful, and generous as you are.
Happy holidays!

CONTENTS

- - - - - ✳ - - - - -

THE UNSPEAKABLE UNKNOWN

1

A KILLER POP QUIZ

A single flake of snow came to rest on the tip of my nose and balanced there weightlessly—one of those tiny reminders of just how subtle and lovely the world can be if you look closely enough. I tried to blow it back into the air so it might continue on its way, but I'd just taken a sip of hot chocolate. Instead of gently nudging the pure white snow-flake into flight, I brutally murdered it with a tiny jet of still-warm fluid.

As if that weren't bad enough, it also meant I spit a little hot chocolate at the person who had just sold it to me. From her point of view, the situation must have been completely bizarre. She'd sold someone a cup of hot chocolate from her little homemade trolley. They'd paid cheerfully, mentioned how lovely the snow was, took a sip, and spit it right into her curly black hair. The look she gave me was a mixture of bewilderment, irritation, and revulsion.

I'm more used to that look than you might expect.

Fortunately for me and any other complete morons wandering the streets of School Town that day, the snow had put everyone in a pretty jovial mood, and after a second, she went on to the next person in line.

Technically, snow was strictly prohibited on school grounds during the week. At most schools, that kind of rule would be a bit difficult to enforce, but when you run a school located under an impenetrable force field, you get to exercise a little more control.

Unless someone hacks the climate control system. Then they get to make the rules for a while.

Just an hour or so before, everyone had gotten an email from Principal Patricia Plaskington reminding us of the School's weather policies:

> *Snow is allowed on weekends, winter holidays, and occasions when the pursuit of science calls for adverse weather conditions. The snow currently falling in town is UNAUTHORIZED, and because of this, students are NOT allowed to enjoy it in any way. If you are caught frolicking, gallivanting, or behaving in flagrant youthfulness in or around the snow, you may be subject to disciplinary action. If you have information that can lead us to the person or persons responsible for the*

contraband weather, you may be eligible for a reward.
Just click the SNITCH NOW link on the administration
home page, and you'll be taken to an online form where
you can betray the trust of your peers in complete
anonymity!

I stepped along a path that led through the central park square, took a second first sip of my hot chocolate, and discovered once again why I was absolutely in love with the School.

The School Town could have been lifted straight out of an unrealistically idealized 1950s movie, with pristine streets, a multitude of fascinating shops, and little parks here and there just begging to be wandered through. The only thing that spoiled the illusion is that the population consists of about 5 percent adults and 95 percent kids, which is not how the fifties were at all, unless I've been reading the wrong history books.

The School is actually called the Plaskington International Laboratory School of Scientific Research and Technological Advancement. It's a long name, so we just call it the School. We're an independent learning community for humanoid aliens called parahumans and other folk who are unusually intelligent and don't get along in normal schools. It's a . . . unique place.

I came to the School following a pretty bizarre string of events that involved my home being destroyed and my dad being kidnapped and taken to some unknown location. It's a long story, and if you're reading this, you probably know all about it. If not, just try to keep up. You'll figure it out soon enough.

All around me, students were having snowball fights, constructing forts and igloos, and creating other snowy monuments. Across a clearing I spotted my friend Dirac Fermion putting the finishing touches on a nine-foot-tall snow tyrannosaur he had made. Its eyes were glowing and smoke was cascading out of its mouth like it might breathe fire at any moment—which wasn't completely outside the realm of possibility.

I stopped to watch a few students who were trying to come up with ways to beat Bob Flobogashtimann down the park's steepest slope. Bob had mounted a tiny jet turbine on his sled, and because of this, he had become the undefeated star of the Tuesday Morning Crystalline Precipitation Racing League. I gave Bob a wave, which he returned as he finished repacking his drag chute for the next run.

Speaking of students who seemed unusually prepared for snow, just then Fluorine Plaskington glided down the street in my direction, carried upon a bright red full-sized sleigh, which was pulled by about two hundred miniature animatronic plastic ponies harnessed to a shimmering web of multicolored ribbons. Sitting at the reins, Fluorine, who was about my age at the time, looked bored and slightly irritated.

Fluorine was by far the smartest kid at the School, and she had been one of very few students on my list of people who might think it a good idea to hack the School's climate *and* the list of students who actually had the *ability* to hack the School's climate. The fact that she had an elaborate sleigh ready to go seemed a bit too coincidental to be dismissed. I flagged her down.

She pulled to a stop next to me and gave me a *What now?* kind of look.

"Is this your doing?" I asked, gesturing at . . . everything.

She looked around, as if taking it all in for the first time.

She worked her mouth around in consideration. "Probably. Rubidia said I was like four years old all last night. When I woke up this morning, there was all this snow, and someone had put this whole crazy sleigh contraption together. I don't remember doing it, but I wouldn't put it past me."

All that might make a little more sense if you knew Fluorine *should* have been about six years old, but she suffered from a condition called Pilgrim Syndrome, which was probably triggered by some unauthorized time-travel activity. This meant she was unstuck in time and tended to change age at random intervals. One minute she was thirty-six, the next she was a toddler. It was fun for everyone except her sister, Rubidia, who never knew if she'd be following orders or changing diapers when Fluorine came home after class.

I wasn't sure I bought Fluorine's paradox memory defense 100 percent of the time. Sometimes it seemed perfectly reasonable—you wouldn't remember things that happen to your adult self when you were just a kid, because those things hadn't happened yet. But there were other times when it seemed she could remember things a little better than she let on.

"Feel like giving me a ride in that?" I asked.

"I would, but something tells me they'll have this all fixed in a few minutes. I should take the sleigh back to the house while there's still snow for it to slide on."

"The principal is going to kill you if she finds out," I said.

"Nah," Fluorine said with a dismissive wave. "Granny knows I'd *never* do anything like most of the things I do."

Did I mention that Fluorine and her sister were the principal's granddaughters? I often wondered whether Fluorine would try half the tricks she pulled if there were an actual possibility that she might face real consequences for them.

A sudden warm, dry breeze told me she was probably right about the weather going back to normal. I was about to say something else, but Fluorine had already given her team of plastic ponies a whistle and taken off back toward the student residential neighborhood.

Apart from Saturday, Wednesday, Thursday, Sunday, Friday, and Monday, Tuesday is my favorite day of the week. For once, I was *not* running late to class, which is more unusual than illegal snowfall. I have my alarm clock set to wake me at the last possible moment, at which time, instead of beeping, it screams, "OHMIGOD, you're SOOOOO late! Get up, GET UP, GET UP!"

Blind panic is a good motivator, I find.

Rhetorical question: If my roommate is female, is it technically considered "objectifying women" if I refer to her as my alarm clock? It's *literally* referring to her as an object, but I mean it in a nice way.

I should probably knock that off.

That was what I was thinking about when the snowperson across the street exploded. I've never studied snowpeople behavior, but I know "exploding" is on the List of Things Snowmen and Snowwomen Don't Do, right below dance contests and tanning. I was about to worry about it when a trash can right next to me also exploded, followed by a large section of the sidewalk immediately behind me.

I was starting to suspect I might be in danger.

We'd been discussing emergent threats and surprise attacks in Electronic Combat class, so we might better protect ourselves in the outside world once we left school. I knew that when faced with a sudden attack, I should follow the Emergent Situation Protocols, step one of which is to seek cover immediately before attempting to analyze the situation further. At the moment, I'd just left the park and was only a few feet from the door of Carother's Clothing Boutique, which was our chemistry laboratory. I ducked inside just as another explosion atomized the sidewalk where I had been standing a moment before.

Inside, I performed an expert tactical roll right into a chair, entangling its legs with mine and just generally screwing up the whole maneuver. While I kicked and cursed at the inconsiderate and poorly designed chair, a middle-aged woman with dark, neatly parted hair and wearing a black suit and tie stood up in the front of the room.

"Young lady!" she admonished. "Class is in session, and you are distracting our work. Please leave!"

"Things are exploding out there!" I pointed out from behind an overturned desk nobody had even been using anyway.

"The weather is not my problem. We are attempting to synthesize polymers, and you are *disturbing* us."

"Listen, lady. You can take your polymers and stick—"

I might have gone on, but that was when the storefront windows became a bigger problem than her by exploding in precisely the way you don't want windows to explode. The shock hit the table I'd hid behind and knocked me farther into the room, and also untangled my legs, which was a plus.

A few younger students who had been carefully stirring flasks of various fluids a moment before stepped cautiously away from their experiments, waiting for the hullabaloo to die down. A few of them yelped in surprise, and a couple giggled and clapped. One of them helped me up, patting me on the back.

Sudden disaster was a regular feature at the School, so students tended to take it in stride, even when it might have been wiser to run away screaming. Some of the kids were wandering to the edges of the room, but most were just sitting there, playing the important role of Potential Victim. I shouted for them to get under cover, and maybe three listened.

Next I followed step two of the Emergent Situation

Protocols and attempted to identify the threat. This was simple because just then the threat swooped down onto the street and hung hovering in the air right in front of where the windows had been. What I saw was a terrifying, compact car-sized mass of tentacles, teeth, rage, and slime. I couldn't believe my eyes, but there was no denying it. I was looking at the disgusting, shockingly terrifying form of an Old One.

If you don't know what an Old One is, I kind of envy you. Allow me to ruin your blissful ignorance. On this earth there are a certain number of nasty, very smelly, and utterly evil interdimensional creatures who call themselves the Old Ones. Because they're old. Clever, huh?

I was one of only a handful of Old One survivors, people who had seen one of them in person and could still feed and dress themselves without assistance. I briefly wondered at the odds that a second Old One had infiltrated the School and was trying to blow up a chemistry class, but just then the Old One roared in a completely animalistic way and thrust its tentacles forward into the classroom. I decided I didn't care how it had gotten in.

As soon as the Old One's considerable form made it into the room, the windows began automatically repairing themselves, sealing us in with it. That's normal, by the way. Most of the important buildings at the School were constructed from materials impregnated with nanoreconstructors, which are millions of microscopic robots that fix things as soon as they're broken (which was often, in my experience).

I thought back to my training, again thanking my good

luck that we had just studied this kind of thing in eCombat class. Step three of the Emergent Situation Protocols was to consider my options—to decide whether to flee from the threat, or to stand and fight it.

Running *was* a possibility. I'd been in the building a number of times and knew the class had a back exit and a hatch that led to the underground tunnel network that ran beneath everything in town. The problem was that the class was filled with seven- and eight-year-old kids, none of whom was able to stand up against an Old One. They had a teacher, but the moment the Old One appeared, the aforementioned teacher had made use of one of the aforementioned exit routes and was gone. *Nice.* I doubted I could get all the kids through a door in less than five minutes on a good day. That meant I needed to put up a fight to give them more time.

Because Old Ones are interdimensional by nature, they can move pretty quickly when they want to, but for some reason, this particular Old One was having trouble moving through the room and kept getting hung up on tables and chairs. No complaints from me there.

The mood in the room had changed, and now *none* of the kids in the class thought *anything* was funny. That was probably because, without protection, they wouldn't last long, and worse, the only protection they had was me.

Back to the protocols. Step four was to assess my assets. I had my quantum agar bracelet, which was extremely useful in most situations, but it didn't generally work against Old Ones.

I also kept my gravitational disruptor on me at all times. It's a small weapon that creates powerful, localized distortions in gravity. It couldn't kill an Old One but could push it around and generally irritate it—so that was something. If I could buy some time, I could make an amplifier and make the disruptor more powerful. But this wasn't an electronics class, so they didn't have anything that could—

It wasn't electronics, I realized. It was chemistry! There must be something dangerous somewhere! As the Old One tried to untangle itself from the same desk that had ensnared me, I ran to the shelves of chemicals lining the walls, searching for something toxic or unstable.

I found hydrochloric acid—not dangerous enough.

A tentacle slid forward and almost got me around the waist, but I ducked under it and dodged another right after that.

Another bottle. Chlorine trifluoride—WAY too dangerous. I wanted to kill the Old One, not everyone in the neighborhood.

Finally, I found a glass canister of golden metallic liquid with a tiny, flaking label that read CESIUM. It would have to do.

I grabbed it and took cover behind the sturdy teacher's desk as another explosion ripped apart the floor in the center of the room. The kids, hunkered down behind overturned tables, shrieked and cried. It didn't sound like any had been injured . . . yet.

Step five: execute the plan. I took the canister, which held about as much liquid as a can of soda, and lobbed it over the top of the Old One. As I had hoped, it caught the canister in one of its many tentacles.

The good thing about gravitational disruptors is that you don't have to be a good shot.

My first shot missed the canister entirely but was still close enough to shatter it. Glass fragments and chunky metallic liquid sprayed all over the Old One. Its skin smoked and bubbled ominously everywhere the element touched.

Here's the deal with cesium. It's an alkali metal, and not one of the friendly ones like sodium or potassium. Alkali metals are fantastically unstable. Every atom has these desperate and lonesome single electrons just begging to hook up with any eligible atom or compound they run into. For instance, when combined with water, alkali metals produce a large amount of hydrogen and heat very quickly in what chemists call a *vigorous exothermic reaction*.

"Vigorous exothermic reaction" is chemistry-talk for BOOM.

The teacher's desk had, among a bank of slider controls, switches, and dials, a single lever labeled SPRINKLERS, which are essential in any chemistry classroom. I pulled the lever, and sprinkler heads dropped from the ceiling and began spraying.

I barely had time to duck when an immense explosion broke out the newly repaired windows, knocked several students against the walls, and reduced the recently sturdy teacher's desk to a pile of scrap wood and sawdust.

I was surprised to find that I was not seriously injured, apart from a few cuts and scrapes here and there. A quick glance through the smoke told me the Old One had been thoroughly vanquished. A shredded, smoking pile of tentacles was writhing on the floor, looking mostly dead.

But . . . something didn't smell right. Or rather, something didn't smell *wrong*. The room smelled like a burning chemistry classroom usually smells, which is to say it didn't stink like Old Ones are supposed to.

The Old Ones aren't really built to exist in our dimension, and so they manipulate our brains to see them as something they aren't. Our brains can't exactly handle the manipulation, which produces a telltale side effect: the impression that you're smelling one of the worst things you've ever smelled in your life. But the Old One twitching and moaning on the floor of the chemistry classroom? This one just smelled like . . . nothing.

Also, the Old Ones are not fragile. I shouldn't have been able to take one out completely with an explosion of any size (at least one that didn't involve plutonium). When hurt, they tend to slip back into that other dimension and return later when the coast is clear. I'd been hoping to drive it out of the area, not kill it.

Still, a dead Old One was a good thing.

Climbing over the remains of the desk, I discovered several of the tentacles were burning and twitching. One was ripped apart, revealing a robotic skeletal framework that reminded me of one of our projects in Creative Robotics class the previous week. I kicked it, and the machinery whirred sadly in reaction. It had been a *fake* Old One? Who would—

Somewhere inside the pile of tentacles, I heard a zipper grumble. A charred and bruised woman climbed out from inside the imitation Old One.

"A little much, don't you think?" asked Ms. Botfly, my eCombat teacher. "Still, you performed well. Let's call it 98 percent?"

"Ninety-eight?" I asked. "What do you mean? *That* was a TEST?"

She nodded, her graying hair falling from the unkempt bun that restrained it. She adjusted the pair of spectacles on her nose, and the spare pair on top of her head slid off onto a burning tentacle, where it melted and joined in the burning. "I *told* the entire class to expect a pop quiz. I've killed six of your classmates so far this morning."

"Killed?"

"Oh, don't be a ninny. They got better. Help me out of this blasted suit, dear."

I pulled her up and out, wondering if she'd meant *blasted* in a literal or expressive way. "You're doing this to everyone in class?"

"That *was* the plan until you ruined my suit. Those take months to assemble, you know. Very expensive."

She was guilt-tripping me? "I didn't ask you to assault me. You're lucky you didn't attack me somewhere with better armaments."

Ms. Botfly threw back her head and laughed, launching

another spare pair of spectacles I hadn't seen before out of the nearly repaired window.

She surveyed the damaged costume. "*You're* lucky I didn't bring my good bombs. My error was that I forgot you have had direct exposure to undisguised Old Ones and can function around them without being reduced to terror. Everyone else ran away, which was the *goal*. A tactical retreat."

I shrugged. "Sorry about the damage."

She shook her head. "I was running low on explosives anyway. I'll have to come up with something better for the rest of the students. Is your generation still frightened of zombies, or are we done with that yet? Oh! That reminds me—"

She whirled suddenly and stuck an accusing finger at a particularly meek student who had been sidling toward the door. "YOU'RE NEXT, MARK!"

Mark, a redheaded kid with freckles and a perpetually startled expression that I vaguely recognized from eCombat class, squealed in terror and fled.

"I've always hated that kid," mused Ms. Botfly. She shook her head as if to clear it. "Incidentally, since you've passed the quiz, you'll be allowed to take the full test, which will occur tomorrow morning."

"Another ambush?" I said.

"No, well . . . not really. You'll get a message later with the details. Now, get out of here. I hear Dr. Filamence climbing out of her hidey-hole, and she will not be pleased that you've squandered her entire supply of cesium on the staff member who bought her Secret Santa present at a dollar store last year."

I left, and before I was more than a few feet down the pavement, the sound of another explosion found my ears—this one vocal in nature. It was the sort that occurs when the element known as an OCD chemistry teacher encounters unexpected damage to her classroom, supplies, and daily routine. I hoped Ms. Botfly had saved a couple of bombs for her getaway.

2

BREAKFAST AT THE IMAGINARY NUMBER

"Goodness gracious!" Hypatia cried the moment she caught sight of me entering the Imaginary Number, my new favorite breakfast joint. At first I thought this was just her reaction to my being several minutes late, but it occurred to me that having been in the same room as a rather large explosion or two might have taken a toll on my personal appearance.

Hypatia started to say something else and then stopped.

"Yes?" I asked, after a pause.

"Well, I don't mean to be insensitive," she said. "Is . . . that just how you look today, or did you have an accident?"

It is probably some kind of comment on my grooming habits that my closest friend and roommate could not discern the difference between "normal Nikola" and "recently survived explosions Nikola." I made a mental note to start spending a little more time on my hair in the mornings and otherwise ignored Hypatia's insulting attempt at politeness.

Honestly, I couldn't take it personally, even if I tried. Hypatia was so compulsively neat that to her, I probably looked like a disheveled slob every day. Compared with Hypatia, everyone in town looked like a tornado victim who just crawled out from under muddy wreckage.

Hypatia herself was looking about four times as cute as a button, although I never understood how the button became the standard unit of cuteness. What was a puppy? Eight-point-four buttons?

I hate describing people, because I already *know* what they look like. So it feels weird to just slip in that Hypatia was just under five and a half feet tall, with long blond hair styled into improbable golden spiraling curls, which bounced adorably whenever she so much as blinked. The whole hairdo situation was ornamented with an oversized ruby-red bow that was nothing short of offensively adorable. At the time, her eyes, which changed color with her moods, sparkled green with faint slivers of violet. She wore a green cardigan over a polka-dotted white skirt, and I noted that the trim on her socks matched the trim on her skirt (of course).

Ugh. I'm serious: you could literally freeze Hypatia on any random day, shrink her down to three inches tall, and place her on your shelf, and people who visited would be like, *Oh my goodness, that's adorable! Where did you get it?*

And then you'd have to tell them about freezing and shrinking some innocent girl, and your friends would probably call the authorities, you sicko. What's wrong with you?

I told Hypatia I'd just taken my eCombat quiz, and as usual, Ms. Botfly had gone a little overboard. This earned me a motherly pat on the shoulder. "Our table is over by the windows. Come on."

As soon as we'd started frequenting the Imaginary, Hypatia had done some calculations and scoped out the ideal table, the location she determined was the best for aesthetic and practical reasons. Her choice of table had *nothing* at all to do with the fact that the boys' ballistic Frisbee team practiced immediately across the street on the town square under the leadership of one Tom Gillman, a human that my parahuman roommate absolutely did NOT have a crush on.

Are you comfortable with sarcasm? If not, huge chunks of this story aren't going to make a lot of sense.

I actually did a pretty good job of not teasing Hypatia on the subject of her human boy crush. In parahuman communities, dating between humans and parahumans is strongly discouraged—not because of some irrational prejudice, of course, but because if things went well and the couple got married, they could never have children, since it would kill the mother and the baby. We aren't exactly the same species, after all. There's also the matter that parahumans live about two to three times as long as regular humans, so weird age differences can arise, and the fact that many parahumans go into long periods of hibernation starting in their midthirties.

I still had a lot more I needed to learn about parahumans, but I hadn't taken the parahuman health class yet.

I was about to give Hypatia a thrilling and barely embellished replay of my heroic actions that morning when a male voice spoke from the entrance. "Did you have that eCombat test today?"

I turned and caught sight of my friend Warner. He took a long, indulgent look at my *lightly damaged* condition, smirking obnoxiously. Knowing Warner, he had probably been planning to brag about how easy the test had been and how only an idiot could have had problems with it.

"Only an *idiot* could have had problems with that quiz," Warner said. "How did you do, Nikola?"

Some of the human kids at the School get a little insecure about their abilities at times since they're, well, human. It can make some of them act like hypercompetitive jerks. There was a time when I figured that was Warner's problem. But over my first few months at the School, as he, Hypatia, and I became better friends, I discovered that Warner was actually a hypercompetitive jerk by nature, and he didn't really mean anything by it. He just couldn't help himself.

"Don't start with me, Warner," I said. "It's been a long day."

Warner ran a hand absently through his dark mop of hair. He always looked like he'd just rolled out of bed, but the kind of *just rolled out of bed* look that requires $22 in hair-care products and forty-five minutes in front of a mirror to get just right. His jeans were torn in strategic places, and his shirt was just wrinkled enough to give the impression that he was the sort of guy who had better things to do than laundry. "It's not even eight AM yet," he said, a bit wearily.

"Right," I said. "That means today is pretty much guaranteed to get even longer, so why make it worse?"

He joined us as a robotic cart rolled past with various breakfast foods for us to choose from. I grabbed a waffle and was about to dig in when I got a clear look at my reflection in the waiter's belly and realized how much restraint Hypatia and Warner had been showing.

Normally my hair takes the form of a brown mane-like halo surrounding my head, where it resolutely refuses to do anything but hang around, making me look like someone trying to hide in a furry shrub. THAT would have been fine. What alarmed me was that I had an actual smoking *hole* in my hair. The hole was about two inches across and ran just past one of my ears. If I didn't clean myself up, people were going to start offering me medical attention. I excused myself and slipped off to the bathroom, half wishing it was socially acceptable to bring waffles into the can.

In the bathroom, the mirror told the whole story. The girl in the reflection might have been a regular, somewhat plain-looking geeky girl in unfashionable glasses on a normal day, but today she looked like she had also been through a war zone or two. I grinned, and the girl appeared to snarl at me, blood between her teeth.

I looked like a madwoman or a homicidal maniac. But my hair wasn't smoking anymore, so that was good, at least.

I dunked my face into the running water, trying to scrub the black smudges off my skin without getting soap in my eyes.

A second later, I straightened up and saw the reflection of a gorgeous girl staring back at me with soulful blue eyes and a distractingly handsome and serene expression. Her glass-straight hair was so blond it was almost silver. Naturally, I jumped and nearly killed myself by slipping on the puddle my shortcut shower had made on the floor.

Another student had lined up behind me. I couldn't see my own reflection anymore because the mirror was a video screen designed to show only one face at a time. They'd been installed in a lot of the girls' bathrooms on campus and were supposed to keep people from crowding around mirrors, which was both sexist and occasionally necessary, in my opinion.

"Morning, Majorana," I said. Majorana Fermion and her twin brother, Dirac, were both parahuman and had been among my first friends at the School.

"Good morning," Majorana replied dreamily. "I like the hole in your hair. Interesting concept."

"Thanks," I said. "It was probably burning shrapnel or a glob of cesium. Can't be sure. You should have seen it. There was this huge . . . "

I trailed off, seeing Majorana had stopped paying attention and was instead rooting in her bag, mumbling distractedly.

This is common etiquette among parahumans and requires some getting used to. If a parahuman loses interest in a subject, they typically just stop listening or walk away, and nobody takes it personally.

But Majorana hadn't gone anywhere. She was searching for something. "I have just the thing here . . . somewhere . . . Ah! Here it is!"

She removed a jeweled barrette with a flourish and affixed it next to the hole in my hair without asking permission. Then she stepped back so the mirror would display my reflection again. Attached to the clip was a small woodpecker. The bird blinked with a faint mechanical *click* and tapped at the hole. *Perfect.*

Back at the table, I found Dirac had joined us as well.

A silvery-blond artist with disproportionately long, slender features and an aloof, disaffected personality, Dirac was every bit a twin to Majorana. His only difference from his sister was that he was male. There was also the fact that they never agreed on anything.

"I ordered for you," he said to Majorana. "You're welcome."

"What *is* this?" Majorana asked, jabbing a fork at a pastry as if some sort of diseased vermin had wandered onto the table and died on her plate.

"It's a bear claw," Dirac said. "Traditional human breakfast. Try it. You'll love it."

"Did you forget I'm a vegetarian?" Majorana asked testily.

Dirac sighed. "It's named for the form, not the contents. See the shape?" To illustrate, he held it up, growled, and threatened to scratch her with the pastry.

It was a little weird to see a group of parahumans all eating something that wouldn't put me in the hospital from severe vomiting. For instance, the previous morning Hypatia had ordered "spicy oatmeal," which was blended wood pulp soaked in concentrated vinegar with chunks of habanero peppers and tapioca.

I'd finished about half my waffle when my computer informed me of a new email from Ms. Botfly. I was momentarily worried that she might want me to reimburse her for the cost of her Old One costume, until I saw Hypatia, Warner, and Dirac had all gotten a message, too.

To all Electronic Combat students:

Those of you who were able to pass the pop quiz administered yesterday and today will have a previously unscheduled off-site practical exam session tomorrow. Our destination is the Ozark Foothills in northern Arkansas and possibly southwestern Missouri (depending on how things go). Please bring the following supplies:

• Human-appropriate winter clothing and any personal camouflage you require. If memory serves, February can be quite cold outside school grounds. Students who freeze to death will need to retake the examination.

- *A lightweight nonexplosive and nonradioactive weapon.*
- *Your tablet and preferred vocal communicator.*
- *Water-resistant boots and any other hiking equipment you wish to bring along.*
- *Money, if you wish to purchase souvenirs. (Note to self: Find out if forests have gift shops before sending this.)*

The bus leaves at 7:00 AM from the courthouse. Be on time or be prepared to walk several hundred miles.

I love you,

Ms. Botfly

P.S. NOT YOU, MARK.

P.P.S. If you do not have one or more of the items on the list, feel free to stop into my store during normal business hours. Mention this email and receive a 2 percent discount!

I looked to my friends, expecting them to be as excited as I was, but they all looked like they had been assigned a month's worth of toilet-related chores.

"Ugh, a field trip?" Warner said. "I was going to study for my Situational Nihilism test tomorrow."

"That's a shame. Can you ask to take it later?" Majorana asked.

"Eh, that test won't really matter anyway. The class was optional," Warner said noncommittally.

At my old school, a field trip was something you looked forward to for months. "You guys seriously don't like field trips?"

Dirac sighed wearily. "Not Botfly's. She's dangerous enough here in town, where she can be supervised. Did you hear about how Ben Rufkin got lost in her store last week? She installed an unlicensed spatial extender to increase her square footage, but it ended up creating a non-euclidean aisle."

I'd never heard of such a thing. "A what?"

"An aisle that doesn't obey the rules of geometry. The south end was accidentally connected to the north end, even though it was straight. Because of that, there was no way out. To make matters worse, it was connected upside down, so every time he went through, he fell on his head. That woman is a serious danger to students."

Ms. Botfly was one of my favorite teachers precisely *because* of how she never got very uptight about safety. "A little risk can be educational," I said.

"I told her I needed an AI calculator for math class, and she tried to sell me a magnetic singularity," Majorana said.

This earned a gasp of horror from Dirac and Warner. The fact that someone somewhere was insane enough to even *make* a magnetic singularity device was the only thing more astounding than the fact that Ms. Botfly had tried selling one to a student.

Hypatia and I exchanged a quick glance. In that second,

we reached a silent agreement that neither of us needed to mention that I'd actually bought one on my first day at the School, without knowing that a magnetic singularity was an incredibly dangerous device that created a near-infinite magnetic force for a short period of time.

In my defense, it was shiny and cheap.

"She was probably testing you to see if you knew what it was," I said. "Magnetic singularities are against school rules, aren't they? I doubt even Botfly would have sold you one."

Majorana scoffed and took another bite of her bear claw, which she had soaked in hot sauce. "That may be, but I'm not sure I trust her anyway."

"How often do we have field trips?" I asked. Being relatively new at the School, I didn't know what a "normal" schedule of field trips looked like.

"They're irregular," Hypatia said. "We only have them when there's a good reason to leave town. That will be two this month, which is pretty unusual."

"Two?" I asked.

She nodded. "The Urban Camouflage class is planning a trip to the mall. *That* one should be fun, at least. It's part recreational and part test, to see if we can blend in without getting spotted. That'll be a cakewalk compared with whatever Ms. Botfly has planned. Sounds like we're going to see some action."

Dirac groaned. "Can't they count my chronic laziness as a disability so I can stay here?"

"It won't be so bad," I said. "Arkansas is lovely this time of year."

"Really?" he asked.

"If you like frigid weather, freezing rain, and mud mixed with snow, you're going to love it."

3

TUESDAY

Just then my tablet beeped so loudly that I almost choked on the last bite of my waffle. A message read: *You have an urgent code-red last-minute emergency French class beginning in ten minutes.*

I clicked OKAY to let Mademoiselle Hernandez know I was on my way.

Personally, I didn't think anything related to French class could be considered an emergency, but I got there in a hurry just in case. When Mademoiselle Hildegaard Hernandez comes up with a great new way of explaining irregular verbs, she needs to let the world know, pronto.

After that, I was back to my normal abnormal class schedule, which was never the same from one day to the next and occasionally had one-off classes I'd attend and never hear about again. That was one of my favorite things about the

School: you never got sick of the daily routine because there *was* no routine.

- - - - - ✳ - - - - -

"Shoes!" Dr. Hoffman cried at each student who crossed the threshold to her Xenopsychology classroom.

Proper shoe removal and storage were Serious Business in Dr. Hoffman's classroom. But then again, many things were Serious Business to Dr. Hoffman. For the world's leading expert in both human psychology and the psychology of alien races, Dr. Hoffman tended to be . . . a little unusual.

According to Hypatia, when Dr. Hoffman was in private practice and running her own research project, she'd invented an empathy generator, which allowed her to *try out* the neuroses and irrational fears of her patients so she could experience them firsthand. Her hope was that it could give her insight into the root causes of common phobias. It was a great idea, but unfortunately, her primary discovery was that irrational fears were far more difficult to get rid of than she had anticipated.

Because I arrived with Hypatia and Dirac, Dr. Hoffman made sure to shout "Shoes! Shoes! Shoes!," pointing at each of us in turn.

"You want all of us to take our shoes off, or just them?" I asked.

"Yes! *All of you!*" she replied with a burning passion I could not summon about any subject that did not mean life or death to me (and several subjects that did).

I went on. Ruffling Dr. Hoffman's feathers had become a favorite sport of mine because she never saw through it or ran out of steam. "I mean, I know every class session, every student needs to take off their shoes, put them in one of those airtight bags, have all the air sucked out of the bag, and then make sure the shoes are kept in the vacuum chamber, where they can be irradiated during class, but I was wondering if today you maybe wanted all but *one* student to remove their shoes."

Dr. Hoffman rolled her eyes from the front of the room, where she stood behind an inch-thick panel of bulletproof polymer. "Your casual approach to footwear is deeply concerning. There are things on shoes you can't imagine! Listening devices, mind-control microbes, spider eggs, GERMS, just all kinds of things!" she said, growing louder and more upset as she mentioned each increasingly horrifying possibility.

"You've got me in such a tizzy! Look at me—I'm shaking!" she exclaimed. "Are my pupils dilated? Margie, dear, can you see if my pupils are . . . NOT so close, please. Mind the line!" Margie had gotten dangerously close to the line that extended 3.14 feet in all directions from where Dr. Hoffman's podium stood. "I don't need your teenager microbes all over the glass. No offense, Margie. I'm sure your germs are lovely."

"Thank you, Dr. Hoffman!" Margie said.

"Not at all, dear." And to me, "Shoes please, Nikola."

Dr. Hoffman looked amazingly well put together for such a nut. That's why I never judge people on looks. Some people who look like they are nice, upstanding, and respectable are actually concealing serious mental issues. But then again, so are some of the people who look crazy. Dr. Mary Hoffman, a parahuman version of the first type, wore a thick off-white cable-knit sweater beneath a formidable light tan scarf that obscured her face below her nose. She'd gotten a haircut recently, and her do was now a dark blond wedge that looked really cute on her, even if the combined effect of her low bangs and the high scarf made her look a bit like Pac-Man. At first I'd thought she was wearing jeans with decorative stitching, but on closer inspection I saw they were covered from the knee up with countless little notes jotted upside down in ink. Tilting my head, I could see that one of the larger notes said, *Buy milk or vitamin D supplement.* Another simply said, *EAT.* So maybe she didn't look *100 percent* normal.

"Who can tell me a mental illness that can be described as a normal aspect of Old One psychology?" Dr. Hoffman asked, once she'd checked the room for listening devices and had ensured her video camera was recording her presentation for analysis later.

"Narcissistic personality disorder!" several students suggested.

"Of course!" Dr. Hoffman said. "While we don't have much in the way of interaction with the Old Ones, thank god, we do know that nearly all of them are incredibly full of themselves. This may be a side effect of membership in a hive mind where every individual shares knowledge and memories. Research has suggested that can contribute to an increased sense of self-importance. Or it might just be them. What else?"

"Sociopathy?" I suggested. That hadn't been in the textbook, but I'd actually met an Old One, and she had been an obvious sociopath with no concern for right or wrong.

Dr. Hoffman shook her head. "It seems like that, but we're only observing that they don't conform to *our* morals and ethics. They may have their own set of rules they adhere to closely, and we just don't know what those rules are. For instance, the Old Ones are reported to consider any kind of independent decision-making to be a grave immorality. Psychology tends to evaluate individuals on their own cultural norms."

Someone else raised a hand. "Psychopathy?"

"Yes, correct. They have no regard for right and wrong and will use violence—"

I didn't usually interrupt, but: "How are they not sociopathic but they are psychopathic?"

Dr. Hoffman thought this one over a moment. "Well, you see. There's a subtle . . . Look, it's not just because I say so. The book says the same thing."

"But you wrote the book," I said, holding up my copy, which had been suspiciously overpriced at the bookstore.

Challenging teachers was not only allowed at the School, it was also encouraged. Despite that, Dr. Hoffman decided she'd had enough. She leaned close enough to her glass wall to fog its surface faintly, even through her thick scarf. "Why are you persecuting me? Who put you up to this? Was it *them?* *The Shriners?*"

"The who?"

"Never mind," she said, flipping her hair with a care-free gesture and returning to her upright posture. "There are subtle but important differences between sociopaths and psychopaths. And that's going to be your next research topic, so I'd rather not spoil it just yet. Now, who can tell me how the Old Ones perceive their individuality?"

Warner, who never sat near anyone he knew, in case they distracted him from his quest to be the best student at the School, had an answer. "They consider themselves funda-mentally linked individuals. Like fruit on a tree. An apple is separate from the tree but is part of it."

"All correct!" Dr. Hoffman said, narrowing her eyes. "Did you know I was going to ask that?"

"Um," Warner said, looking slightly less triumphant than he had a moment before. "Maybe? It was in the reading."

"Oh, the *reading!*" Dr. Hoffman exclaimed, tossing her head to one side with a breathy laugh. "I'd forgotten about that. I'm sorry." She glanced around the room, addressing us all in general. "Do you still like me? *Please say you do.*"

Warner turned beet red, and a few scattered students nodded.

Fortunately for all of us, Warner knew his way around Dr. Hoffman's tangents and went right into the next topic. "So . . .

they're individuals, but not. As long as they stay connected to the hive mind, they're part themselves and part other."

"And what happens if they get disconnected?" she asked. "What happens if one of those apples is cut from the tree?"

"They lose their memory and die, or go into hibernation."

"Very good, Warner. You're always prepared for whatever might come up, aren't you?" Dr. Hoffman said, her eyes narrowing.

She made a mark in her book and went on. "It is rumored the Old Ones forcibly disconnect individuals as a punishment on occasion. It's said to be their harshest form of punishment, their version of the death penalty. I'm going to assign a supplemental reading I came across recently. It's an account of the only known *capture* of an Old One. Although technically, it was more like managing to transport one without waking her up. Still, she talked in her sleep and . . . I don't want to ruin the surprise."

------*------

His nose sufficiently browned, Warner was slightly more insufferable than normal for the rest of the day. In literature class we were comparing the poetry of Robert Frost and Blackheart Murdergrace-Deathperson Jones, a famous parahuman poet of the same time. Warner could not shut up about how dark Frost's work was compared with Jones's, like everyone didn't already know.

He was even worse in Spontaneous Engineering, where

he insisted he could do a group project better if he was allowed to work alone and openly scoffed at the talents of the other people at his table. The challenge had been to create, during class time, a device that could locate water and bring it back to the lab. He'd done pretty well. As soon as it was switched on, his machine scurried out into the park on its six wheels and immediately started drilling for groundwater. He'd have taken home best project once again, if my project with Hypatia had not been a machine specifically designed to destroy and steal water from whatever Warner made.

We only got 80 percent credit because Dr. Dell *reckoned that went against the spirit of the competition.* "It should be a zero," he said, "but I'll be darned if I don't love seeing one machine bust up another."

One thing I'd learned since coming to the School was that even though classes didn't assign grades, they were still keeping score, and our scores on tests and assignments seemed to have a direct effect on our schedules. Even so, it was worth getting partial credit if only to take a bit of the wind out of Warner's sails.

"You're always trying to take the wind out of my sails," Warner complained that night at dinner with Hypatia and me.

"That's ridiculous and self-centered," I said. "You should be *ashamed* to accuse friends of treachery like that!"

Here's the thing: Warner *needs* a good friend to undermine him from time to time. When I first came to the School, almost nobody would speak to him, precisely *because* he was the best student in school. He was so competitive that you couldn't talk to him about anything without him trying to beat you at something or reminding you of something he'd already beaten you at. One time he defeated Hypatia at a conversation about the weather. But I like to think I've been able to challenge and derail his self-serving egotism here and there. I haven't been the best at everything, but losing once in a while has actually made his personality a bit more tolerable.

"Yeah, okay. Sorry," Warner said. "I think I'm catching paranoia from Dr. Hoffman."

"I'm not very offended," I said. "You can make it up to me by lending me your extra fusion transmitter for the field trip tomorrow."

Warner and Hypatia both looked shocked. "You can't take a fusion transmitter into the woods!" Hypatia said. "You'll start a forest fire for sure."

"Ms. Botfly only said to bring a nonnuclear weapon. I'm sure she'd allow it, since it's *technically* nonnuclear."

Hypatia shook her head. "If you judge what is and is not a good idea based on what Ms. Botfly thinks, you'll be dead before you're twenty."

She had a point. "Fine, I'll just bring my disruptor. What are you guys bringing?"

Hypatia's eyes lit up like only hers can, because they can literally light up and glow a bit when she's excited. "I got this last week—look!"

She produced a pastel-pink cylinder with a few buttons on the top.

"It looks like a water bottle," Warner said.

"It's a superstring slicer. Very subtle. It creates a wave of anti-energy and temporarily immobilizes the target by making them fail to *exist* for a short period of time."

"Whoa!" Warner said. "I've heard of those! Can I see it?"

"Careful, I tried it on Nikola after I got it, and—"

"WHAT?" I asked, unaware I'd been a test subject.

"And it . . . it . . . didn't work," Hypatia said, taking the slicer back from Warner and hastily concealing it in her purse.

Something occurred to me. "Was that why they canceled last weekend?"

"What?" she said, flustered. "I don't know, but we should be thinking about heading down to—"

That wasn't going to work. "I should have known they didn't cancel Saturday and Sunday. You literally blasted me into the next week!"

"Okay, yes! But it was YOUR IDEA!"

"I think I'd remember *that*," I said.

"Yeah, but I also think you'd remember a weekend you spent hovering over the kitchen floor inside a localized semi-existence bubble I couldn't figure out how to deactivate. But you don't remember *that*, do you?"

Sometimes you just have to decide you can trust a person.

"Fine . . . What are you bringing to shoot at whatever we're supposed to be shooting at?" I asked Warner.

"Plain old zapper. No need to get fancy. We probably won't run into anything too bad, and there will be a lot of us. Why don't you just bring your quantum agar thingy? That counts as a weapon, right?"

I should explain. Quantum agar is a special material that is especially prone to quantum events, which allows it to be controlled simply by making certain observations about it. Most of the students at the School are pretty good at controlling it with computers by creating complex mathematical equations to describe the form and properties they want it to take on. For some reason that I've never really understood, I'm able to control it by just thinking about the form I want it to take. That can make it a pretty powerful weapon in my hands.

I glanced at my agar, which I usually kept in the form of a silvery bracelet with a thin, faintly glowing blue streak running around its length, and made it shiver a bit. "I don't have a lot of it left. Most of it was lost along with Tabbabitha, remember?"

Back when I first came to the School, our Practical Quantum Mechanics teacher, Mr. Dolphin, had given me a substantial amount of agar because he owed my dad a favor or something. Unfortunately, *someone* helped an Old One named Tabbabitha gain access to the School Town so she could kidnap or kill me. Because of the School's security system, she couldn't walk right in, so she used time travel to go back to just before the School was established and hibernated until I came along. We never actually figured out who helped her, although the principal had been pretty eager to blame it on my friend Bob Flobogashtimann.

Anyway, I ended up using almost all my agar to knock Tabbabitha into an interdimensional void where nothing could exist, which meant most of it was gone, too. On the upside, my bracelet was a lot lighter.

"Looks the same to me," Warner said.

"Yeah, but there's not as much there," I said, removing it. "Here, feel it."

Warner moved the bracelet from hand to hand. Something seemed to occur to him, and he stared hard at it for a while. I could tell he was trying to make it do something and failing. For the heck of it, I made the bracelet turn into a pair of handcuffs that jumped out and locked his wrists together.

"Ah! Very funny," he said insincerely.

A second later, the handcuffs slipped from his wrists like they were made of milk, and the agar slid back across the table and leaped onto my wrist, again taking its familiar form.

Hypatia's tablet made a noise, and she consulted it briefly. "You're both coming to my volleyball game tonight, by the way. Jill Green-Eleven Nuclei is sick, so I get to start. It'll be the first time I actually get to play."

Warner consulted his tablet. "Yeah, I'm really sorry. I have a lot of work to do. I'm sure Nikola can make it."

"Actually, Hypatia . . . I would *absolutely* come, but I don't want to," I said.

"Oh no," Hypatia said, pointing her finger angrily at me. "You're coming. Nikola, you owe me one, *remember?*"

She was talking about our orbit trip. Some weekends, the School has an optional activity where they launch a few students into low earth orbit so they can experience weightlessness, being in space, and all that. As soon as I heard of it, I knew we had to go, despite Hypatia's protestations that "space is dumb."

When the time came, it was Hypatia, me, and six kids from the preschool class crammed into a tiny, multicolored space capsule that operated on an electromagnetic thruster so we didn't need a giant rocket to get us up there. The thing was automated, so there were no adults, just a screen with a cartoon version of the School's pangolin mascot wearing a space suit who spent the whole time jovially telling us "fun facts" about space. It turns out that for students who have been at the School since they were little, going into orbit is a lot like going to a petting zoo: something safe and dull that is a good adventure for little kids.

Here's a space travel fun fact: seasickness and car sickness have *nothing* on space sickness. Here's another fun fact: in space, nausea is *very* contagious, especially because when you're experiencing microgravity, vomit pretty much just drifts around in the air. I should have been worried when I noticed all the walls of the space capsule were covered in rubber.

"Fine," I said reluctantly.

- - - - - ✱ - - - - -

At the game, I got the distinct impression that the School's version of volleyball operated on a set of rules that had little in common with normal volleyball. I could be wrong, though; I'm no expert on sports. The game's final score was Brown Dwarves: 214.999 repeating, Malaria Mosquitoes (Hypatia's team): 322.5, and Tyler Ruffin: 400. According to Hypatia, this made it the second game that season won by a member of the audience.

When we met outside the auditorium after the game, I'd been prepared to console Hypatia on her team's loss, but she was *thrilled* with the results. "It's about having fun, not winning," she said.

Her positive outlook surprised me a bit. Perfectionist that she was, I'd assumed losing the game would be upsetting to her.

"Besides," she said, "audience members aren't allowed in the playoffs, so we're still ranked number one. Did you see how I set up that hundred-point spike that landed right in the triple-bonus anti-penalty zone? I was like, 'Get that ball in the air, and let someone do something with it!' "

"Good thinking," I said. "I've always thought volleyball was just like chess, but without the similarities."

"You're totally right," she said, actually spinning there on the sidewalk with her arms outstretched. "Did you save a program?"

"Do people usually do that sort of thing at sporting events?"

Hypatia rolled her gray eyes and kicked a rock. "When it's someone's first game, maybe. It's not a big deal, though."

"Because I got one just in case," I said, handing her the program/rule book, which was about the size of your average paperback novel.

Hypatia jumped and spun, and generally did the sorts of things you expect a puppy to do.

"What has gotten into you?" I asked. "Do I need to find my tranquilizer darts?"

"You're a stick in the mud, and you can't handle the fact that I just have a little joie de vivre!" she said as she tripped on a rock and almost fell joyfully onto her beaming face. "Besides, I'm not headed home, so you don't need to tranquilize me."

"No?" I asked.

She kicked at another rock. This one turned out to be a lump of gray slush left over from our temporary winter earlier that day, and it splattered all over my left pant leg. "Tom asked me to meet him at Garden Supply for coffee. He wants to talk about *my performance on the team and how I can improve*," Hypatia said, taking no notice of the gross splotches she'd left on my jeans.

I wondered if she had caught on to the fact that the meeting probably wasn't going to be positive. But Tom could offer to sneeze in her salad and she'd be thrilled, so I just nodded.

"Sounds like fun. Don't stay out too late," I said.

Hypatia's eyes and cheeks turned a bright shade of pink. She punched me on the shoulder. "You goof! I'll be home sooner or later."

I might have said something funny, but she was gone before I could come up with something good.

4

UNIVERSAL RECYCLED
BULK NUTRIENT MATTER

Coming home without Hypatia was deeply weird, and I wasn't sure I liked it. You know how things can change, and you don't really notice it? Going home alone made me realize that in my few months at the School, Hypatia and I had been pretty much inseparable. Our little School-provided bungalow was eerily quiet. For the first time, I could understand why some of the older students still chose to live in the large dorms downtown instead of in houses in the residential neighborhood.

I used to *love* being alone. Back in North Dakota, I liked being around my dad and nobody else. Dad was always a presence, if not an especially paternal one. Don't get me wrong—we got along fine, but he wasn't exactly one for hugs or playing catch in the yard. We didn't even have a yard; we had a parking lot. His idea of showing emotion was to arrange for dinner to be delivered for us (*Nikola! Make food happen!*), and we'd sit around discussing how to make unstable actinoid metals stop decaying, ways of transferring human memory into computer memory, or whatever it was he was working on at the time.

Six months ago, things were boring, frustrating, vaguely depressing, and familiar. Now Dad was missing, kidnapped by the Old Ones, and being held in some underground place, if the little information I'd gotten from Tabbabitha was to be believed. Meanwhile, I was studying everything I could ever hope to learn, getting three meals a day, and had all these actual friends coming out of my ears. In short, everything was lovely for me and terrible for him. I don't blame myself for what happened, but I can understand how people *do* blame themselves for things like that. The whole situation felt extremely, painfully unfair to me. I almost wished I *could* believe it was my fault. Maybe I'd feel a little less helpless about it.

I flopped into my chair and pulled a book I'd been reading from my desk drawer. In doing this, I bumped the desk, and a single framed picture slid onto its back and threatened to topple off. I lifted it and leaned back in the chair, inspecting, for what must have been the billionth time, my favorite (and only) family picture.

In the photo, I was wearing a black T-shirt with a picture of a vest and bow tie printed on the front of it, and Dad had on an oxford-style shirt that was so threadbare you could clearly make out the short-sleeved T-shirt he wore beneath it. I'd worked so hard on getting the photo set up that I'd completely forgotten to do my hair that day, and it was an absolute mess.

It was amazing the effort that had gone into that image. The photographer had made me sit on a wooden crate that was very uncomfortable and low so it was out of frame. She stood my dad behind me and said, "Okay, Dad, hands on shoulders."

So, just as requested, he put his hands on his own shoulders and smiled.

She thought he was being clever, so she said, "Very funny, Dad."

To which he replied, "Young lady, I think you may have me confused with someone else. I am *not* your father. Do you have a history of early onset dementia in your family?"

Eventually she had needed to physically place his hands on my shoulders when he hadn't quite understood the pose she was trying to describe to him.

When the image was finally snapped, I was smiling at the camera, and he was looking just to the left of the lens, wearing a bewildered, almost angry expression. This was because on the wall behind the camera in the photo studio, there had been a sign that said, DON'T FORGET YOU'RE VALUABLES! and he was having a hard time not correcting it in some way.

We were there on a coupon that promised one free photo, and I'd kind of assumed we'd do more than one pose (as had the girl taking the pictures), but the moment the flash went off, Dad considered his obligation fulfilled and left the building. We stopped for ice cream on the way home that day, and I listened to him expound on how the one free photo was "how they get you."

This was the one copy of that one free photo.

I stared at it for a while, feeling wistful, sad, and lonely all at once. On a whim, I tried to cry, because that's supposed to make you feel better. But it wasn't happening, so I gave it up. Then, for practically no reason at all, I decided to check in with the Chaperone.

The Chaperone is the School's all-purpose artificial intelligence system. She's wired into most of the structures in town and serves as the class scheduler, security coordinator, residence monitor, and pretty much everything else a rational adult might be needed for, since rational adults were pretty rare at the School. I guess a lot of people find the Chaperone's semiomniscience a bit creepy, but she's never bothered me. It's probably because my dad designed her, so she sounds exactly like the security system at my old home.

"Yo! Chaperone!" I said.

There was a faint buzz in the air, letting me know she was "present."

"Good evening, Nikola," the Chaperone said in her oddly reassuring voice. "You have no homework assignments due tomorrow because of an all-day Electronic Combat field trip. According to your schedule forecast you have four assignments due the following day. Would you like details?"

"No, thanks," I said. "Homework is best done at the last minute."

There was a single *click* sound in the air, which I knew

meant she disapproved of something. "That is an unwise, shortsighted, and childish belief. You should make a point of reexamining your lackadaisical attitude in regard to your education at your earliest convenience."

"Yeah, okay," I said, suddenly feeling a bit silly. "Say, I was wondering—"

"When will that be?" the Chaperone interrupted.

"When will what be?"

Another click. "When do you plan to reexamine your priorities in relation to your schoolwork?"

"Oh," I said. "Probably at the last minute."

The Chaperone responded with another click, this one a bit louder.

"Has there been any news on my dad?" I asked.

"Melvin Kross has been the subject of an exhaustive search for some time now. Were you expecting news?" the Chaperone said, sounding a little less stern.

"No. Well, I spoke with Dr. Plaskington a couple months ago, and she said she'd let me know of any developments. I haven't heard anything recently, so I thought I'd . . . you know . . . check in?"

"Of course. If you'll wait a second, I can ask the principal if there's been any news."

I really didn't like the idea of having her contact the principal at—I checked the time—9:00 PM. "Oh, you don't have to bother her now. I can ask tomorrow. I was just—"

But there was another faint buzz in the air, signaling that the Chaperone had "stepped out."

About two minutes later, there was another buzz. "Nikola, I'm connecting you to Dr. Plaskington's line."

I was about to tell her she didn't have to when I found myself talking to the principal, her voice emanating from nowhere as if she were an invisible person standing in the middle of the room. "Nikola, dear! How are you holding up?" Dr. Plaskington said in her not-quite-chipper grandmotherly voice.

"Ah, pretty good, I guess," I said.

"Excellent, excellent, that's so good to hear! It's very important to me that every student feels valued, challenged, and well cared for. At the Plaskington International Laboratory School of Scientific Research and Technological Advancement, we have always prided ourselves on ensuring an unparalleled . . ."

I picked up my tablet and checked my email as she spoke. There had been a new message from Ms. Botfly reminding us of the impending field trip, and Warner had sent a close-up photo of his bent arm that was supposed to look like a butt.

" . . . but the opinion of my students is what truly matters. So what do you think?" Dr. Plaskington asked.

"Oh, sorry, the line cut out a bit," I lied, setting my tablet back down on the desk quietly. "What were you asking?"

"I was just wondering how the cafeteria food has tasted lately. Has it seemed at all artificial or synthetically replicated from universal recycled bulk nutrient matter?"

"Um . . . no?"

"Wonderful!" Dr. Plaskington crowed. "Because that's

just the sort of cost-cutting measure I would *never* stand for. Can you imagine how the parents would react?"

I nodded, even though she couldn't see me. "Speaking of parents, I was wondering if there was any news about my father."

"The Chaperone filled me in. As it just so happens, I've only recently gotten a message from him!"

My jaw dropped. "You have? When? Just today?"

"No, no, let me think," Dr. Plaskington said. "I'd say it came in about . . . six weeks ago?"

I leaped to my feet, banging my legs against my desk, which almost tipped over. "SIX WEEKS? AND YOU DIDN'T SAY ANYTHING?"

"Well, I've been very busy, young lady," the principal said, a bit testily. "Running an educational community isn't all daisies and jalapeños, I can tell you that! All this month I've had the Parahuman Food Safety Board breathing down my neck about—"

"How did you get the message?" I asked, summoning every ounce of patience I had.

"Well, they just marched in with a search warrant and—"

I gritted my teeth so hard I'm surprised they didn't break. "NOT . . . THEM! How did you get the message from my DAD?"

"Oh, *that*. It seems he's being held in a mixed detention facility of some sort. There are a few other humans and parahumans who come and go on occasion."

"They come and go? Like they're free?"

I heard papers shuffling on her end of the line. "Yes, the Old Ones are known to collaborate with willing traitors from time to time. I hear they pay quite well. It seems your father was able to attach a tracking device to one, and as soon as he left the facility, it went online and transmitted a message along with his coordinates."

My eyes must have almost bugged out of my skull. "So you know where my dad is!"

Dr. Plaskington made a disappointed *tsk* sound. "Unfortunately, no. That's turned out to be a dead end. We were able to apprehend the individual your father tagged just outside Boise, Idaho, but our readings indicated he had recently passed through an interdimensional gateway we can't trace very well. They must be using a kind of transportation we aren't familiar with yet. He could have been sent from anywhere in the known universe."

"Oh," I said, suddenly overwhelmed with a sinking feeling. "Were you able to ask him where he'd come from?"

"Another dead end. It seems the Old Ones installed a security device of some sort in the individual, and his brain melted before the security team was able to ask him any questions."

"His brain . . . melted?"

"Yes, poor fellow. I understand he was very upset about it."

I shook my head. "You mean his brain literally melted? Like ice cream?"

"Oh, it's not as horrible as it sounds. I've seen a video of the interrogation. One moment he was asking who they were, and the next . . . Well, if I'm being honest, it actually was pretty horrible."

"So what did the message say?" I asked.

"It says that I'm supposed to read it aloud to you. However it is getting quite late. Do you mind if I forward it to your email?"

"Yes! I mean, no! Go ahead!" I said, relieved I wouldn't have to stay on the call much longer.

"Right-oh!" Dr. Plaskington said cheerfully. "It's on its way now! Have a great evening."

There was a last faint buzz in the air, and the room was silent. A moment later, my tablet *dinged*.

My finger hovered over the new message. The subject line read, *Fw: Kindly rescue me at your earliest convenience.*

According to the header information, it had been sent from my father's personal email account to at least fifty email addresses, including some at the NSA, the FBI, the CIA, and the various armed forces. Weirdest of all, almost all the remaining email addresses were just long strings of numbers with the suffix *@USCIRF.gov*. Here's an example of one: *2382 50494025152102152085180453154914702089 19@USCIRF.gov*. I googled it, and the domain name belongs to the United States Commission on International Religious Freedom.

I should probably ask about that at some point.

The final address on the list was the only one that was familiar to me, Patricia.Plaskington@PILSSRTA.org.

Here's what the message said:

Hello, friends, acquaintances,

and emergency personnel,

My name is Melvin Kross, and I'm currently being held captive by hostile forces whom I've been repeatedly ordered not to mention in open, unencrypted communications. If you're getting this message, I think you can probably guess who. The facility where I'm being held seems to be located deep underground, and I've unfortunately been unable to get any idea of its location beyond that. I'm being treated reasonably well and am almost never tortured, unless you count the food, and also the literal torture.

Most of you will have some idea of what they have me doing down here, so I won't bore you with details, because the details are somewhat less interesting than you might expect. I honestly wonder how they get anything done. Very little supervision, no peer review, and apparently unlimited funding add up to a lot of waste and nonsense. It's simply ghastly.

Anyway, to get back to the matter at hand, I'd like to be rescued. I know I can't give you a lot to go on, but I'm doing my best. I'll be attaching a tracking and message delivery device to one Paul Merchar, one of about a half dozen "visitors" who are able to come and go as they please. If he does not notice it before he leaves here, you should get this message, along with an emergency beacon alerting you to his location. You may be able to press him for further information.

Press as hard as you like, by the way. He's a real jerk, in my opinion. Wouldn't even bring me a decent ink pen. All they have down here is blue ink. Like I said, ghastly.

Patricia, this last part will be sent to you only. I'd like you to convey a message to Nikola. You might recall that I arranged for her to be misled in regard to my whereabouts. I cleverly informed her that I had gone on an unexpected vacation, so she would not worry about me. Since I've been gone for as long as I have, she may be starting to doubt that explanation. Please read the following aloud to her:

Hello, Nikola!

Vacation was wonderful! I had the time of my life, but not such a good time that you should be jealous I did not bring you along. It rains a lot here, there are no children your age, and it's actually quite dull. I'd tell you where I've gone, but the name slips my mind at the moment. It's irrelevant, really.

My friend Carter Reagan and I have decided to set up a research facility here. Because of this, it is possible I won't be back anytime soon. In my absence, please continue to apply yourself to the best of your abilities. I hope you do not miss your old school too much, but if you do, it is no excuse to "take it easy," as you young people say.

As always, please remember that I hold you in high
esteem and hope that you think fondly of me. With luck
we can meet again quite soon.

Warmest regards,
Melvin Kross (Father)

Just a few minutes before, I'd found it difficult to cry. Suddenly it came easily. I could never handle it when Dad got all emotional and mushy like that.

I read the message three more times, at first just taking it all in and eventually considering all the information. I searched the email addresses, but apart from what I already mentioned about the agencies, none of the names seemed to match up to anyone of any interest. Something told me they were aliases.

There was one exception. The person he'd attached the device to, Paul Merchar, was apparently a famous shipping magnate who was heavily involved with politics and philanthropy. There were about a million articles that mentioned his name in passing, and a handful that spoke of his death. According to his obituaries, he suffered a traumatic head injury while skiing on his private ski slope and had died before help could arrive.

I spent close to an hour studying him and learned a great deal, but nothing especially useful. Paul Merchar was just your average superrich guy. He donated lots of money to various causes and donated many, many times that amount to politicians. He was quoted in articles talking about things like regulatory policy and new technologies to make container ships more efficient.

None of the information I found suggested whether he was human or parahuman. In his pictures, he just looked like a normal guy, if normal guys were always having their picture taken in front of helicopters and gigantic sea vessels.

I might have done some more research, but just then I heard the front door open and ran to fill Hypatia in on the news so I would have someone to speculate with.

5

THE OZARK MOUNTAIN CREEPER

That night, I slept fitfully. Every time I woke even slightly, my brain hammered into overdrive trying to process every minor detail of my father's message. I hadn't come up with any new insights, but that didn't stop me from trying. The next morning, when Hypatia woke me at 4:45 AM to weigh in on her choice of outdoors garb, I decided to give it up and started getting ready for the trip.

I had located a warm coat in my school-supplied wardrobe and was dressed and ready to go more than an hour early, which was something of a minor miracle for me. There was also the fact that I didn't want to miss my ride. Something told me Ms. Botfly wasn't kidding when she said missing the bus meant walking several hundred miles.

After six months at the School, I was starting to wonder if the outside world was still out there. I didn't think it had ceased to exist or anything, but . . . You have to understand, nobody watches TV at the School, and it's not like newspapers deliver to Nowhere, Iowa. Sure, we have Internet and all that, and I'd been up to orbit and back, but life in the School Town can make a person feel pretty isolated.

When people want to see their families, the parents usually travel to the School Town, rather than the other way around. It makes sense from a safety angle, but the fact is some students remain in town for *years* at a time, apart from occasional brief summer vacations. Some even settle in town after they're done with school, because it's one of the largest parahuman communities in the world and anyone can live there free if they agree to teach at least one class. Initially, that had seemed like a great deal, but I was starting to realize that if I spent too much time here I might lose my mind.

Plus my dad was out there somewhere. If I'm being honest, that's at least part of why I was excited about leaving. Sure, he'd want me to leave him to his own devices, but Dad's *own devices* are easily distracted and prone to malfunction. I pictured him sitting in a cell, hoping his desperate ploy to send an SOS had worked, not yet knowing it had failed.

What I'm trying to say is that after months of doing nothing, getting *out there* and keeping my eyes open was at least slightly more than nothing.

------*------

As we walked toward City Hall, I imagined what the School's bus would look like. Amazing contraptions floated in my imagination—flying saucers, luxury trains with mechanical spider legs and a special dining car, high-speed blimps where we all got our own beanbag chair and a private room with really great Wi-Fi and free snacks.

When I finally saw it, I made a mental note that I probably shouldn't allow myself to get excited like that very often. The School's bus sat idling in front of City Hall, looking like any one of the millions of grimy yellow student freighters you might see rumbling down the road on any random school day. Apart from large black text on the side that read PILSSRTA, nothing marked it as belonging to the School or being special in any way.

I won't deny I was a bit disappointed at first. But then Hypatia and I stepped onto the bus and I got a look inside. The moment I saw where we'd be riding, I went from mildly disappointed to completely depressed. It *was* just a normal school bus, down to the creaky floors, the rows of seat belt-free fake leather benches, and the twin lines of windows you can just tell are all messed up so you can't open them properly. I smelled rust, plastic, and the faintest trace of vomit.

"You're twenty minutes EARLY," the driver growled when Hypatia and I climbed aboard. "In *my* day, kids were disrespectful and irresponsible about punctuality."

The way she said it was a lot like how you might point out that someone else in your elevator was covered in dog poo. As it turns out, both school buses and school bus *drivers* are crappy and inhospitable wherever you go. Now you know.

"We didn't want to keep anyone waiting!" Hypatia said in

a voice that made me want to poke her in the back of the head with a pencil.

"My roommate is pathological about things like this," I added. "We won't be any trouble."

"Ow!" said Hypatia.

"Except for that," I said, slipping my pencil back in my bag.

The only good thing about arriving early for a field trip is getting to snag the back seat of the bus. At my old school I'd always been a bit of an outcast (shocking, right?), which meant being relegated to the single seat just behind the driver. Or worse, sharing a seat with the teacher. Now that I attended a school made *for* oddballs *by* oddballs, I could claim the cool seats without having to worry that my classmates would use that as an opportunity to sharpen their best insults on me.

Hypatia had already started going over the checklist. She'd polished and charged her superstring slicer and let me know that the battery still showed a 99 percent charge. I had my own gravitational disruptor in my pocket, not because I'd thought ahead, but because I never left home without it. You run into the Old Ones a couple times, and it can make you paranoid pretty fast. I'd also brought my agar bracelet, which I never remove, even when I sleep.

Hypatia, always prepared, had a pretty sizable pack with camping gear, a pup tent, emergency flares, a drone helicopter with remote and camera, bear deterrent spray, a water purifier, about twenty granola bars, spare clothes, and two military MREs.

I had a thermos filled with hot coffee from the Event Horizon, heavy on the cream and sweetener, and two spare pairs of socks in my bag, in case things got muddy.

"Why don't we pool our supplies in case one of us comes up lacking something?" I suggested.

Hypatia nodded enthusiastically. "Great idea! Can I have a drink of your coffee?"

I poured her a tiny sip, and she gave me a dirty look.

"This is all the coffee we have," I said, grabbing the only peanut butter granola bar for later. "Can't have you guzzling it all."

Some people just don't understand cooperation and sharing.

We had twenty minutes to wait, so I took the time to download some reading materials before we left town, since accessing the Internet from a school computer when off campus was strictly prohibited.

Then it hit me.

A gigantic water balloon collided with my face, exploded, drenched my tablet, soaked all of Hypatia's supplies, and left us both sopping wet. My tablet sparked once and winked out. I swallowed a huge, choking mouthful of water and looked up to see Warner and Dirac giggling madly at us from behind a row of seats.

I sprang to my feet. *"OPEN CASKET OR CLOSED?"*

"Wait, wait, wait!" Dirac said hastily, tapping at the screen of his phone. "It's reversible. We made them last night. When I activate it, all the water will be sucked back out of your clothes, and it will return to balloon form. It's the world's first recyclable water balloon."

Let me tell you, their invention worked perfectly, but it's only fun if you haven't swallowed any of the water.

-----*-----

The School has wormholes it can direct to any location on Earth in an instant. But how does our group of twenty-five students get to Arkansas? A grimy yellow bus with a top speed of fifty that needed new shock absorbers about three hundred thousand miles ago. Apparently, transporting more than a few people by wormhole is a security risk of some sort, so old-fashioned *have this machine physically carry us there* travel is still the best option.

And you know what? It wasn't that bad.

The worst part was at the beginning. As the bus trundled down the road, I became aware of a low humming, and before I could wonder if there was something wrong with the tires, I saw that we were entering the bees' territory. The School's last line of defense, the bees are several million autonomous attack drones designed to kill any unauthorized intruders by poking them with stingers filled with special toxins that can hurt even the Old Ones.

One by one, the bees stuck themselves to our windows, until the interior of the bus was as dark as midnight, except for a small space so the driver could see. Everyone behaved like this was normal and not gravely terrifying. I knew they were just checking us out, as they did with every vehicle entering or exiting school grounds, so it didn't make me nervous at all. I might have chewed on my knuckle a bit, just until it started bleeding a little, but that was mostly because I was bored.

At the window next to my head, a twitchy little bee with a small brown spot on one side used his front leg to point at one of his bulging eyes and then at me, before drawing it along his "neck" in a threatening gesture. I was pretty sure it was Bzzlkrullium, a specific bee I'd tangled with shortly after coming to the School, but bees can be hard to tell apart from one another.

After a minute, they concluded we were not much of a threat and dispersed.

I shuddered. "Do they have to do that *every time?*"

"You get used to it," Hypatia said.

After that, we passed through the gap, which is the School's primary defense. It's kind of like a dome that stretches over the whole school, but instead of something solid, it's made of a very thin sheet of unreality—a hole in the fabric of space-time where nothing exists. If you were to try passing through the gap without permission, you wouldn't regret it, because you'd have vanished into nothingness before you had time to process regret. It's also a great way of killing an Old One, if you ever find yourself in a jam.

For a while, I passed the time playing around with my tablet, not really paying attention to anyone else.

"What game is that?" Warner asked, pointing at my tablet.

"Nothing," I said, shoving it into my bag.

"Let me see," he said, deftly snatching the tablet from my fingers. "Is it a contraband game? I downloaded one where . . . What is this?" he asked, flipping through the pictures in my photo album.

Hypatia, now keenly interested, snatched it from Warner and took a gander herself.

"Is that your dad? Why are you both posed the same way in every photo?" she asked.

"I only have the one picture of him, so I edited the image to look like different places," I said, grabbing the tablet back from Warner and closing the image on-screen of my dad and me in front of Big Ben in London. It seemed like the sort of place he'd take me to visit if he were around.

Warner looked slightly abashed. "Sorry, I didn't mean to get all grabby."

"Don't sweat it. I got this email from him and . . . I feel a little guilty, you know? Because things are going so well here, and I know he's . . ."

Hypatia sent a copy of my dad's email to Warner so he could read it (and maybe to shut him up for a bit).

Hypatia patted my knee. "I've heard how clever he is. I'm sure he'll figure out how to get away from them sooner or later."

I nodded in agreement, but I had to wonder if his attempt to signal the outside world had gotten him in trouble. The Old Ones must have known *someone* had done *something*, because they'd had to melt that Merchar guy's brain. Maybe there were loads of people wherever my dad was being held who were capable of smuggling out an emergency transmitter, but somehow I doubted it. My dad and the guy obviously talked sometimes, so they must have known my dad at least had the opportunity to plant something on him.

What would they have done if they'd figured out it was my dad? Was he being tortured or held in solitary confinement? Maybe they'd decided he was too much of a risk and had opted to cut their losses by . . .

Hypatia pulled me over and leaned my head on her shoulder with her arm around mine. A ring of her perfect curly golden hair sprang into my nose, tickling my nostril a bit. She didn't say anything. Sometimes Hypatia knew exactly the right thing to do.

Then I sneezed in her hair, and the moment was over.

-----*-----

According to Hypatia, most school trips are usually pretty straightforward, but most school trips aren't run by Ms. Botfly, who insisted on stopping at every mildly interesting tourist trap along the way. We had funnel cakes; visited an antique mall in Cuba, Missouri, where I bought an Eiffel Tower figurine; and hit up about nine gas stations, where I made a point of stocking up on gum and candy to take home. Let me tell you, it was nice to go shopping somewhere I didn't have to worry about accidentally buying peach-onion-gunpowder-flavored bubble gum.

After a couple hours on the road, we arrived at our destination—a random dead-end gravel path off a random dirt road, which was off a random, unnamed country highway somewhere in northern Arkansas or southwest Missouri. (I'd quit paying attention a few hundred miles before.)

Incidentally, the fact that our drive should have taken the better part of eight hours, but my tablet said it was barely 9:30 AM suggested that perhaps the school bus might not have been 100 percent normal after all.

It wasn't until the bus pulled to a stop just behind a stand of trees that I started wondering why exactly we had come. All the way I'd kind of assumed the reason for going would be obvious once we arrived. But the only obvious thing was that there didn't seem to be a lot going on in that particular corner of the world. For all I could see, it was your basic forest, albeit an unusually dense and cold one.

Ms. Botfly gathered everyone in a clearing once the bus had abandoned us. She was dressed in jeans and a thermal jacket complete with matching hat, and held a baby wrapped in a blanket on one hip. It threw me for a loop until I realized the baby was Fluorine.

There was a bright flash, and a tall, slender woman in her midthirties was sitting on Ms. Botfly's hip where the baby had been a moment before. Ms. Botfly was ready for it and dropped her on her full-grown butt the moment the change occurred. Adult Fluorine was perturbed by this rough treatment and wondered aloud whether school employees should be throwing people around all willy-nilly.

I doubted the School would drag me along on field trips if I had a similar problem, but being the granddaughter of the School's owner and principal meant a little more special treatment than the rest of us could expect. A good example of this was the fact that Ms. Botfly helped Fluorine to her feet and apologized. If Ms. Botfly had dropped any other student, she would have just chastised them for falling and moved on.

"Ladies and gentlemen," Ms. Botfly began, speaking in her loud official voice. "Everyone open your FieldTrip app and make sure your tablets are recording sound and location data for evaluation later. This will be a major examination and counts as roughly thirty percent of your grade in my class, so no slacking off and no funny business. I'll be watching."

She made a point of issuing a free supplemental warning sneer at everyone before continuing. "As some of you know, at the School we get about ninety percent of our students through enrollment of children born to known parahuman families, and the other ten percent are regular humans we hear about from testing, grade reports, science fairs, and things like that. HOWEVER, from time to time we have a student who does not come to our attention via our traditional processes. We find these students through rumors, satellite data, and reports in human media. Recently we started seeing articles in local papers like this one."

She produced and held aloft a copy of the *Ozark Mountain Times Shopper*, which was emblazoned with two-inch-high letters spelling out one of the most amazing headlines I'd ever seen: MIRACLE MULE BARKS LIKE A DOG.

"We can't take him!" I cried. "THAT MULE BELONGS IN A MUSEUM!"

"Not that, dummy," Ms. Botfly snapped. "Look here . . . ," she said, leafing through the paper until she found the article she was seeking. "Read that aloud to everyone, won't you, Princess SmartButt?"

I didn't hate Princess SmartButt, as far as nicknames went, so I didn't correct her.

Third Ozark Mountain Creeper Sighting Raises Concerns

by *Shopper* Staff Reporter Kitty Willis

The Tomahawk County Sheriff's Office today issued its first official statement on the Ozark Mountain Creeper phenomenon that is sweeping the tri-county area. Speaking with reporters yesterday afternoon, Sheriff's Deputy George Willis said, "We have no evidence of anything unusual happening up in them woods. There's plenty of animals, but we don't have any creepers, or prowlers, or howlers, or Wookiees, or anything like that. Anyone who says they saw some big, weird animal or whatever is probably remembering things wrong. Every animal looks bigger and scarier in the dark."

Despite the official position of denying growing public concern, the Sheriff's Office has investigated several reports of a creature some have described as something between "a big worm and a moose." So far no creatures have been captured, and miraculously, no citizens have been killed or eaten alive.

When pressed to account for his organization's stunning failure in protecting the public from an unknown menace, Deputy Willis grew defensive. "Darn it, Kitty, your mom didn't raise you to go throwing insults at family like that. You probably heard someone hunting off season or doing something they shouldn't be doing. You shouldn't be going up in there anyway. Besides, you never even saw it. It got cold, there was a shooting star, and you heard a noise and reckoned whatever made it must look like a moose worm. What the heck kind of sound does a worm make, anyway?"

The press responded with a chilling imitation of the sound many have heard over recent months, eliciting laughter instead of grave concern from the ALLEGED public servant. Officials have recommended that if encountering an unknown animal—

"Okay," Ms. Botfly interrupted. "You can stop there. The long and short of it is that people around here have been complaining about strange noises in the forest, unexplained lights in the sky, and a marked change in typical conditions. These are the classic signs of uncontacted parahuman activity. At the School, our Chaperone artificial intelligence system monitors all manner of news reports from across the nation, looking for just this sort of article. Once reports indicate someone might have run into a parahuman or one of their projects, we do further research.

"Last week satellite and drone observations determined the presence of a small antimatter reactor and some quantity of extraterrestrial genetic material within the target educational age range. We can therefore conclude that the source is at least one parahuman and that they should be attending school instead of goofing around in the woods."

"How do you know they're school-aged?" I asked. "Carbon dating or something?"

Ms. Botfly shook her head. "The angst readings are off the charts. It's a teenager for sure."

"Is that common?" someone asked. "For parahumans to live on their own, without knowing there are other parahumans out there? It seems like they would have gotten caught by now."

"It's not terribly common, but it happens," Ms. Botfly explained. "In certain places, we still come across small groups of parahumans who exist in relative isolation. Some are aware of the rest of us and prefer to go it on their own, and others think they and their family are alone in a world filled with normal humans. The reason they're here doesn't matter. The goal today is to contact the school-aged student and to bring them back with us to begin a proper education."

Warner raised a hand. "What if they don't want to come? Attending the School isn't mandatory."

"True, Warner," Ms. Botfly said. Warner was one of the few students whose name she could remember on a regular basis. "The issue is the technology. They can live out in the normal human world, and they can build antimatter reactors humans haven't invented yet. But we'd *prefer* they not do both at the same time. The last thing we need is for them to be discovered and cause a national panic. Whoever this is, we know from the fact that they're making headlines that they won't stay hidden long. If the wrong humans discovered even one parahuman, it could start a panic. They'd be using genetic tests to weed us out for research and interrogation in no time. That's why when we see someone doing interesting things and getting attention for it, we let them know they shouldn't do that and offer them a chance to learn how to *fly under the radar*, so to speak."

Something didn't add up for me. "So we're here to pick up one kid? And we've brought two dozen armed students just to say hi?"

"Yes!" Ms. Botfly exclaimed cheerfully. "The thing you need to remember is that many uncontacted parahuman families believe they are alone in the world and live in fear of outsiders. They assume they may be attacked or imprisoned if they are discovered, which isn't far from the truth. This one appears to be alone. Because of that, there's a pretty significant chance they will attempt to flee or murder us all when we approach. You should see what they did to my drone.

Horrifying. Speaking of which, did you all remember your weapons?"

Everyone nodded.

"And everyone brought boots suitable for hiking?"

Again everyone nodded.

"Fantastic! And everyone brought energy-dampened body armor capable of repelling a one-point-twenty-one gigawatt thermal inversion stream weapon?"

Nobody nodded.

"Hello! Earth to class?"

Hypatia raised her hand. "You just said to bring warm clothes. The email didn't say anything about body armor."

Ms. Botfly looked around to the other students before consulting her handheld. "Is that right? I could have sworn I told everyone that . . . No, here's the email. You're right, Hypatia. I said nothing about body armor. Hm. Well, you should be fine without it."

Several students raised their hands, apparently concerned that the possibility of being murdered was even a thing, but Ms. Botfly charged forward intrepidly. "Now, every indication of parahuman activity has been within five miles of this location, which gives us a relatively small area to search.

"I want you to divide yourselves into teams of three or four, spread out, and find the source of those readings. It might look like a research facility, or it might look like a tree stump with wires coming out of it. It could be a small house, a shack, or even an inhabited cave. There's no telling what we might run into, so the moment you spot any sign of habitation or development, please alert the class using the FieldTrip app. That will give the rest of us your location, so we can approach our rogue parahuman en masse, thus minimizing the possibility that they will put up a fight.

"Everyone got that? Great! Let's go!" she said, bravely unfolding a camp chair. A second later, she had produced a fat paperback novel and a narrow aluminum thermos and appeared to be quite comfortable.

Then she noticed that the rest of us were still hanging around.

She took a gulp from her steaming thermos and grimaced, waving us away like we were flies trying to land on her. "What are you all waiting for? Go on! I'll maintain base camp. Call if you have problems. Git!"

6

DOWN IN THE HOLLER

Winter in northern Arkansas isn't quite as bad as winter in North Dakota, so it wasn't as miserable as I'd expected. There wasn't even a lot of snow on the ground. To be honest, I wouldn't have minded a little more ice and snow. Wind almost cold enough to bite chapped my cheeks, and spongy, snowy earth grasped my feet with every step—it was nice to experience the real outdoors again.

For once, I wasn't the one complaining. Hypatia, an indoors cat if I've ever met one, was absolutely outraged that there weren't sidewalks or even gravel paths for us to follow. She and Dirac both complained about how "they" kept it so cold in the forest. "I should have brought Majorana's portable microclimate generator. That would straighten this right out. Why don't they keep it at least a little drier?"

"*They* don't set the temperature, you know—it's a climate thing," Warner pointed out.

Hypatia looked perturbed. "Of course the humans don't set the *temperature*—we're not idiots. But this is a state preserve. I just think it's a bit inconsiderate they haven't made an effort to . . ."

She trailed off as we crested a hill and found ourselves looking down on a humble wooden cabin. Situated at the foot of the hill, it was about thirty feet down a steep, densely wooded slope. Our viewpoint allowed us to see only the roof and a windowless back wall. A tin chimney no wider than a soda can extended from the roof and emitted a slender tendril of white smoke. The faint smell of baking bread hung in the air, making my stomach rumble.

It could have been anyone's cabin—a hunter's shack or even a full-time home—but something told me it belonged to our mysterious parahuman. Maybe it was the lack of a car or other means of normal transportation, or the absence of a road anywhere nearby. It could have been the weirdness of an almost perfectly tidy cabin in the backwoods connected to no power line or propane tanks. Or maybe it was the blinding shafts of vivid green light flooding out of the front and sides of the house at random intervals, like somewhere in that little shack a thermonuclear rave was going down.

"Get down!" I said on instinct. That was a bad move because Warner, Hypatia, and I all knew I meant "Take cover and conceal yourselves," while Dirac assumed it meant "Let's get down there!"

He took two steps forward, noticed we weren't following, and turned to see what the holdup was. Before he could say anything, he slipped on the muddy slope and tumbled backward down the steep incline. Instantly putting his parahuman grace and physical ability to work, he grasped a tree as he tumbled past and slipped around the trunk like a gymnast on the parallel bars. The young tree, rooted in shallow, rocky soil, struggled to support his weight and tilted precariously down and out from the slope, threatening to come loose altogether. In the end, it brought Dirac to a rest just a few inches above the top of the cabin. If he had hesitated even a millisecond, he might have crashed through the roof. Instead, he lowered himself soundlessly to the shingled surface and became our forward scout.

Warner, breathing a sigh of relief with Hypatia and me, booted up his FieldTrip app and pressed the SEND NOTIFICATION button. Hypatia used her computer to scan for heat and electromagnetic signature changes in the area that might indicate some kind of alarm or response had been triggered. A buzz in my pocket told me the other students had also gotten Warner's message and would be on their way shortly. We just had to stay still and quiet until the cavalry arrived.

Then a shrill squeal erupted from all four of our tablets.

"ATTENTION, CLASS, PLEASE CONVERGE ON THE POINT I'M TRANSMITTING TO YOUR UNITS IMMEDIATELY," Ms. Botfly's voice blared from each of our devices.

"USE STEALTH TO ENSURE OUR TARGET IS NOT ALERTED TO OUR PRESENCE AND AWAIT FURTHER INSTRUCTIONS!"

Shockingly, broadcasting our plans to be stealthy out loud to the whole valley did not help. Immediately, the green light went out. As the last remnants of Ms. Botfly's orders echoed back to us from an opposing hill somewhere, a door clattered open on the front of the cabin. It was on the side facing away from us, so I didn't get a look at whoever was there, but they were also unable to get a look at us. I motioned to Dirac that he should get down, and once I saw that he was laying flat and well hidden against the roof, I got behind a sturdy log that offered the best position and cover. Before long, Warner and Hypatia joined me, and we assessed the situation.

"How long before the others get here?" Hypatia asked in a whisper barely loud enough to carry above the slight breeze.

"The nearest group is about half a mile away, so it could be a while," Warner said, consulting his phone.

Hoping his phone was muted, I jabbed out a quick text to Dirac on my phone: *See anything? How many?*

A second later, he replied: *One young female, maybe thirteen, alone. Looking around the cabin. Stay low.*

"She's alone," Hypatia said. "What are we scared of again? Let's go talk to her instead of storming the house like the Marine Corps."

"She could still be a threat," Warner said. "She might think we're the NSA or something."

"Nonsense," Hypatia insisted. "I'll go alone and make it clear we mean her no harm."

"And then blast her if she gives us any trouble?" I asked.

"Um . . . no?" Hypatia said, probably wondering if we'd missed her point.

"Bad plan," Warner said. "She could take you hostage, and we wouldn't have the option to take her down, or she could kill you before we had a chance to intervene. I say we wait for the others, and let Ms. Botfly talk to her."

"Oh, THAT sounds like a great idea," I said.

"She's done it before," he said.

"Maybe that's why some have attacked. She almost killed me and the Basic Chemistry class yesterday."

Warner rolled his eyes. "It was *pretend*."

"*I* didn't know that."

"I'm just worried that if we have the whole class hanging around, someone will get trigger happy the moment she sneezes," Hypatia said. "They'll probably blast her if she blinks."

"That doesn't sound very neighborly," said a voice just over my shoulder.

"Ha-ha," I said, trying to sound like I hadn't noticed the voice was a new one. My disruptor was still in my pocket. *Why hadn't I bought a holster?* I moved my phone into the opposite hand and ran my newly freed hand up my leg casually, like I hadn't heard anything out of the ordinary.

"Darling," the voice said with a deep southern drawl. "You're going to a bad place right there. Why don't you keep looking that way and lift your hands up by your ears where I can see them? That way nobody loses any body parts for the time being. You, too, twinkle toes."

"Okay," I said, seeing Warner and Hypatia following suit from the corner of my eye.

My phone buzzed, and before I could react, it was snatched from my hand. Whoever she was, she moved *quickly*.

For just a moment, my agar bracelet twitched on my wrist, like it was dying to do some work. I could have used it to restrain her, but something told me she wasn't a threat right then.

"Someone named Dirac wants you to know he can't see me anymore. I'm just going to let him know he should sit tight. That all right?"

I heard the keyboard on my phone clicking as she typed out a response.

"Which one of us is 'twinkle toes'?" Warner asked.

"Shut up, Warner," Hypatia and I said in unison.

Once the message was sent, our new acquaintance stepped between Hypatia and me, and hunkered down in the grass in front of the three of us, her weapon (a ramshackle assortment of various electronic components mounted to a board) trained on me.

She was a girl with clear umber skin. Her eyes gleamed bright golden-green from between thick braids that parted like curtains around her face and ran down over her shoulders and back. Obviously tall, even crouching in the grass, she wore faded blue jeans and a flannel shirt over a plain white tank top. She smiled warmly, still smelling of the bread she'd probably been baking when we interrupted her. She tossed her head, sending a cascade of braids over her shoulder, improving her peripheral vision.

The wind shifted, and despite the whole firearm situation I was looking at, my mouth watered at the smell of baking bread in the air. "Tell me who sent you here. Do you work for the family?"

"No," Hypatia said cheerfully. Apparently her initial fear had passed. "The School sent us. And we're just students. We came with our class and teacher, Ms. Botfly."

"Thanks, sweetie. Keep going. How many are you? What kind of threat are we talking about here?"

Warner answered this one. "There are twenty-five of us, but not all of them will make it very soon. Maybe about half. And of those, only three or four are really worth anything in a fight."

Little more info than she needs to know, Warner. I threw him a glance, hoping he got the point. Was he trying to gain her trust?

"Your turn, darling," she said, fixing her big eyes on me. A second later her expression turned quizzical. "You're a tough cookie, aren't you? I'll ask you easy questions to start with. Did *they* tell you I was here?"

"Who?"

"That's a question, not an answer. How did you find me?"

"Newspaper articles, police reports of strange animal sounds, drone readings, and—"

"Yeah, I got it. That drone was pretty obvious. Should have known y'all were coming. Do you know my name?"

"No. All we know is that you're an uncontacted parahuman, and we're supposed to tell you about the School and invite you to attend."

"The School is one of the things I *do* know about. I don't remember a lot about it. That was another life, practically."

"Well, they want you there," I said. "It's pretty great, to be honest. Do you have family around here?"

"Well, my sisters ditched me and left me for dead. They'd probably kill me if they could find me."

"Oh," I said, not sure what to say. "Sorry about that?"

"That was months ago. I'm over it now. Getting back on my feet and all. Are you telling me the truth? You really think you want me at your school?"

"Yeah, I . . ." She looked directly into my eyes, leaning forward. The smell of fresh-baked bread flooded my senses. I could almost taste it. My mouth watered involuntarily. Was the house on fire? Did she have bread perfume?

"What's your deal?" she said, giving me the stink-eye. She turned suddenly to Warner, who was sitting patiently, waiting to be helpful. "Is she lying?"

Warner shook his head. "No, that's the deal. You can come to the School with us. That's why we're here. They want you."

"No, they don't," she said, standing and dusting herself off.

"You're all alone out here. What are you going to do?" I asked. "Hang out in the forest? Hide in your cabin until some normal people find you and call social services? You going to fight them off or run? How long can you run? Do you really want to?"

She leaned close and her smile faded. "I have no other choice, darling. Once the family disowns you, you either die quick or hide till someone kills you later. I figured out the basics. I can blend in, I can walk and talk, and I got a few more tricks up my sleeve. Don't I?"

I wasn't sure who she was asking, until both Hypatia and Warner turned their heads to me.

"If she's lying, she's dying," Hypatia said in a distinct southern drawl.

"And she ain't dying, 'cause she *ain't* lying," Warner said in the same sharp lilt.

"I'm sorry," I said, raising a hand. "What the—"

But I stopped asking because suddenly I understood.

It was the smell that told me, that and an almost imperceptible vibration in the air. As soon as she made eye contact with me, I caught it again, more intense than before. We were too far from the cabin to smell anything from there. It was *her*. I hadn't caught it, because they usually smelled awful.

I looked at the girl again—not like you usually look at someone, but *really* looked. It's hard to explain, but the trick is letting yourself observe what your eyes see, not what your brain *thinks* it is seeing. I'd learned the difference from Tabbabitha, having seen her in disguise on a couple of occasions and once in her true form.

It was instant—the girl wasn't there at all. But something else *was*—a writhing mass of tentacles of a color we don't have a name for swirled and twitched around a central body whose shape broke several rules of geometry but vaguely resembled one of those stout street-side mailboxes. The girl wasn't the same as the other Old Ones—but she was right, she was a member of the family.

"Oh," I said.

"*Yeah,*" she replied slowly.

I took a breath to compose myself and worked hard to see the girl again, instead of the being that made my brain hurt. "They disowned you? What is that? I thought the Old Ones had a hive mind, like they all shared the same memories and everything. How could they kick you out?"

"When they kicked me out, I was nothing more than a pile of goo and tentacles for a while. I almost died. No mouth to eat or drink with, no eyes to see where I was going. I was sure I was dead. That was till this lady came by and happened to sit and have a bite to eat right where I was dying, and because of that I was able to figure out how bodies work. I suppose I look like her when she was younger. After that, I hung around, eating leaves and drinking rainwater till some hunters came along . . ."

"You didn't . . . kill them, did you?"

"Nah, but I did make them teach me how to talk and some other basic stuff. I had them bring me here, too. Then I had them forget the whole thing after. I *was* pretty set here, till you all came poking around. I can make *them* forget they found me," she said, gesturing at Warner and Hypatia. "But it isn't working on you. Why is that?"

"I'm not a hundred percent sure," I said. "I've run into another Old One in the past, so I guess I'm used to what the disguise and suggestions feel like, maybe?"

"You mean," she said, holding out her arms, "you can see—"

"Yep, but I'm looking at the girl now," I said.

She smirked at my barely disguised shudder. "Maybe that will teach you not to look at things you don't want to see. How's my disguise, by the way?"

"Good," I said honestly. "Actually, it's impeccable. I'd heard only the most powerful Old Ones could pull off a really convincing human suit. You're a lot better at it than the other one I met. You don't look weird or misshapen or anything."

"It's probably because, since my memory was wiped, I've only ever known humans. They're all I have to go on. I blend in pretty well, huh?"

"Yeah," I said. "But people will question why a kid is hanging around alone out here. Can't you look like an adult?"

"Long story short, no. It's easier if we pick a look closer to our developmental age. Besides, most of blending in is acting natural, you know?" As if to illustrate the concept of acting natural, she pulled a cigarette from behind her ear, popped it into her mouth, and chewed it thoughtfully.

"Um," I said. "You're doing that wrong, I think."

"Am I? Those hunters tried to explain them, but they got a little confused at the end. I should have known I was doing it wrong. Why would anyone do that on *purpose*?"

"You can skip the tobacco stuff altogether. It's bad for you. Well, it's bad for humans. I don't know if—"

"Done. Listen, I don't mean you any harm, and I don't want any part in your school. I wouldn't hurt a fly, which is probably why my sisters kicked me out. I just want to be left alone, so I can go to work and live my own life."

I had to ask. "Go to work?"

"I just got a part-time job at the Dairy Shed in town. You've probably heard of them; they're a *Fortune* Ten Thousand company. I landed an entry-level frigid dairy formation and customer-service specialist position. I really don't want to pick up and start over somewhere else when my career is just taking off. Can you—"

"You're a what?"

"I make ice cream cones, and if someone wants a waffle cone or a mix-up, I get a manager and—"

With a flash of silver, Dirac dropped from a tree and landed softly on his feet, seeming to simply *appear* directly in front of the girl. He was training his ridiculously oversized blaster rifle directly on her heart.

"Drop the weapon. Now," Dirac said, his voice calm and very, very serious.

I waved at him. "She's okay, D. She's not a threat. It's a—"

"I was listening, Nikola. She's an Old One, and she got in your head. It only *seems* like she's harmless." To her, he said, "Now, drop that weapon, *or I drop you*." Behind the sights of his raised weapon his eyes were ice-cold stone.

"No," the girl said.

"Okay," Dirac said cheerfully. He handed her the blaster, sat down next to Warner, crossed his legs, and closed his eyes.

"God, that's creepy," I said. "You know it messes up people's brains if you do it too much, right?"

"Yeah, I always stop before they get damaged. Learned my lesson with those hunters. Now, where were we?"

"You were going to ask me nicely not to tell anyone you're here?"

"Good summary," she said. "You're sharper than a light bulb. So is that cool with you, or do I need to skip town?"

"It's fine," I said. "What's your name, by the way?"

"Well, the family took my old name, so I had to come up with a new one on my own."

"They took your name? How does that work?"

"We have a name people like you couldn't understand or pronounce. It's pretty difficult to explain."

"Okay, so what are you called now?"

"You can call me Darleeen."

"Darlene—that's nice," I said, wondering what it's like to have to pick out your own name.

"No," she said, shaking her head, sending her braids swirling around her. "You're spelling it wrong. It's Darleeen, not Darlene."

"That's what I said."

"You said it right, but you're spelling it wrong."

It took me a moment. "You're saying that when I pronounce your name out loud, I'm misspelling it in my head?"

86

"Yeah, I can tell. It's D-a-r-l-e-e-n." Then she did something I didn't see coming at all. She tossed Dirac's weapon, set down her own weapon, took out a felt-tipped pen, and wrote an email address on my arm. "I check my email pretty regularly at the library after work, so do me a favor and drop me a line if you hear of any trouble headed my way."

"Yeah, okay. Well, it was nice meeting—"

"Honey, you don't have to do that. No need to be polite. You want to do me a favor? Go back to your people and tell them I got away. These three will remember whatever story you make up like it really happened, so they won't rat you out."

"Can you let them remember it?" I asked. "I trust them, and I'll probably tell them anyway, so you'd be saving me the trouble."

She rolled her eyes. "Ah, fine. They'll remember . . . after a while. Fair enough?"

"Fair enough," I said.

With that, Hypatia, Warner, and Dirac stood up in unison and started trudging back toward our rendezvous point. I made to follow them but had to ask one thing.

"I've always wondered—you Old Ones can slide into other dimensions to move around or to protect yourselves from harm. Why didn't you just hide from us somewhere . . . else?"

Darleeen shook her head. "See, I was supposed to die when they abandoned me. But when I didn't, they started looking for me, hoping to finish the job. Anytime I do something that you might call unnatural, it makes noise. Not actual noise, but it's a kind of signal they can home in on. Think of it like trying to catch a lightning bug. Every time it blinks, you can get a little closer, even if it's basically invisible the rest of the time. If I were to cross over for even a second—it'd be like a lightning bug you could see from ten miles away."

"How do you know they're looking for you?"

"I'm not connected anymore, but I can still listen in, sort of."

"So wait," I said. "You just basically rewrote my friends' memories. Won't that lead the Old Ones here?"

"Nah, stuff like that isn't so obvious. I can get away with a little here and there, but I can't do it too often or do really big stuff, like crossing over or absorbing energy from people. That's also why I need the gig at the Dairy Shed. I have to eat, and soft-serve ice cream is the least gross thing you all make."

"How do you get to work from out here, since you can't slip into another dimension? Do you have a car stashed somewhere?" I asked.

"I look about thirteen. Would you give me a license?" she asked.

"Probably not. So how do you get around?" I said.

"I usually bum rides or hitchhike. That's where I use my abilities most often. I just make people want to help me out, when their natural instinct is to steer clear."

I was about to ask something else, but Darleeen interrupted me. "Speaking of getting around, your friends went over that ridge a couple minutes ago, and they might be a bit disoriented. You should probably keep an eye on them."

I might have argued, but we'd crossed a pretty healthy

stream not long before we'd found the cabin, and the mental image of Warner, Hypatia, and Dirac stepping zombielike into an ice-cold bath convinced me I should probably catch up.

Just as I went over the top of the hill myself, I turned back to wave at Darleeen one last time. I could be wrong, but I think I heard her say, "Don't come back, now."

7

PISTOL-PACKIN' PUPPY

A nd then," Warner said, his eyes growing wide, "she let the dog off his chain, and *he* had a gun, too."

Marie, the pretty red-haired girl Warner had been regaling with his tale, gasped in astonishment. "No! You must have been terrified."

He leaned back expansively in his seat, as if trying to take up as much room as possible. "Nah, I've been out there in the real world before. Once you've stared down death, not much can scare you anymore . . . not when you've looked into . . . *the void*."

I took a big, fizzy gulp of Ridgeline Condensate and bit my tongue. Whatever programming Darleeen had planted in my friends' heads seemed to involve them agreeing with one another no matter what, so as soon as one of them embellished the story even a little, the other three remembered the fib as completely accurate.

DeShawn Foster's head appeared over one of the tall bus seats in front of us, wearing a puzzled expression. "The dog had a gun? How does that even *work*?"

"It was in a harness over the dog's back, like a backpack. One pistol on each side," Hypatia chimed in. "Like a service animal *OF DEATH*!"

"How does he shoot it without opposable thumbs?" Marie asked, somehow able to apply scrutiny to the tale only when it wasn't being told by Warner.

"It was sound activated, so it would shoot whenever he barked," Dirac said. "That dog barks at you, and you're *dead*."

Marie seemed to believe this, but a fourteen-year-old Fluorine popped up over one of the other seats, and her face made it clear that she was *not* buying it. "Dogs bark all the time. You're telling us these people have this animal hanging around the house, and whenever he barks, whatever he happens to be looking at in that moment gets shot? That doesn't seem safe to me. And do they reload their dog every day, or just when they think harmless students might stop by? Why would you need a dog holding the guns anyway?"

The story was spinning out of control fast. "Look, maybe they have bulletproof pants, Fluorine. I don't know. We didn't even get a really good look at the dog. I mean, it *looked* like guns, but he might have been wearing something else. I didn't stick around to find out. We hid behind some brush, and we heard them get into a van and leave. Then we went looking for everyone else."

Fluorine rolled her eyes and was about to argue further when there was a flash, and a second later, she was about forty-seven years old. The change in her level of interest was obvious.

She gave me an understanding smile. "That's lovely, dear. I'm sure you were very brave."

-----*-----

Back at school, the four of us went straight for Fleming's Sub Shoppe to discuss what had happened. I picked the place because it was right by where the bus dropped us off, and because their blue cheese sub was my new favorite food that week. Over the course of the two hours we'd spent in the bus, Darleeen's brainwashing had faded noticeably. I had seen the realization that they had been lying about *something* creep over each of their faces in turn.

"So, there wasn't a gun dog?" Warner asked before taking a heroic bite from his hoagie.

"No," I said. "I'm pretty sure that was your own idea, but you believed it as soon as it was out of your mouth."

Hypatia was shaking her head. "No, I wasn't lying. I still remember it, clear as day. It just doesn't feel one hundred percent solid. Like—"

Warner and Dirac were nodding in agreement. I held up a hand to stop them. "Let's try something: on the count of three, I want each of you to say *what kind* of dog it was. One, two, three!"

Warner said, "German shepherd."

Dirac said, "Bloodhound."

And Hypatia said, "Chihuahua."

Ignoring the physics involved with a Chihuahua discharging firearms strapped to its body, I said, "Okay, does that seem odd to you, that all three of you remember a dog, but not the same dog?"

"A bit," Hypatia allowed.

"Makes sense, I guess. I think I'd remember being able to do a spinning backflip," Warner said, looking a bit disappointed.

I patted the back of his hand, feeling sorry for him. "I'm sure you could do a backflip if you really needed to and also had the physical ability."

He smiled, then lost the smile a bit. "Thanks?"

Dirac, on the other hand, was nowhere near a smile. "So, we ran into a genuine Old One, and you didn't fight her? You just let her mess with our brains?"

I shrugged. "Pretty much, yeah. She seemed okay to me. They kicked her out, after all, so she can't be *that* bad. Besides, you threatened her. It was self-defense."

"She seemed *okay* to you? That's the most preposterous—they're *all* bad, Nikola," he said, his anger rising. "They've killed people I love. Everyone here knows someone who died because of one of them. The only good Old One is a dead one."

"You can't claim to know them all because you've had bad experiences with some," I pointed out.

He rolled his eyes. "Leave it to a girl to get all softhearted around a deadly predator."

"Leave it to a boy," I said without thinking, "to get all softheaded the moment he gets his hands on a weapon. What the hell were you thinking? You were going to blast an interdimensional creature? You might as well have thrown a napkin at her."

"It's more than you were doing!"

"Yeah! Because I was talking to her, Dirac!" I could feel my cheeks getting hot. "They kicked her out. She said they took her memories and her name. She's not one of *them* anymore."

"What do you know?" he said. "You're just as brainwashed as the rest of us, except that *you* don't know you're lying. We need to take this to Ms. Botfly. She wasn't affected. She might be able to call in an airstrike or something. Maybe she can have the humans test a nuke there like they did to that hive in New Mexico way back."

For some reason, knowing Dirac thought I was lying or just being foolish really got to me. I could see Hypatia signaling to me that maybe we should leave or perhaps have a bathroom conference, or maybe she was trying to say I had something in my teeth—I hadn't memorized all the signals yet. I figured it didn't matter because Dirac was going to realize he was wrong and apologize at any moment.

I said, "I *told* you—she couldn't mess with my head for some reason. If she had tried to kill us, I could have stopped it."

"You'd have saved us?" he asked, his eyebrows climbing ever closer to his hairline. "Just like you saved *them* at the football field last fall?" He was pointing at Warner and Hypatia. "Oh, no wait, you blasted them yourself, and once they were out cold, you tried to run away, right?"

I was momentarily taken aback. It didn't surprise me that the other students had heard all about what happened when Warner, Hypatia, and I had confronted Tabbabitha, but I didn't expect I'd have to defend my actions.

"She was controlling them, Dirac. Knocking them out made her stop before she could make them hurt themselves or—"

He stood suddenly, which, given his superhuman grace and speed, was almost too quick to see. "Or you? A lot of people didn't like that you tried running when your friends were down. I told them you were probably trying to lead it away, but maybe you thought it would leave you alone if you gave it someone to eat. Seems like you don't think the Old Ones are all that bad."

I could feel my face reddening. A weird feeling washed over me, like a dizzy tingling behind my eyeballs inside my head. Did Warner and Hypatia think I'd abandoned them?

"Dirac, I *know* what their lies feel like. I'm not wrong; I'm certain of it. *Please* don't tell Botfly. I like her, but she's nuts. She might hurt innocent people trying to get an Old One. Remember when she booby-trapped her desk with a live grenade to catch whoever was stealing her gum?"

Dirac drew a deep breath, let it out slowly, and brushed

away the tendrils of air-light silver hair from where they had fallen in front of his face. He looked about to say something and changed his mind. Silently, he gathered his things and turned to the door.

"Dirac," I said. "I'm sorry. I should have told her not to mess with you guys. I'm . . . I'm just sorry, that's all."

He threw me a sardonic, angry smile and left without another word.

"That went well," Warner said around a half-chewed mouthful of hoagie.

"He won't tell anyone," Hypatia said. "He's just embarrassed that he was fooled so easily. It's not a wonderful feeling."

"Hey," I said, "you guys don't think I was . . ."

"No!" Warner and Hypatia said in unison.

"You did what was best," Hypatia said. "It's so creepy, remembering when Warner and I tried to . . . to . . ."

"When you tried to 'get me'? Yeah, I remember that," I said, suppressing a grin at how weird the memory was.

"You smile, but it isn't like being remote-controlled. I really wanted to do it. Like, I felt like I was unquestionably right to grab you because she asked. It's really unsettling to think about. I don't know how it doesn't bother you."

"It does bother me," I said. "But I know none of it was real. That helps."

Hypatia went on. "We'd *all* be dead if you hadn't shot us."

"You can't blame people for being skeptical. It *is* a pretty unlikely story," Warner said. "I looked it up and can't find a single account in history where someone has been as close

96

as you were to an Old One in their true form and come away from it without dying or suffering permanent psychological damage. If I hadn't been there myself, I'd be sure you were lying about something."

"Thanks," I said.

"Hey, don't blame me," he said. "We're all supposed to think like scientists here. Skepticism is our native language."

"Yeah, yeah," I said. "So is Dirac going to tell Ms. Botfly?"

"No, I'm sure he won't," Hypatia said.

"He might," Warner said. "He gets pretty headstrong sometimes."

"Try it," Hypatia said, flagging down a girl who had been on the way to refill her drink. "Tell Radia here what you saw today."

I threw Hypatia a *what are you doing?* glare, but she ignored me. "Go on. Try."

Radia tossed a sheet of deep violet hair over her shoulder and smiled at Warner, waiting.

He grinned a little goofily. "Well, the three of us went to the forest today for eCombat and ran right into a . . . I mean, we saw this . . . What's the word for . . . You know, when there's a . . ." He seemed to lose his train of thought. "What were we talking about?"

"See?" Hypatia said. She dismissed Radia with a flick of her hand, which is a common parahuman gesture that means *Go away now* but isn't counted as rude. I've never been comfortable with it myself.

"I couldn't tell her," Warner observed shrewdly.

"Nope. I tried earlier and couldn't. We don't believe it anymore, but whatever she did to stop us from telling was a little more permanent."

"Wait, *you* tried telling?" I asked.

"Yeah, it's the law, Nikola. Hiding the existence and location of an Old One is a serious infraction. I hope you decide to tell someone as soon as possible."

"Darleeen is *not* a threat, though. Why can't anyone understand that?" I said.

Hypatia sighed. "She didn't brainwash you, but that doesn't mean she told the truth. Dirac has a point there. It's not our call to make. The authorities might decide to leave her be, once they hear she's not part of the family anymore."

"Do you really believe that?" I asked.

Warner shook his head without looking up from his phone. "Of course she doesn't believe it. They'll probably imprison her somehow, which is the best move. Better safe than sorry. I bet they use one of those inverted gap fields like we invented to deal with Tabbabitha. We should have patented it."

"Well, I'm not telling if they're going to be so irrational about it," I said.

Warner pursed his lips. "That's why you *should* tell. If people find out you aided and abetted an Old One—imagine if she hurt someone, and it got out you knew she was out there. Even if you didn't get in trouble, people would always assume you might be on their side."

"I can't believe how suspicious you all are about this stuff. Is it common for people to change sides and help the Old

Ones?" I asked, remembering what Dr. Plaskington had said about willing traitors.

Hypatia's smile was sad but frank. "Sometimes they force cooperation with torture, blackmail, or capture like with your dad. Sometimes they brainwash people for extended periods of time if they don't need their minds or information. And sometimes they lure them over to their side with the promise of money or power. That's most common."

"You can't be serious," I said. "People willingly help them?"

Now it was Warner's turn for exasperation. "God, you're naive. Have you noticed how many of the kids here just happen to come from extremely wealthy families? Think that's coincidence?"

"I just figured their families have patents, or that parahumans are just naturally more successful," I said.

"That's part of it," he said. "But another part of it is that every wealthy family has their own turncoat somewhere in the family tree, and that money hangs around. You sell a secret to the Old Ones, and they'll make you fabulously rich. They'll make you so rich it carries over to your children, grandchildren, and so on. Even the best and most honorable parahuman families have a little blood money in the bank they don't like talking about."

I wondered for a moment if any of my dad's money had come from disreputable ancestors, but I remembered that, as humans, we didn't exactly have a long history of excellence in the family. I'd never met my grandparents, but according to Dad, they had been Christmas tree farmers.

"So where do the Old Ones get all *their* money?"

"You can make a lot of money when people will believe anything you say. They tend to be really successful in business, law, and politics, jobs where dishonesty can really pay off," Warner said.

"Politics? You don't mean—"

"God no," Hypatia said. "We've never had an Old One president or senator or anything like that. They like to hide in the shadows. Usually they work behind the scenes, acting as advisers, laundering illegal contributions, encouraging war and pollution, fighting to keep poor people poor and blaming each other about their troubles, and fostering discord in general. Anything that will slow down progress and encourage conflict. Conflict is good for business, after all."

"Wow," I said. "You know, people always talk about how bad the government is, but I never knew—"

Hypatia popped a candied oak leaf into her mouth and chewed thoughtfully. "It's not that bad. Most of the people running things are just regular, flawed people who are actually trying to do a good job and get it right sometimes. The Old Ones intentionally spread the message that they're all corrupt so they can turn people against one another. If you make people believe working together causes corruption, they're less likely to try it."

Without warning, I came to a decision on something I hadn't even known I was considering.

"I'll go tell Ms. Botfly about Darleeen tomorrow morning," I said. "People should know, and I don't want to break any laws."

Hypatia appeared to be momentarily taken aback but recovered quickly. "Oh. Well, it's what you *should* do." She stood up and threw her bag over her shoulder. "I really should stop by the synthetic animal sanctuary before going home. I need to return a hummingbird before they charge a late fee. Meet you at home?"

"Okay," I said, wondering what was behind the abrupt departure and why Hypatia had rented a hummingbird in the first place.

Warner pulled out his tablet and started playing a game, and I grabbed my own.

"You really going to tattle?" he asked without looking up.

"I said I'd tell someone, and I will. But I never specified *how many* people I'd tell." I typed out a quick email.

Darleeen:
   Really sorry about this, but I've just found out that it's a little bit illegal for me not to inform someone that we saw you, and a couple of the kids who were there are anxious about keeping it a secret. I'm going to spill the beans tomorrow morning, so you might want to make yourself scarce.

                              Sorry for the short notice,
                                        Nikola

I sent the message and took a deep breath. Something felt wrong. It took a minute to realize what was bothering me. I had been honest with Darleeen and I was coming clean to

Botfly, but it felt a bit like I was lying to Hypatia. I decided to tell her I'd warned Darleeen as soon as I saw her again. The moment I'd finished making that decision, my tablet buzzed to alert me of a new message.

The email was from the same disposable email address I'd sent the warning to a moment before.

> Dear Snitch,
>
> I already know. The blond Cabbage Patch Kid you had with you just emailed me. Thanks for the heads-up. :)
>
> Deee

"That deceptive little fink Hypatia went behind my back!" I told Warner.

Warner had his face planted firmly behind his screen and only chuckled in response.

8

EXISTENTIAL QUESTIONS AND THE SNAILS WHO ASK THEM

The next morning's conversation with Ms. Botfly went roughly like I'd expected, which is to say it went nothing like what I'd expected.

"So you're saying you met an Old One while you were out, and you forgot to mention it to anyone until just now."

"Yeah," I said, realizing I probably should have worked out my story before stopping in to see her. "Kind of slipped my mind."

Ms. Botfly was standing behind the counter of the Bookstore Bookstore, fondling a dangerous-looking slab of angular metal and exposed circuitry with polished spikes extending in random directions. To say it looked dangerous was an understatement. "You just remembered an encounter with an Old One, a terrifying interdimensional monstrosity, this morning," she reiterated.

"I did," I said, trying not to think about what it would feel like if I happened to touch one of the thin rivulets of electrical current that danced between the spikes on the device. "But there was so much going on yesterday. I bought that Eiffel Tower figurine at that gas station . . . It's all a blur, really."

"Very peculiar," Ms. Botfly said. "I've known since last night and haven't been able to think about anything else. I wondered how it came to be that some of my students encountered an Old One and didn't tell anyone, and I wondered if they had been compromised in some way. You know what we have to do if a student has been compromised mentally?"

She pressed a button on the device, and the spikes jittered back and forth and stabbed outward threateningly as a surge of electricity thrilled through its surface. Somewhere on the device a speaker beeped out a shrill, electronic version of "When the Saints Go Marching In."

"You torture them with that thing and leave them for dead in the middle of nowhere?"

Ms. Botfly only chuckled. "What? This thing? It's supposed to help with the bags under my eyes, but I just can't bring myself to stick my face into it. Why don't you try it first?"

She thrust it abruptly in the general direction of my face.

I dodged to the left just in time. "No, no, no! That's fine. I like bags under my eyes," I said. Somehow, knowing it was a beauty device made it seem *more* dangerous.

Ms. Botfly looked me over appraisingly. "They actually work on you. Makes you look diligent."

She placed the device gently on the counter, where it

hummed a Chopin tune and sparked ominously. "What I was saying is that if I found out that one of my students had been mentally compromised, I would have to turn them over to the authorities so *they* could torture you and leave you for dead somewhere. They don't pay me enough for that kind of work."

"Oh."

Ms. Botfly went on, making pointed eye contact. "Fortunately, nobody was compromised that I'm aware of. I bet *you didn't even speak to the Old One or encounter her directly.* You probably just saw some signs of habitation that you've only now realized must have been *signs* of an Old One. *Isn't that correct?*"

She was giving me an out. "Yeah, that's right!"

"Very good," she said. "Don't forget that's what happened, in case anyone asks. One of my old friends works in the Department of Defense. I'll have her arrange for a malfunctioning missile to accidentally blast that part of the forest to splinters."

"But she's not *one of them*," I said, dropping the ruse.

Ms. Botfly nodded and picked up the torture device again. "Doesn't matter. As a rule, we can't trust the Old Ones, no matter how trustworthy they are. Trustworthiness is one of their most useful disguises."

"How did you know we met her?" I asked.

"You know that monitoring app I had you all activate on your tablets? It's surprisingly good at *monitoring* things: audio, video, temperature, background radiation, police radio bands, heart rates . . . very comprehensive. Something about your story seemed just a little bit cockamamie, so I went through the recordings. You really have a way with the Old Ones, don't you?"

"Guess so," I said, feeling a bit ashamed that I hadn't remembered the FieldTrip app was listening the whole time.

"Honestly, I don't know what this orphan act she was putting on was supposed to be, but I'm not terribly interested. It may even be true. I've read accounts of an Old One being exintegrated and living. Although calling them *accounts* is a bit generous. *Legends* and *rumors* might be more accurate," Ms. Botfly said, typing something on her computer terminal.

As if an idea had occurred to her, Ms. Botfly stopped typing and looked at me over the rims of the pair of glasses that were on her nose at the moment. "Question: What did she smell like?"

"That was one of the weirdest things about her!" I said. "She didn't smell bad at all. She smelled like fresh-baked bread. It made me hungry, more than anything."

Ms. Botfly frowned appraisingly. "Whatever the case, she'll be vaporized about ninety minutes from now, and we can forget all this ever happened. Make sure not to talk to anyone about this. If word got out . . . that's more than enough time for someone to get away. Worse, if she happened to leave behind a tentacle or tooth she wasn't using, the cleanup crew would find biological traces of her and conclude the strike was a success. Do you understand?"

"Okay," I said, trying not to sound surprised. She was

giving me another out. I was starting to suspect Ms. Botfly might be a reasonable person.

"You said she was exsanguinated?" I asked.

"No, *exintegrated*. It's a word for when they banish one of their own from the hive mind. Exintegration is an unspeakable horror for them. It's like having their memories ripped out of their head, being forced back into infancy, and abandoned with no way to fend for themselves. Almost makes me feel sorry for her."

"What was the legend you heard?" I asked, hoping my sympathy for Darleeen wasn't too obvious.

"It's our oldest legend," Ms. Botfly said. "Long ago one such Old One is supposed to have become the first parahuman. But it's been a few hundred thousand years since then. Maybe there have been more. Who knows?"

I had more questions, but she flapped her hand at me dismissively. "You'd better get to class. Also, could you please try not to commit any felonies for a while?"

I grabbed my bag and headed for the door. "I'll do my best, but I can't promise anything."

"At the very least, don't get *caught*," she added. As I left, I could hear her muttering something about "rookie mistakes."

- - - - - * - - - - -

After I left the bookstore, I fired off a brief email to Darleeen suggesting she might leave an old tentacle at her cabin. (I just assumed that was an option for them.)

Then I had Comparative Reality Studies with Mr. Moravec, a class I'd never even heard about until just then. We worked with computer-simulated universes as big and as complex as the actual universe we live in. It was tons of fun at first. Everyone created their own big bang, and you got to wear virtual reality goggles and go zooming through whole simulated galaxies at triple-infinite speeds.

The goal was to locate simulated planets where simulated intelligent life had formed and built little simulated civilizations. We were then supposed to make observations about what their simulated cultures turned out like, and whether they ever figured out science, art, sitcoms, taxes, and other things like that.

I was overjoyed to be the first person in class to discover an intelligent species. They looked like snails with flexible bony shells that could turn transparent to soak up the sunlight if they got hungry.

They had just discovered radio a few generations before, so I tuned into their radio chatter and got to hear them wondering about their place in existence and debating whether there was other intelligent life in the universe. They even had radio programs about snail-things from the stars who came to attack them with laser beams and high-tech salt cannons.

That was a little weird, so I sped up time until they were building spaceships and supercomputers. On a whim, I looked up a research institution where a group of simulated snail-things were actually using their *own* supercomputer simulation to look at their own *even smaller* simulated universe.

"It looks so real!" one of the snail-things said in snail language that my computer translated for me. "Do they know they're not real?"

A bigger snail-thing slurped and burbled condescendingly at such a silly question. "Certainly not! Their universe is as real to them as ours is to us," it said.

The first snail-thing discolored its lower thoricatellum pensively. "Do you think it might be possible that we're simulated like they are?"

Well, that must have been the funniest thing any of the snail-things had ever heard because they all burbled and *glormph*ed with absolute glee at such a silly concept.

"Don't be absurd! I think we'd know if we were a simulation," said the bigger simulated snail-thing.

The first snail-thing agreed it was being silly. Then it looked up at the ceiling where I was looking down on it invisibly, almost like it was looking right at me.

Just then, I got a notification that it was time to delete our simulated universes and report our findings.

I took off the headset and looked up at the ceiling of the converted tanning salon that served as our classroom. Nothing was there.

"Do you have a question?" Mr. Moravec asked.

"Not one I want an answer to," I said.

My second class was Creative Nucleonics, where we were supposed to be making francium do unnatural things like not decay instantly, and where I was able to apologize to my temporary lab partner, Dirac, for not listening to his advice the day before. (Although I *did* fail to mention that both Hypatia and I had warned Darleeen.)

"I'm glad you came to your senses," he said. "I was sure she had gotten into your head. Every one of them is a potential threat, and pretending otherwise is just foolishness."

"Yeah, but everyone everywhere is a potential threat," I said, feeling strangely perturbed and a bit insulted at his unwillingness to trust my judgment over his own preformed opinion. "*Potential* is a pretty big word."

"I guess, but we're safer if we follow the rules, and the rule is that they're all a danger. You can't just go around making friends with rogue Old Ones. If one of them is being nice to you, it's because it wants something."

I was in the process of formulating a response when a tap on my shoulder interrupted my train of thought.

The person tapping my shoulder was Ultraviolet, Hypatia's archnemesis and general fancy-pants bad egg. She was holding a neutron stabilizer and looking very pleased with herself. Dirac and I had been sitting at the back of the room, so I'd assumed we could talk with some level of privacy. Unfortunately, I'd forgotten some of the supplies were stashed in a bin right behind us. How long had she been standing there?

Ultraviolet flipped her hair and smiled. She was a gorgeous human girl who was at the School mostly because her superrich parents had hired some parahuman doctor to perform quasilegal genetic engineering on her before she was born. I guess it's possible for very rich families to pay to ensure their children turn out genetically perfect. I wondered if being an awful person was a side effect of the treatment.

"What are you two talking about?" she wanted to know.

"Ah, you know . . . francium stuff . . . ," I said, once again proving that I'm not very good at lying under pressure.

Ultraviolet arched her perfectly formed brows. "Is that so? It sounded to *me* like Dirac was saying you shouldn't have made friends with an Old One. I heard you all came back from that field trip with a lot of pretty wild stories, but I couldn't have imagined you were covering for something like *that*."

At least I knew how long she'd been standing there. "Listen, Ultra, you probably misunderstood. We were just talking theory, you know? Sometimes when you eavesdrop on people, you hear things out of context. Right, Dirac?"

I looked to Dirac to back me up, but he only sighed grouchily and went back to the atom he'd been working on. *Thanks for the help, pal.*

"Oh, you're probably right. Context is so important," Ultraviolet said in a kind, understanding tone that told me I was in serious trouble. "I'm just a kid. We should probably let the authorities sort this out."

Crap, crap, crap. "Wait a sec, Ultra. It's not like—"

Ultraviolet raised her hand. "Mrs. Perey! Please come quick!"

Mrs. Perey, a very elderly parahuman with long dark hair and a serious unibrow shuffled over as quickly as she could.

"Yes? What is it?"

Ultraviolet shot me one last gleeful smile and put on a deeply concerned expression that almost could have fooled me. "I was just back here getting some supplies, and I overheard Dirac and Nikki talking—"

I'm just going to stop the story here for a moment. Under no circumstances possible in this world or in any possible universe is anyone ever permitted to call me Nikki.

Ultraviolet went on. "And what I heard, well, I'm *frightened*, Mrs. Perey. I think we may need to call the principal."

Mrs. Perey looked very tired and faintly irritated. "About what?"

"Dirac told Nikki that she shouldn't have . . . Dirac was saying it was bad that she . . . Oh! You know what I mean. At some point, possibly during the field trip yesterday she . . . What's the word for one of those . . ."

I'd heard the same kind of speech before when Warner tried telling Radia about our meeting with Darleeen. She'd put a bug in his brain that stopped him from telling anyone about it, but Darleeen hadn't been anywhere near Ultraviolet. Had Ultraviolet somehow caught the same mental block just by overhearing the information? Maybe Darleeen made it so if one of them slipped up and someone else overheard, the new person couldn't tell anyone, either.

Mrs. Perey was looking significantly more tired and irritated than she had a moment before. "Go on, girl. Spit it out. I haven't got all day. Someone's probably irradiating themselves as we speak."

Ultraviolet shook her head, trying to clear it. "I think Nikola made contact with . . . She found a . . ."

I wondered if the other part of Darleeen's mental tampering had transferred as well. Only one way to find out. "Ultraviolet, are you talking about how I found a deer turd in the forest and brought it back home to study it, but you mistook the turd for a chocolate muffin and ate the whole thing?"

"Yes! That's exactly what I remember! *I ate the whole thing!*" Ultraviolet said, overjoyed. She shot me a triumphant look that meant something like, *Ha, I sure showed you.*

A few students giggled but were immediately silenced by a truly radioactive glare from Mrs. Perey. "*Why* are you telling me this?" she asked angrily.

If Ultraviolet's reddening cheeks were any indication, she was starting to realize that loudly confessing to eating a deer turd in front of an entire class really wasn't *showing me* anything. Her face had fallen, and she looked deeply confused. . "I . . . I'm not sure."

Mrs. Perey shook her head with deep disapproval. "That makes two of us. I'm ordering you to report to Dr. Foster this moment for a full drug test."

"I'm not on drugs!" Ultraviolet cried.

"You could have fooled me. Go!"

Ultraviolet stormed angrily from the room without

so much as another look in my direction, and Mrs. Perey returned to the front of the class, where one of the students actually had succeeded in irradiating himself.

- - - - -✱- - - - -

After the best Creative Nucleonics class ever, I winged a test I hadn't studied for in Metabotany, discussed themes of alienation and internal conflict in Gerard the Excessively Moderate's choose-your-own-autobiography in Parahuman Literature, and learned about meromorphic functions in math class, which would have been drastically boring if Fluorine Plaskington hadn't started time-jumping like crazy in the middle of class, switching from baby to teenager to adult and back to infant over and over again. You know that game babies love where you hand them something like a pencil and they throw it and laugh maniacally until you go get it for them? Fluorine could play that game on her own.

A younger student dressed in a bright orange sari moved next to me and asked me about it. "Do you know what caused that? Was she breaking rules?" she asked as her eyes widened in delight. Something told me this one liked gossip.

"She doesn't remember, so nobody knows. Must have been a big one, though, because paradox effects usually aren't supposed to last more than a couple days and this has been going on for months."

Her deep brown eyes got even wider, and her dark hair kind of shivered a little bit. She was a parahuman, I realized. "If she was time-traveling when she lost her memory, why didn't she just stay in the past or the future? How would she know to return?"

"How should I know? Maybe she sent a cell phone or a sports almanac back in time and that caused it."

I saw that under the table she was scribbling furiously in a notebook without even glancing at it. She saw I'd noticed what she was doing and set it on the table. It was filled with equations, temporal math, bizarre conversion formulas, and theorems I'd never seen before.

She tilted her head curiously. "If she sent a cell phone or an inanimate object back in time, wouldn't that affect the person who found and used it?" she asked. "In Temporal Management class—"

"What's your name, kid?" I asked.

She offered a hand and I shook it. "Sophie Ramanujan, theoretical editor of the School's theoretical theoretical journal. We love unexplained phenomena like this. I've been thinking about her predicament for some time, and I just can't figure it out."

"What's to figure out?" I asked.

"Paradoxes affect people based on the Hot Potato principle. When a paradox is caused by sloppy time travel, the person closest to the event is the one affected. If she sent back an animal or object, the paradox would affect whoever found it, not her. If she sent a person, it would affect that person. If she sent herself, she would probably have gotten stuck because of her amnesia. The math only works if she was involved in sending someone who is immune to paradoxes—"

Just then I noticed the teacher had become aware that Sophie and I were chatting about something other than Riemann surfaces. I waved my hand rudely at Sophie in that familiar dismissive gesture parahumans used with one another when they were done interacting. As if by magic, she stopped talking and went back to her work.

- - - - - ✳ - - - - -

The first couple weeks after our field trip were the busiest I'd ever had while at the School. I'd meant to talk to Hypatia about Darleeen, but life, classes, and Hypatia's huge list of extracurricular activities kept getting in the way.

I finally decided to fill her in over dinner at Forbidden Planet one Friday evening when we were actually done with classes at a reasonable hour and neither of us had anything planned. I was mustering the courage to bring it up when Hypatia couldn't take it anymore.

"I can't take it anymore!" Hypatia cried, flapping her hands madly in the air. Her eyes took on the pale color they usually had when she was panicking overdramatically about something.

"Are you talking about that salt-and-vinegar lima bean smoothie?" I asked, pointing to the half-finished cylinder of pea-green goo sitting on the table before her. "Because I don't know how you've gotten as far as you have, to be honest."

"No, that's delicious. I've been *lying* to you, and I have to come clean!"

She stood, sat back down, and grasped the edge of the

table like she was afraid someone might try taking it by force, staring at me with frightening intensity through almost pure-white eyes. "Promise me you won't be mad!"

Fortunately, Forbidden Planet was mostly empty at the time. Most Friday nights the School projected a movie on the sky over the whole town, so it was a great time to get some work done or have a conversation if you weren't into the movie because everyone else was lying around on the lawn in the park.

"I promise I won't be mad!" I said, feeling a little relieved. If she'd been lying to me about something, she might not be as mad at me for not telling her about my email to Darleeen.

"But if you are mad, you have to promise to be honest and tell me!"

"Okay!" I said. "I promise that if I break my promise to not get mad, I'll be sure to tell you."

She shook her head, and her curls swung in a golden vortex around her head. "And if you do get mad and you don't tell me, will you promise not to secretly loathe me?"

I shook my head. "Hypatia, at that point, I'll have already broken the first two promises. I'm not sure you could trust my word in that situation. How about we make it a bet so if I end up hating you, I have to pay you twenty bucks? You'll at least get something for your trouble."

"How do I know you'd pay me?" she asked.

"Because I promise to pay you if I start breaking promises. You can't lose. Unless you lose the bet; then you lose. But if you win, you can't lose."

This seemed to perplex her a bit, and I was starting to wonder if it made sense myself.

"So what's the big lie?" I said.

She leaned forward. "I did something awful . . . treasonous, really," she said.

I leaned in close. "*This sounds good.* Are you spying for North Korea?"

"What? No. Nothing like that. Remember when I convinced you that you should report that Old One we found in the forest?"

"Darleeen. Yeah, I remember," I said. "Is this about how you tipped her off that she should clear out?"

"I couldn't stand knowing that if she wasn't really evil maybe we were doing an awful . . ." She trailed off and cocked her head to one side. "You knew?"

"Yeah, I was just about to tell you," I said. "I emailed her right after that, and when she wrote back, she said you'd warned her first."

Hypatia's voice went strangely flat, but her eyes took on a vivid shade of glowing red I was starting to know well. "I've been feeling guilty about that since we got back. I wrote you, like, four letters and then shredded them. I even tried to make an appointment to see the school therapist to talk about it, but he was booked out for eight months."

"Well, let me tell you, I'm not mad at all."

"Well, of course you aren't!" she said, her voice rising again. "Because you did the *same thing* and didn't bother to mention it. Were you ever going to tell me, or were you going to just let me wallow in my own guilt and self-recrimination?"

I leaned back a bit to keep myself out of spittle range. "Listen, Hypatia, I meant to tell you, but in my defense, I didn't bother to think about your feelings at all and pretty much forgot about the whole thing after I brought Botfly up to speed and my own part of the problem was solved. Plus I've been really busy."

"How is that *in your defense*? That's what I'm mad about. You should have told me."

"Well, since you're already angry, I suppose it's a good time to mention that you basically owe me twenty bucks, since I didn't get mad and resent you."

"Oh, *that's* rich!" she said.

"I'll make you a deal. How about you forgive me, and in exchange I'll apologize and agree to feel guilty about it for a while? I'll also let you keep the twenty bucks you owe me as a sign of good faith."

She thought it over for a second. "Yeah, okay," she grumbled.

"Great, I'm glad that's settled," I said. It really was a load off. Having Hypatia mad at you is no fun. Every time you see her, her eyes get all red and glowy, and she insists nothing is wrong. To make matters worse, she doesn't even drop little verbal barbs in conversation or slam doors like people are *supposed* to do when they aren't admitting they're angry about something. It's intolerable.

Fortunately, one of my favorite quirks about parahumans is that they can be bargained with emotionally, and once you strike a deal where they agree not to be angry with you, it's done completely.

Hypatia took a deep breath and blinked, and her eyes went from bright orange to a cool pastel violet. "You want to go home and clean the kitchen?"

As fun as that sounded, I had other ideas. "Or . . . I just got a new video game. We could play that. *It's banned in Australia.*"

"How about we meet halfway? Let's camp out on the sofa, turn on a reality TV show, and make catty comments all night?"

I have to admit, she found the perfect midpoint.

9

FREE CANDY!

One morning the following week I awoke to the most terrible realization I can imagine. I was up early. Worse, Hypatia was already out of the house, so there was nobody to blame but myself. One strong cup of tea later, I figured out what my mistake had been. I'd properly set my alarm for the last possible moment the night before but had missed the fact that my 8:00 AM Basic Macrosociology class had been canceled at some point the previous day. My next class, Precision Horology, wasn't scheduled until "noonish" according to the schedule forecast. Unable to get back to sleep, I showered, dressed, and did the unimaginable. I tried to think like a morning person.

Unpleasant discovery number one: morning television is nothing but boring infomercials; bad reruns; chipper, vapid newscasts with recipes I'd never make and reviews of movies

I'd never see; or grave, substantial newscasts with real information that I really didn't feel like burdening myself with that early. The newscaster had just begun describing some endangered condor the president had promised to "wipe off the face of the earth as soon as possible" when I switched it off.

Unpleasant discovery number two: there was nothing to eat in the kitchen, apart from a lot of gross, unappetizing stuff I'd ordered from the School's grocery delivery drone. Wheat germ chowder . . . what had I been thinking? In my defense, it sounded good at the time, and getting your groceries delivered by a drone is super cool.

The lack of edible food led me to unpleasant discovery number three: I'd have to leave the house. At least it was something to do.

A few minutes and one stomach-churning trip through our kitchen wormhole later, I was sitting in a dark corner booth at Forbidden Planet, working on a bowl of breakfast flakes with cranberries, a cup of parahuman-strength Turkish coffee steaming fragrantly on the table. I'd gone over my homework list, and to my surprise there was nothing needing to be done and no assignments I'd slacked my way through that needed doing properly. That is, except for my French homework. But I was starting to feel a good mood coming on; I didn't want to ruin it by diving into the only class I could never seem to get ahead in. Why did we have to study French anyway? There were loads of other, cooler languages, and everyone had a perfectly good real-time translator app on their tablets anyway. I just couldn't bring myself to do it.

Out of desperation, boredom, or both, I checked my email and discovered exactly what I was going to be doing that day.

The very first message in my inbox was a frantic communication from a *world-class scientist* who had found an amazing way of both improving my vitality and supercharging my investment portfolio. (That wasn't the important one.) The second was from Warner and looked like it had something to do with his beating my high score on one of the games at the Event Horizon. I skimmed the message without reading it completely and replied, *No, you didn't. Check again.* The other new message was from Darleeen.

There was a fleeting moment when I wondered whether someone was playing a joke on me. Spoofing an email address is such basic hacking that I cringe to even think of it as hacking, but when I opened the email and found a much longer message than before, I also detected a faint whiff of baking bread in the air. It was all the proof I needed.

I made a mental note to find out how that worked. Imagine the money you could make in advertising if you figured out how to send someone an email containing pizza coupons and the *smell* of a large pepperoni pizza.

Dear Meddler:

Remember how you ratted me out and then kindly gave me a warning that I should make myself scarce for a while? Well, right after that, one of your pals dropped a cruise missile on my cabin and turned all my worldly possessions into splinters and ashes.

Gotta tell you, I'm a little sore about that.

But that's not why I'm writing you. I'm writing because I need a ride. A couple days after you all obliterated the tiny patch of ground I once called home, one of my ex-sisters started sniffing around town, trying to pick up my scent. Maybe they didn't buy the whole "accidental military strike" gag. Whatever the reason, she's here, and she's going to find me before long if I don't skip town pronto.

Normally, I'd just stick out a thumb, temporarily brainwash some random schmuck, and have an easy ride wherever I wanted to go, but that's not an option anymore—she's too close. The moment I mess with someone's head, she'll know where I am and what I'm up to. I can't hitchhike or bum a ride honestly because regular humans have a kind of natural aversion to me if I'm not counteracting it somehow.

I tried to buy a bus ticket, but I only had twenty bucks on me when your friends nuked my home. Even better, my work uniform was incinerated, so I got fired from the Dairy Shed.

I'm a little sore about that, too.

So here's the deal. You and me had an agreement, and you broke it. You tried to do right by me afterward, and I appreciate that, but you still broke your promise. You owe me. What I need is a ride out of this town and to somewhere at least a few states away. Maybe West Virginia or South Carolina. I haven't decided yet. I'd have

you wire me some money, but the Shed was paying me
under the table because I don't have a bank account.
They don't hand out bank accounts, birth certificates,
Social Security numbers, and official identification to
nonhumans without parents, relatives, or any proof that
they actually exist. Imagine that.

    You seem like an honest girl who tries to do the right
thing. So prove it. I'll be hanging around the Tomahawk
County Public Library every day from open till close, and
I'll be in the dumpster behind the building after hours.
Figure out a way to get me out of this town, and I'll
consider us square.

Your innocent victim,

Darleeen

I had to hand it to her—the girl knew how to lay down a guilt trip. I read the email a second time and looked around Forbidden Planet's spacious dining room, like the chairs or decorations might give me a clue about what to do. No such luck.

The first thing was obvious; I did owe Darleeen a debt. Maybe Ms. Botfly would have called in a strike even if I hadn't ratted Darleeen out, but she had known for hours before I talked to her and had waited to request the "accident" until I was able to pass along a warning. Even if I managed to convince myself there was nothing I could have done, it didn't change the fact that I'd promised to keep her secret and hadn't. Plus I did feel a little sorry for her. I happen to know a thing or two about feeling alone in the world. I couldn't

imagine not having *anyone* to turn to when I needed a friend.
I had to help.

Sending money was out. I might have been able to send
money to someone else in her town if Darleeen had any close
friends, but it didn't sound like that was the case. I considered
overnighting a couple hundred dollars cash to the library, but
whoever received it might just hang on to the money, especially considering Darleeen's claim that people had a natural aversion to her. In the end, I decided there was probably
a simple solution I wasn't considering, and the best course of
action was to bounce the idea off someone else.

-----*-----

"There's not just some *simple solution* to this," Hypatia said
after I'd filled her in.

We'd met at Eastside Park, which was next to Big Roy's Big
Muffler Shop, which was where Hypatia's 9:00 AM Android
Health and Maintenance class was held.

"Come on, you've lived here longer than me. There must
be some way around the rules. Maybe a way to sneak out?"

She sighed and checked her watch for the third time. Her
class didn't start for fifteen minutes, but the whole time we'd
been talking, she had been inching toward the building. I
wondered if she knew she was doing it.

I went on. "It only took us a couple hours to get there the
other day. What if we—"

Hypatia held up a hand. "Just stop right there."

"What?"

"Look," she said, "I know you've heard it before, but getting back in once you've gone outside the gap is impossible without permission, and *nobody* is going to grant you permission for that."

"Well, *obviously*. But this is a school filled with teenagers. You're telling me nobody has *ever* come up with a way of sneaking out and back in again?"

"Yes, that's exactly what I'm telling you. The Old Ones have spent years working on ways to get in. You think some kid like you or me has come up with something *they* haven't tried?"

I had an idea. "What if we used the kitchen wormhole—"

Hypatia shook her head, frustrated. "Oh, you can stop that idea right there. Wormholes aren't *magic*. They're extremely trackable and traceable. That kitchen wormhole is only allowed because I spent about two months filing paperwork on it. I had to have it approved by a teacher who is a certified wormhole regulator, and every year I have to have it inspected for continuity and alignment. If we moved the exit three feet to the left, the Chaperone would alert the authorities in about two processor cycles. Never mind what would happen if we aimed it at *another state*. Even if we got out in the three milliseconds before anyone noticed what we'd done, they'd drop us in a containment chamber at the Wormport the moment we tried to get back in."

That was a new word. "Um . . . Wormport?"

Hypatia took another step toward her upcoming class. "Most students use wormholes to come and go, but the School can't allow open gateways that anyone can just walk through. The place would be crawling with Old Ones. Anyone traveling into the area via wormhole is automatically routed to the Wormport, which is on the outskirts of town, just outside the gap. You show up, and you're locked in this room that is outfitted with all kinds of instruments to detect if the people showing up are humans, parahumans, or something else, whether they have any contraband, and whether they've been brainwashed. They don't let you through the gap until they're sure you're okay."

"What happens if they detect an Old One?" I asked.

"The containment chambers are supposed to be able to kill one. I'm not sure how."

"Well, that sounds pleasant," I said.

"It's not, but you never lose your bags, you don't have to wait in line for a metal detector, and nobody pats you down or makes you take your shoes off. The snacks are reasonably priced, too."

I had about a dozen more questions, but by the time I decided which to ask first, Hypatia had sped off toward her next class, barely eight minutes early.

"That's the dumbest thing I've heard all day, and I just came from a lecture on using poetry in combat situations," Warner said without looking up from his tablet.

"Hear me out," I said. "What if we . . . I'm sorry, you said poetry in combat situations? How would you—"

"You wouldn't. The whole point was that it's completely useless unless the other side is also fighting with poetry. Still, I guess if I *had* to fight in a war, that's the one I'd sign up for."

I shook my head to clear away a question about the tactical viability of haiku vs. sonnets and steered myself back on track. "What about field trips? Are any classes going to that part of the country soon?"

"You could check with the Chaperone. She'd know."

"She'd tattle, duh."

Warner shook his head. "She has a confidentiality filter. If you ask her to keep something private, she has to, unless you're in danger or breaking a serious rule."

"I'm literally talking about breaking one of the most serious rules there is, for the purpose of putting myself in danger."

"Yeah . . . then you probably shouldn't ask her." Warner's tablet started blinking, and whatever game he was playing suddenly became more important than what we were talking about because he was out of commission after that.

I needed to find someone less ethical than my friends, someone who didn't mind breaking a few rules, someone who wouldn't rat me out. Fortunately, I knew just the person.

- - - - - ✳ - - - - -

I still had "about an hour or so" before Precision Horology when I sat down next to Fluorine outside the health center. She was about seventeen at the time and sporting a green

Mohawk. Dealing with teenager Fluorine was a lot easier than when she was a baby, who wouldn't understand anything, or a full-grown adult, who would understand even less.

"Paradox therapy," she said. "Since you're going to ask. Also, no, I'm not cured. They say my prognosis is good, once they figure out what caused it in the first place. And no, I don't remember what it was."

There was a tiny black box with little blinking lights protruding through a hole in the shoulder of her leather jacket. When she saw me studying it, she explained, "I made it to stabilize the time shifting so I only fluctuate between about five and thirty years old."

"Cool. But that's not what I wanted to know," I said. "I was thinking of—"

"Here's the deal, kid. I'll do your homework for you, but it'll cost you two hundred dollars. I can guarantee a perfect score on any assignment in any class up to and including graduate-level work, but I get eighty-five percent of the money if you patent anything. You keep the credit. If it's a doctoral thesis, you have to give me six hours' lead time, eight if you want more than three hundred pages."

"That's not what I want, either," I said.

This finally got her attention. As if in response, Fluorine seemed to glow and flicker briefly. The gadget attached to her shoulder clicked and buzzed faintly, and when she stopped glowing, she looked to be almost exactly my age. She was dressed in a plain black T-shirt and jeans and had a full head of straight dark hair.

She blinked and shook her head, not remembering why we were sitting together. Finally, she said, "Paradox therapy, since you're going to ask. Also, no, I'm not cured. They—"

I held up a hand. "Stop, we already did that. I'm thinking of doing something stupid."

A grin flashed across her face, and she quickly hid it. "How stupid?"

"*Really* stupid. Dangerous. Major rule breaking. Like—"

She held up a finger decorated with a fat electronic smart-ring that looked like it was displaying a series of explosions. "Hold on."

From a canvas backpack (which had been a spiked leather purse a moment before), she produced a piece of blue hard candy wrapped in cellophane.

"No thanks," I said, assuming she meant to offer it to me.

Ignoring me, Fluorine unwrapped the candy, set it gently on the concrete, stood, and stomped it ferociously under one pink rubber boot. Instantly, every neon sign on both sides of the street went out, and the streetlight above us turned itself on and politely died with a shiver of electricity. My own tablet flickered, sparked, and went black.

"Piezoelectric EMP," she said by way of explanation. "Everything will repair itself in about five minutes, so talk fast while the Chaperone can't listen in. I doubt she's monitoring us now, but if something goes wrong later, I don't want them finding anything weird in the logs."

I knew I'd come to the right person.

As I'd hoped, Fluorine had no qualms about helping me

provide aid and comfort to an alleged enemy. "She might be okay; she might not," was all she had to say on the topic.

According to Fluorine, my idea was indeed stupid, not to mention catastrophically dangerous. "I sure wish I could come with you," she added, "but this anti-time-shifter thing only works when it's linked up with the network here, so leaving town would give me away in a heartbeat."

I asked why it didn't die when she zapped every other electric device in the neighborhood, but she only replied with a stare that seemed to mean *How stupid do you think I am?* So I dropped it.

Fluorine consulted her handheld, which had also somehow survived the candy EMP, and gave me the details. "I've added a new unescorted field trip to the official school schedule. That should take care of getting you past the bees and through the gap both ways. It also takes care of transportation. The bus leaves tonight at midnight from the bus lot behind the maintenance building. It will get you home by 7:00 AM, assuming you don't stop at any tourist traps."

Then she handed me a compact spring-loaded umbrella. "You'll be leaving after curfew, so the Chaperone will be watching for anyone out and about. Stay under this at all times, and she won't notice you. Careful you don't hit that button till it's time to go; the charge only lasts about an hour."

I stowed the umbrella carefully in my bag and stood. "Listen, I really appreciate this. Just so you know, I'm a hundred percent certain it's the right thing to—"

Fluorine scoffed audibly. "If you get busted, I had nothing to do with any of it. If you don't, I want my umbrella back after. Oh, and you have to tell me all about it sometime, even if I'm too young to remember helping."

I had to ask. "Is that *really* true? Sometimes it seems like you remember more than you let on."

Fluorine eyed me studiously for a moment. "Okay, sometimes I ham it up a bit. Can you blame me? It's like a get-out-of-jail-free card that renews every ten minutes or so. But if I go from being ten to twenty, the thing that happened five minutes ago for you happened ten years ago for me, so it's not *totally* fake."

"So . . . do you really not remember what caused it in the first place?"

Fluorine produced a juice box from her bag, stabbed it with a straw, and took a long, puckering sip before responding. "Kind of . . . I remember it a little more every day."

"Oh yeah? What was it? Did you go back in time and hang out with Isaac Newton or something?"

Fluorine took another sip and tossed the box into a nearby trash can. She folded her arms, like she was hugging herself, and sighed. "Did you know my parents joined the Old Ones? Willingly?"

"Oh," I said, not knowing how to respond. "I . . . I hadn't heard that."

Fluorine was looking straight ahead like she was talking to the empty street. "It doesn't surprise me. People don't usually talk about that stuff. It's a bit rude, you know? Pointing out that so-and-so's folks are traitorous rats . . . Plus Granny keeps it pretty quiet."

I went to put a hand on her shoulder, but Fluorine flinched away like I'd threatened her with a hot poker.

"Granny says they were kidnapped, but . . . You know how sometimes the truth can be so awful that you'd rather force yourself to believe a lie? Rubidia saved the note they'd left. I found it in her room." Fluorine shook her head. "It was all the garbage people who join the Old Ones are always spewing. 'It's humans against parahumans. They're going to wipe us out. We parahumans should be in charge. Think of what we could accomplish . . .'"

"Jeez, Fluorine, I don't know what to—"

She shook her head and went on. "I was six, but I was smart enough to understand that my own parents had abandoned us to go be terrible people. That's a hard thing to have in your brain, you know? But . . . I still wanted them back."

I had no idea what this had to do with her being unstuck in time, but something told me I shouldn't ask. I just nodded.

Fluorine went on. "I liked to pretend that maybe Granny was right, and *maybe* the Old Ones would just let them go someday." She paused and stared straight up at the clouds. "Let me ask you a question. If someone told you they could bring your dad back, but first—"

The box on Fluorine's shoulder clicked and buzzed again. She glowed for the briefest moment, and then she was suddenly about five years old.

She seemed to notice me for the first time and gave me a wide grin. "Hi, Nikola! I'm waiting for my paradox therapy appointment. I'm not cured yet, but they say—"

- - - - - ✳ - - - - -

Hypatia brought her fist down on the table almost hard enough to convince me she meant what she was saying. "You can't go. That's all there is to it. I can't believe you'd even think of it. If anyone found out . . . well . . . I don't know what they'd do, but you'd *hate* it, I'm sure."

I leaned in close. Fluorine had given me a handful of her instant privacy candies, but there were still students all over the Event Horizon. "They *won't* know. It's simple. We can do it all in one night, and nobody will be the wiser. I already sent Darleeen an email to let her know we're coming."

"Well, I'm glad you have confidence, at least. They'll be sure to knock a few years off your solitary detention sentence since you're so—I'm sorry, did you just say '*we*'?"

I shrugged. "Well, I just assumed you'd want to ride along, in case there's any fretting or worrying to be done."

Warner snickered, his gaze locked on his game of solitaire.

Hypatia harrumphed. "I just think it's awfully presumptuous to assume."

"You don't have to come if you don't want to. Like you said—"

"*Well, of course I'm coming!* I just don't want you to go around assuming this is the kind of thing I like taking part in!"

"Noted," I said.

Out of curiosity, I stole a bite of Hypatia's sauerkraut fudge cookie. It was less horrible than I'd imagined. She studied my expression while I chewed.

"*FINE*," Warner said out of nowhere.

"What?" Hypatia asked with a start.

Warner peeked under a card that had been lying face-down. *He was cheating at solitaire. Who does that?* "I'll come, too. You don't need to keep hinting about it."

"Thanks, Warner!" I said, patting myself on the back for knowing the best way to get him to come was not to invite him. "We'll stop by your place at about 11:30. Don't talk about it at all after this, and don't tell Dirac. He wouldn't approve."

"Ya think?" Warner said.

10

WHAT'S IN A NAME?

Hypatia had quadruple-checked that her new superstring slicer was fully charged and re-re-recounted the three large bottles of water she was bringing. "Do you really think we'll need weapons?"

"I sure hope not, but if we run into any trouble, being able to make someone stop existing for a while and forgetting we were ever there could turn out to be useful," I said.

I had my own bag packed and was bringing my agar bracelet, Fluorine's umbrella, my school tablet, my gravitational disruptor, and my slightly used magnetic singularity.

"Don't bring that," Hypatia said as I was taking inventory. "If you set it off by accident, it would crush the bus with us inside."

"I doubt it even works. I've never charged it, and it looks

pretty banged up," I said, which reminded me to check the charge on my disruptor. It read:

85% CHARGE
PLEASE KILL RESPONSIBLY

Good enough, especially since the odds were slim I'd have to shoot anything.

"Leave your tablet, too," Hypatia said.

"Why?"

"Because it's a major security risk, that's why," Hypatia said. "You should never bring one unless the class requires one, and even then, you shouldn't use one unless you absolutely have to."

I figured she knew something I didn't, so I left it charging on my bedside table.

At the door, I pulled out the umbrella Fluorine had lent me and pressed the button. It sprang up and opened over us. From the edges dropped a delicate and nearly invisible reddish lace that hung down almost to our ankles. I felt it thrum faintly, and a light on the handle turned green.

I reached through a gap in the lace and opened the door, and Hypatia and I stepped out into the night.

"This is breaking curfew," she said.

I couldn't help but laugh. "Ohmigod, Hypatia, I had no idea we were going to violate curfew. Should we go back?"

She pinched my arm in retaliation. "You're turning me into a criminal, you know. I never would have dreamed of doing this kind of thing before you corrupted my innocent sensibilities."

"What are you talking about? You were practically begging to be corrupted."

She moved her head back and forth. It was dark, but I knew her *I'm not going to argue but I'm pretty sure you're wrong* gesture without having to see it.

"You sure the Chaperone can't hear us under this?" she asked a minute later as we approached Warner's house.

"That's what Fluorine said. It's a full-spectrum Faraday cage with active noise canceling, so it keeps any electromagnetic waves from getting out and dampens sound. From the outside, we're just a silent dark spot walking down the street."

"That's not suspicious at all," she said.

"To a machine, we're invisible."

At Warner's house, I tapped once on the door, nowhere near hard enough to kill an ant. Immediately, the door was thrown open in a completely unsneaky fashion to reveal Warner grinning mischievously at Hypatia and me.

"That thing is the coolest! You guys look like the ghost of a shadow," he said, still making no effort to be quiet.

"Quit your croaking, toad. Get under here," I hissed.

Thankfully, the umbrella was wide enough that the three of us could walk somewhat comfortably without having to crowd together like we were in a phone booth. "Dirac drank half a cup of maple syrup and salt before bed. That always makes him sleepy, so he was out cold. There's nothing to worry about."

"I was more worried about the Chaperone," I said.

"She doesn't listen unless you call her or she has a reason to, and even then she announces herself. Besides, she can't be everywhere at once."

"I'm not so sure about that," I said.

"It's true," Hypatia said. "I heard she can only be in nine or ten places simultaneously before her processor starts getting overloaded."

"Better safe than sorry," I said, not quite convinced.

When we were less than a block from the central square, Warner kicked a rock and sent it skittering down the sidewalk and onto Main Street, where it hit a smaller rock, jumped into the air, and ran right into the side of a lamppost, making a frighteningly loud *DING* sound.

"Ow!" he said when someone pinched him.

From where we had stopped, we could see half the square, including the front door of the City Hall administration building.

I didn't see anyone moving around, and it didn't seem like we'd tripped any alarms. I grabbed Warner's collar and whispered into his ear, "What if someone heard that?"

As if in response, a faint buzz seemed to sound from nowhere. The Chaperone's calling card. All three of us drew together against the closest building and froze.

When she spoke, her voice was quieter than I was used to hearing.

"You are out of your home after curfew. This is a violation

of several rules of conduct. You are ordered to return home immediately."

Before I could start pleading innocence and ignorance and asking for mercy, someone else spoke up.

"No, I'm not," a woman's voice said.

On the lawn in front of City Hall, a shadowy figure rose to her feet. She had been sitting on the lawn, leaning on the memorial that had been erected in memory of the sonic cannon, which had been a perfectly harmless device used to announce class changes until it tried killing me and several hundred other students.

I squinted and had almost given up trying to see who it was when a floodlight came on, highlighting the woman in the center of a column of illumination. The woman, perhaps twenty, was sporting a rather surly expression, which went nicely with her green Mohawk and multiple spiky ear piercings. It was Fluorine.

The Chaperone was unconvinced. "You are in violation of curfew. Return home immediately or you will be reported for insubordination."

Fluorine blew a disrespectful raspberry at the air. "What rule am I breaking, exactly?"

"You are in violation of rule 361.55, which states that—"

Immediately, Fluorine produced a tiny gadget from her pocket and pressed a button on it. The device emitted a shrill electronic chirping sound, and the Chaperone was silent.

Fluorine spoke clearly and quickly. "Enable administrator

override console, commit. Get enforcement action three-six-one-dot-five-five enabled equals false, commit. Drop table evening violation log, commit. Run script reboot with system check and full holographic defragmentation, commit."

In response, the Chaperone made a double *beep* sound I'd never heard before and was silent. Fluorine then gingerly picked up a soda she had been drinking and strolled away across the courthouse lawn.

The three of us were silent for a moment. Hypatia was first to speak. "Did she just . . ."

"Yeah," Warner said.

"Let's keep moving," I said. "Stick to the plan."

It was 11:57 when we finally reached the bus lot behind the maintenance building. The lot contained five or six full-sized yellow school buses and one half-sized bus, which was idling with its lights on. Hypatia, Warner, and I shared a collective sigh of relief and climbed aboard.

What I hadn't expected was the bus driver.

The moment we stepped on, the driver peered confusedly at our umbrella device, poking at it tentatively before waving a hand at it, like she was trying to clear out a puff of smoke. Without knowing what else to do, I pressed the button on the umbrella, and it folded itself back up in less than a second.

The bus driver stared at us. She looked tired and very, very unamused.

We stared back at her.

Time passed.

Finally she spoke. "This is an official school field trip? Exit and reentry both registered in the log and approved?"

" . . . yeah?" I said.

"And I get overtime for this?" she asked.

" . . . yeah," I said.

"In that case, stand there with your mouths hanging open for as long as you like. If you wanna go, you might wanna have a seat instead."

We sat.

The bus driver swung the door closed, and we were off.

"Tell your little friend I owe her one less favor," the bus driver said as we passed through the gap several minutes later.

-----*-----

After forty-five minutes, a road sign announced that we were entering Tomahawk County. It should have been a seven-hour drive. The weird thing was that it didn't feel like we were moving any faster than the rest of the traffic. In fact, other cars passed *us* on occasion.

"How is it so fast?" I asked.

"Spatial folding. The graduate engineering class just invented it a few years ago. It's still extremely top secret, so if the bus breaks down anywhere, it will probably self-destruct," Warner said, typing something on his tablet.

I made a mental note to stand as far as possible from the bus if one of the tires went flat. "How does it work?"

"It's like a wormhole but much less cool. The bus just skips forward a bit when there aren't any obstacles ahead. It's much faster when there's less traffic at night, and it doesn't give off the big obvious signatures wormhole travel does."

"Well, I don't think it's much less cool. You don't even notice it happening—hey!"

"What?" Warner said, looking distinctly guilty.

"How come you have your tablet? Hypatia said they were a risk."

"They are!" Hypatia piped up. "Warner, you should be ashamed! The School's firewall can't protect your computer from cyberattacks out here."

"Pleeease," he said. "The only risk is viruses and phishing attacks from the Old Ones, and those are blatantly obvious. If your email asks you to log in when you aren't expecting it to or someone instant-messages you and asks for money or your GPS coordinates, you just ignore it."

I turned my head to look at Hypatia, who wore the fervent expression of a true believer.

"I thought you said the Chaperone could track us with them."

"I didn't say that. I said it's a risk, and it *is* a risk. Good cybersecurity begins with good habits."

I rolled my eyes and leaned back in my seat, thankful that at least we were almost there.

The Tomahawk County Public Library was not what I expected. Instead of the quaint brick building I'd been envisioning in my head, it was a sleek modernist construction of angular stainless steel and huge sheets of glass, complete with a built-in coffee franchise I dearly wished was still open. The bus parked at the outer edge of the lot, and the driver threw the doors open with a grunt.

"You kids do what you gotta do. I'm going to go fill up, and we can be off. Shouldn't take me more than twenty or thirty minutes," she said.

"This thing folds space-time so it can travel at ridiculous speeds, but it still burns gas?" I asked.

"That's a stupid question," the driver said, marking the mileage down in a tattered notebook. "Runs on diesel."

"Oh," I said. "That should have been obvious."

She grunted in what I supposed was agreement.

Once the bus had left us, the library somehow seemed a lot less welcoming. In the dark, there was a certain foreboding presence about the place. I sniffed deeply, checking the air, but detected nothing apart from a faint whiff of roasted coffee beans. "She's supposed to be in a dumpster in back," I said.

There were three huge rusty dumpsters arranged in a line behind the library. One was green and filled with bags of paper, cleaning supply containers, and other recyclable materials. The second had a lot of food waste, soggy paper cups, and all the gently used coffee grounds you could ever wish for. The third held a small bed, alongside a comfy-looking wingback chair, complete with a tiny bookshelf and reading light. A framed needlepoint stuck to a spotlessly clean metal wall read, DUMPSTER SWEET DUMPSTER. There was a smell of potpourri in the air.

"This must be her dumpster," said Warner Goss, boy genius.

"She's not here," Hypatia said, almost as observantly.

"Maybe she's still inside," I said. We tried the back door to the library and found it locked. I made my quantum agar bracelet into a simple lock-picking kit, and we were inside about thirty seconds later.

Next to the door, a security terminal glowed feebly. Its screen read, DISABLED. "Either they don't turn on the alarm at night or she's in here somewhere," I said.

"It could be the Old One you said was looking for her," Warner said.

I gripped my gravitational disruptor in my pocket, confirming it was ready to go, not that it could do much more than slow down an Old One. Just in case, I switched it to 100 percent power, which was disabled for students who didn't know how to reprogram their weapons (aka not me).

Inside we were greeted by a smattering of security lights and cameras. There was a level of silence in the room most libraries can only dream of attaining during the day. Around us, tall stacks of books loomed in the darkness, creating dim canyons of near blackness between them. We crept slowly up an aisle lined with cookbooks and how-to guides for everything from building a deck to tending a garden. Despite the drab carpet silencing our footsteps, it felt like we were generating an amazing clatter by breathing and occasionally brushing against a protruding book.

At the end of the aisle, we found ourselves in an open space with electronic card catalogs, an information desk, a coin-operated copy machine, and several banks of computer terminals, all but one dark. A few additional security lights and the secondary glow of the parking lot coming in the front windows made the area slightly less foreboding. I rushed over to the lit computer.

On the screen was the email I'd sent earlier that day, which read, *We'll be there tonight. Sincerely, Meddler.*

"It's her, Darleeen," I whispered to my friends. Warner was about to offer what was probably another brilliant deduction when something clanged faintly behind us. The sound must have come from somewhere behind the circulation desk. We crept closer, and a wave of anxiety fell over me. Something didn't feel right. Every instinct told me I was walking into a trap, but what else was there to do?

The ventilation system kicked on, startling me when it tousled my hair and ruffled my shirt. A bit of movement caught my eye. One of the security cameras was swiveling to follow our progress across the lobby. No, that wasn't correct . . . Every security camera was following us. I spied at least three, and each of them was trained in our direction, panning slowly along with us. I should have been worried, but I wasn't. My instincts had stopped screaming at me, and I was feeling a lot better about things. I wondered if I should point the cameras out to Warner and Hypatia.

Nothing to worry about, I told myself calmly. *Just need to get through this.*

As if to confirm my fears were unfounded, I detected the first whiff of baked bread in the air.

Hugely relieved, I strolled straight to the door behind the circulation desk, pushed it open, and found Darleeen sitting at a tiny table in a brightly lit break room, chewing up the unpopped kernels from a discarded bag of microwave kettle corn. She was dressed in a library janitor's uniform with her thick braids bound together above her head with a large metal binder clip.

"Hey, you," she said with a final crunch as I entered. She saw me looking at the bag. "Best thing I could find. I don't want to make it too obvious that I've been hanging around, and they're pretty good about locking up the coffee shop."

"But not the back door?" I asked.

"They are, but it opens for those little access cards. Librarians are easy to pickpocket. It's the cardigans."

Warner and Hypatia sidled in behind me, surveying the tiny break room.

She grinned widely. "Twinkle Toes! Goldilocks! The gang's all here. Wish you'd brought Slim, too. He was kinda cute."

Warner grunted, displeased either at being called Twinkle Toes or at not being afforded the "cute" designation.

"Shut that door," Darleeen said. "We don't want the light getting out. The cops drive by every night about this time. Mind if I finish my dinner?"

"We brought a school bus, and the driver is getting gas now, so we have a few minutes," Warner said.

Hypatia closed the door and walked over to one of the vending machines. "You want anything?"

Darleeen frowned. "I already tried, but I can only get my arm about halfway to those cookies on the bottom row before the lid inside closes. Tried shaking it, too, but it's all in there pretty good. It's almost like they don't want people grabbing things out of there."

"Have you tried money?" Hypatia asked.

"Oh, yeah! Money works every time!" Darleeen said, leaping to her feet. "I spent my last buck a couple days ago, so I guess I got myself into a nonmonetary frame of mind."

While Hypatia and Darleeen chattered about which vending machine snacks had the best-tasting artificial preservatives, I took another look around the room. My sense of dread was creeping back, and my mind was racing. What was bugging me? There was this weird feeling of faint panic in the back of my mind that I just couldn't shake.

There's no rush. Relax.

I surveyed the room, looking for any detail that might be alarming me. Darleeen had a ratty green bag on the table next to a cup of coffee and a copy of *Country Living* magazine locked in a red plastic binder. Elsewhere in the room were a microwave, a few chairs, a soda vending machine alongside the snack machine Darleeen and Hypatia were browsing, a coffee maker that was turned on and about half empty, and a mini fridge decorated with a Post-it note that read *STOP STEALING MY FOOD* in all capital letters.

"What is it?" Warner asked me quietly.

"Huh?"

"Something's got you worried. What's up?"

"Don't know," I said. "Just feeling wary. How long do you think the bus will be?"

"Not sure. Couple more minutes," he said. "You sure you're okay?"

There was a moment where I again considered mentioning the cameras in the lobby, but that hadn't been a big deal or anything.

He doesn't want to hear about that.

"Yeah," I said.

Out of curiosity and general restlessness, I pulled open the fridge and discovered a single Tupperware container filled to the brim with something furry and blue, covered lightly with plastic wrap and stinking to high heaven. Warner's face twisted in disgust, and Hypatia coughed faintly.

Darleeen stopped discussing the chemical composition of chocolate mini cookies for a moment. "That moldy thing was going to be my dinner tomorrow if you all hadn't turned up. Oh! Buy those! Captain's Wafers! Sounds important!"

Relief washed over me. I'd been picking up the smell! Of course something stinky would trigger sudden anxiety when I was worried about running into the Old Ones.

Simple, silly paranoia. Perfectly normal.

When I shut the door, I saw someone else had written on the Post-it, but in much smaller writing. It said, *Sorry. A girl's gotta eat.*

Finally, I was able to think clearly again. Darleeen had retrieved her Captain's Wafers and was sitting at the table, munching happily and offering up detailed commentary on the subtler points of the crackers' flavor profile between bites.

I wondered what we should do next. I didn't want to spend one unnecessary minute in Tomahawk County.

My friends should go outside and wait for the bus.

"Hypatia, you and Warner go back out the way we came and wait for the bus. Tap on the front window when it gets here," I said.

Hypatia stood, but Warner didn't move. "We'll hear it in here for sure," he said.

He was right, but I had to *get them out, have them wait.* "You'll see it coming before we hear it. We don't have any time to waste. We'll be out as soon as she's done eating. Go on!" I gave him a light shove in the right direction, which seemed to get the message across.

After they'd left, I sat down with Darleeen, shoving my hands into my pockets.

"Something you wanna talk about?" she asked.

"Huh?"

She dangled her half-empty packet of crackers between her thumb and forefinger. "Crackers are portable. We could go with them, but you want to stick around. What's eating you?"

"There's trouble coming," I said on a whim. I hadn't really meant it, but I was suddenly sure I was correct.

"Yeah?" Darleeen asked, not looking all that concerned.

"Do you know which of your former sisters is hunting

you?" I asked, pulling my gravitational disruptor out of my pocket and peering at the door. It was open a sliver, but I couldn't see anything moving in the lobby. Darleeen and I were alone.

I realized again that something was wrong, but it was *nothing to worry about.* I just needed to *relax, let go, and say what comes naturally.*

"I told you," she said with a shrug, "I don't remember my own name, let alone any of theirs. Probably not one of the big dogs. Whoever it is, she's close. You're right about that. She's been zeroing in on me for days. I'll feel about a million times better when I'm a few hundred miles away and can use some of my old tricks again. Talking to people is such an inefficient way of getting what I want. Such a pain."

Hearing one of the Old Ones had been closing in didn't really surprise me, but *it's always good to be prepared.* I opened the settings menu on my disruptor and cranked it up to 200 percent power. I needed to *be ready for anything.* The disruptor beeped angrily and displayed a message that said, DO NOT FIRE. POWER CONVERSION OVERLOAD WILL CAUSE FATAL CORE RUPTURE. DO NOT FIRE.

Nothing to worry about. Maybe a bomb will come in handy.

"What's it matter, anyway?" Darleeen asked.

"Doesn't matter at all," I said, feeling calm again as I laid the disruptor on my lap, but without taking my finger off the trigger.

Her dark eyes narrowed slightly. "Seems like it matters.

You asked which of my former sisters is after me, and now you've got your little ray gun ready to go. I'm not bamboozling you, if that's what you're worried about."

"I know that," I said truthfully. I was sure she meant me no harm.

Darleeen pursed her lips. "You know something I don't, Nikola?"

I was about to say no when I realized I did know something important. Something she wanted to know, but I wasn't sure what it was. I realized I just needed to *relax, and let the words come on their own.*

"*Yeah,*" I said.

She leaned back in her chair and slipped a cracker into her mouth whole, chomping down on it. "Well, go on. No need for theatrics."

All the pieces were fitting together. I finally knew what I was trying to remember. As soon as I relaxed, the information just came to me. "*I know who's hunting you. Do you remember Jakki?*"

Darleeen's cool exterior disappeared in a heartbeat. She sat up straight; her wide eyes bloomed wider. She was scared, and it was funny, in a way. I had to suppress a giggle.

Darleeen looked around the break room as I had done a few minutes before. "Jakki—how do you know that name?"

"I just know," I said. "It's hard to explain. *You remember her now, don't you? Queen Mother, you called her. You swore fealty. Eternal loyalty. You must remember.*"

I must have had a frog in my throat because my voice

suddenly sounded older, more melodic and confident than my normal speaking tone. It actually sounded a little better, I thought.

Darleeen was really scared now, and I couldn't help but giggle a little. When I laughed, she shot to her feet, the chair sliding back into the wall. Once again I saw her true form hiding behind her earthly appearance. She was going to evaporate, to escape into the dark places. *She had no business going there. She was not welcome there anymore!* Just the thought of it infuriated me. I gripped the disruptor and laid it on the table, carefully so as not to accidentally press the trigger . . . *not yet.*

"Stay where you are. Sit. This toy is set to overload. It will take out the whole building. You're nowhere near strong enough to survive it."

Darleeen did not sit, but she grew more solid. "Nikola, listen. She's gotten in your head. She's powerful. She can do it from almost anywhere. As soon as you said her name . . . Oh god, I'd never have asked for help if I'd known she—"

Darleeen would have protected me? *A likely story. A lie!*

"Oh, will you shut up, please?" I said. *"You can't hold your tongue, can you? That has always been your problem. You can't just shut up and listen."*

"Nikola, you're strong. I felt it before. You're different. Push her out. You can—"

"Do you want to know your name? Your True Name?" I asked.

That shut her up.

"I can tell you, if you like. At least you'll remember yourself at the end. Consider it a parting gift."

"No!" she said, terrified. "Jakki! No! The girl didn't do anything. You'll break her mind if you do it. They can't handle—"

I didn't know why she was calling me Jakki, but I didn't hate the name. Ever meet someone that looks like a Biff but their actual name is Skyler? I wanted to think about it more, but Darleeen was still going on and on about me not hurting someone . . . or someone not hurting me. It was hard to understand—kind of like she was talking about both at the same time.

Then I remembered. *She was talking about that girl's mind.* Worried I was going to ruin it. I had to laugh again. *"Darling, seriously. What is the point of preserving something disposable?"* I asked her. *"It will all be over for both of you soon. Does it matter if I make a mess in the process? Not one bit."*

Well, right away Darleeen was blubbering and pleading for mercy and *yadda yadda yadda*, offering me her life in exchange, as if her life had worth. *Offering me my own property as a trade. Insulting. Best to just to get it over with and end them both.*

So I told Darleeen her name.

The feeling was different from inside a human. The normally straightforward, subtle transfer was disgustingly . . . biological. Revolting.

Darleeen had been right; just sharing her name tore the

girl's mind apart. I had to use it all, force it through a door far too narrow to admit it without breaking. But it went, and Darleeen received it, not that she could have refused. Her face quivered and contorted as it began to take hold. I could see her memories returning—it wouldn't take long. I waited. Once she was restored to her full self, I knew I could finally end her and her troublesome name.

"What are you doing?" the boy asked. "What's wrong with Darleeen?"

When had he come back? I didn't look up.

Darleeen tried to send him away, stupid thing, but she was far too weak to do anything more than gibber.

The boy was touching my shoulder. My hand tensed on the weapon. Not yet, it hadn't taken hold completely yet. The name had to die with her, or I'd have to deal with it again and again. Why hadn't I just killed her outright in the first place?

"Leave!" I commanded him. "I'm sparing you for the moment. Get out!"

"Nikola," the boy said. "Think about why you're doing this. Really think about it for a second."

What a stupid question. "I'm cleaning up a mess. Taking out the garbage."

"What mess?" he wanted to know. "Why?"

The last thing I needed was a distraction. "Get out of here, or you'll be killed, too. Go on, go wait for the bus like I said."

He didn't leave. The door opened again, and the other girl was in the room. "What's going on, Nikola?"

"It isn't Nikola," the boy said.

I didn't like that. "*Yes, I am.* Get out of here. You'll die, too."

"Nobody is going to die, Nikola," the girl said, putting her hand on my other shoulder. "Let go of that."

Enough. I swept into their minds. It was like stepping through a curtain, much quicker and easier than this one had been. Familiar and uncomplicated like minds should be. I tried to make them stop touching me and leave—

But I didn't want that. I didn't want to be in their minds. I wanted to leave my friends alone. *I was back and they were still touching me. Their hands were warm and nice and awful. I tried to make them leave again, but I couldn't get out.*

No. Stay here.

I tore myself from her mind, ripped myself out. The boy could pull the trigger just as well once this one was ruined. He slid aside, and I was in. I reached for the weapon, but I was already holding it, because I was back. The boy stumbled but did not fall. "Let me out!"

No. Stay here.

I reached for the other girl—the blond one—but I was stopped. Held. Restrained. I tried to flee, to go back to my own form. I was close. I could come back quickly and deal with them in person.

No. Stay here. I won't let you.

"Take my disruptor, quick!" I said, *without my permission.*

The boy reached for it. I squeezed the trigger, but my hand wouldn't move. What is this? I can't move my own

157

finger? I squeezed and was stopped again. I still held the weapon.

You don't want to do that. You're here.

The little insolent wretch. "I'll leave and you'll die!"

You can't leave. I'll hold you, and you'll die with us.

"LIAR!"

Try.

I fled again with all my strength, pulled away. I was out . . . in the dark . . . free. But a force, a great force brought me slamming back. The body shuddered in the chair like it had been thrown down. I was trapped.

See?

I screamed, my voice cracked, and what came out was only a whisper. "Let me go! Let me go! Stop it! It hurts! Make them stop touching me! Stop it!"

I'll let you go, but you have to let me talk first.

"No." *My voice was barely a whisper. I was hardly making a sound.* "I won't let you."

Actually. You don't have to let me talk.

"I can do it myself," I said in my actual voice, feeling like someone who had just come up for air after too long underwater.

Hypatia stuck her face in front of mine. "Nikola! What is happening? Are you back?"

The Old One was hurting me, trying anything she could to get out. My head twitched hard at Hypatia and delivered both of us a solid head-butt. Really, it was more of a face-butt.

"Ow!" she said.

"Sorry. She's still in here."

Then Warner's head was in front of my face. I head-butted him, too, but managed to hold it back, so it didn't hurt that badly. Everything else was blurry. She was using my eyes; I didn't have them completely.

"Can you . . . kick her out?"

"She *wants* out, but I'm holding her," I said. "If I let her go now, she'll come straight here in person and catch us. She's too close. Is the bus back?"

Hypatia glanced over my shoulder out the door. "Yeah, but what do we—"

"I'm bringing her with us."

"WHAT?" they both asked.

"Blindfold me. Don't talk about where we're going. She's seeing and hearing through me, I think. Once we're far enough away, I'll let her go, and she won't be able to find us."

NO! a voice screamed in rage inside me. It was almost strong enough to come out of my own mouth . . . almost.

"Can it. You're a guest, so behave like you have some manners," I said out loud with some difficulty. Everything I said felt like talking after you've just swallowed a giant drink of water.

Jakki didn't like that. She fought me, but the more I talked and thought, the more I realized that I was the one calling the shots.

"Was that you talking to her?" Hypatia asked.

"Yeah. Let's hurry this up. Having her in here is awful. Is Darleeen okay?"

Hypatia checked her out. "She looks like she's sleeping. What happened?"

"Metaphysical stuff. Come on, blindfold me. Tell the bus driver where we're going, tell her not to say anything, and let's get out of here. Warner, can you carry Darleeen?"

He couldn't carry her, but he was able to drag her pretty well. Hypatia found a stack of paper bags under the checkout desk and slipped one over my head. Jakki was flooding my mind with an endless string of violent thoughts and urges. To my credit, I only socked Hypatia in the gut once when I wasn't paying attention because I was trying to climb the stairs onto the bus.

I want you to take a moment to imagine something. Imagine you're a bus driver and you're making a little extra overtime on the sly for a slightly shady acquaintance. You drop three completely healthy-looking kids off at a closed library in the middle of the night, and when you come back thirty minutes later, they come hobbling out the front door. One has a badly swollen eye that looks like it's taken a serious blow. Another has a lighter injury on his cheek. One is wearing a big brown paper bag on her head and is twitching uncontrollably to the point where she needs help walking, and they're dragging along a third girl you've never seen before and who is clearly unconscious. What do you say?

What our bus driver said was this: "That's why I get all *my* books on the Internet."

------*-----

The bus had been on the road for an hour when I turned Jakki loose. I'd gotten more used to the feeling of having a hostile personality inside my head, but that's not the same as being comfortable with it. Imagine taking a drink of spoiled milk and having to hold it in your mouth without swallowing it for an hour.

At the very least, she eventually gave up on trying to make me hurt myself and others and focused her energy on simply causing me physical pain, promising to get her revenge in various creative ways and insulting certain aspects of my personality and appearance.

When I let her go, she was in such a hurry to get back to herself that she didn't bother to harass Warner or Hypatia at all. To be honest, I'm not sure she could have messed with them if she'd wanted to. Being that far from her own body seemed to weaken her. Letting her go was less like releasing a balloon and more like releasing one end of a stretched rubber band.

A minute later, feeling about a million times better, I took the bag off my head and spent some time studying the scenery. According to the signs, we were just leaving Atlanta.

Shortly after that, Darleeen woke up in a dead panic, threw me on the floor beneath the seats, and demanded I leave myself alone. We were able to convince her it was really me, but not before I'd gotten a good lump on the back of my head.

Warner, Hypatia, and Darleeen all had questions about

how I had captured Jakki in my head and what it had been like. I answered them as best I could, but there wasn't really a good way of explaining it.

"It felt like remembering something important, like when you go to the store and repeat what you need to buy over and over in your head, because if I stopped remembering to remember she was in there, she could get away or start controlling me," I said.

What I didn't tell them was that as awful as it had been, it also felt good. I was able to hurt an Old One, one of the monsters that had kidnapped my dad. At one point I even tried to get into Jakki's thoughts to find out where he was, but all I got before she blocked me out was an image, somewhere dark and muddy underground. I already knew that much.

- - - - - ✳ - - - - -

Darleeen's new home, which I had rented for the remainder of the off-season from the North Carolina State Parks' website before we left school, was a little cabin nestled in a clearing of a national forest that was almost completely unoccupied during the winter and spring. I didn't think my dad would mind the charge on the credit card, since it was going to a good cause. It was simple, but there was a working refrigerator and a microwave. Since it had electricity, she wouldn't have to make her own generator, which was what had caused all the problems in the first place.

The cabin seemed a bit spartan to me, but Darleeen was over the moon about it, going on and on about how she might save up for a chair to put by the bed once she found a job. Before we left town, we had the bus driver take us by a twenty-four-hour discount store, where, over her protests, I bought her some basic supplies as well as a poster of a well-known TV family I spotted her admiring repeatedly for some reason.

Once she was all set up and it was time for us to go, Darleeen called me aside. "Listen, I meant what I said back there. I never would have called you all if I'd known—"

"I know. It's fine," I said. "All's well that ends well, right?"

She wrapped her slightly too long arms around me and gave me an actual hug. "Keep telling yourself that. I owe you one now, so give me a call if you ever need anything. You got my number."

She winked when she said that.

11

DRIVEN TO DISTRACTION

D id you see," Hypatia said between sips of her smoothie, "that we have another field trip tomorrow? To the *mall!*"

"Oh god. Can't I get out of it somehow?" I asked. "It feels like we had to go to Arkansas and North Carolina just yesterday, and next week I have that Metabotany final. I'm supposed to be able to cold-sequence a viable new species from scratch. I just want a quiet Saturday at home to slack off, do a little studying, and kill a few aliens. I'll go to the next one."

Hypatia's mouth dropped open. "How could you?!"

"What? Oh!" I said. I hadn't suspected she might take it personally. "In video games, is what I mean. Bad aliens. Like the Old Ones, not friendly, peaceable aliens like you."

"Heh, you didn't bother me," she said, but I could tell she was underplaying it a bit. "Although, I should point out that for a civilized race, you humans are awfully violent. Have you ever noticed that pretty much all human entertainment centers on either killing or mating?"

"I hardly think that's true," I said.

"Try to come up with an exception," she said, tenting her fingers.

I said the first thing that popped into my head. "Okay. Snow White. Girl goes into the forest and makes friends with dwarfs."

"Because a witch tried *killing* her. Not to mention that she nearly succeeds with poison, but Snow White pretends to be dead, until a sufficiently attractive person performs a human *mating* ritual that persuades her to quit faking it. Is that the Snow White you're referring to?"

"Snow White was *not* a hypochondriac. That kiss *cured* her."

Hypatia rolled her eyes. "So human kisses allegedly have medicinal properties when they're being administered by someone who is wealthier or better looking than average?"

"It wasn't a medicinal kiss; it was a magical kiss," I said.

"Magic is either unexplained science or trickery. The whole magic-kiss-from-a-handsome-prince thing sounds like a myth perpetuated by wealthy, good-looking people in order to get kissed more often—not that they have a hard time of it," Hypatia said.

I decided to let it drop.

"So what are you wearing to the mall tomorrow?" she asked. "Remember, you have to blend in."

Hadn't we already discussed that? "I told you, I'm not going."

"But it's not optional. It's an *exam*—look at your schedule."

I groaned in frustration. That was just the sort of thing I needed, mandatory shopping trips. Sure enough, according to my handheld, a large portion of Saturday was blocked off and labeled URBAN CAMOUFLAGE AND DETECTION AVOIDANCE CLASS (PRACTICAL EXAM).

"I've never even heard of that class before," I said, "and I haven't studied at all."

"Stop complaining. You just have to spend four hours at the mall without anyone calling the FBI or NSA on you. You can do that."

It didn't make sense to me. "So even *human* students need to prove we can blend in with humans? Shouldn't the test be for parahumans only?"

Hypatia was about to answer when the front doors slammed violently open and in walked Tom. Well, he was only *kind of* walking. His legs were walking. I mean, they weren't his legs he was walking on. They were homemade legs.

Here's what I mean: instead of shoes, Tom was wearing long metallic stilt-like things that appeared to be somehow bolted to his calves. I'd have thought of them as stilts, but they had knees—the kind that bent the other way, like birds' legs. As they flexed and moved, the joints creaked menacingly and emitted steam in high-pressure jets, in precisely the way that birds' legs don't.

The stilts, undoubtedly some kind of device to help a person travel faster or jump higher, were in the process of causing all kinds of problems for Tom. They kicked and convulsed violently, their metallic feet skittering out of control on the slick tile floor. Look up a video of a deer or horse walking on ice, if you want to know what it looked like.

Tom made an admirable effort to stay on top of his homemade mechanical disaster, pivoting athletically this way and that, maintaining balance against all odds while trying to maneuver the legs and himself back out the door.

A few seconds and some creative hand-flapping later, he managed to get the legs settled. He smiled in satisfaction before realizing that everyone there was staring at him.

"Oh, uh, sorry," he said. "Prototype."

I guess cybernetic legs hate being called prototypes, because they immediately shivered spasmodically and smashed his entire body against the ceiling several times before dropping him unceremoniously to the floor. A second later the legs kicked over a couple of tables, shoved the door open, and stormed out, dragging a frightened-looking Tom behind them.

As soon as this was done, the tables stood themselves upright, and the students who had gotten clear of the danger reclaimed their seats, sorted out whose homework was whose, and went on with their meals as if nothing had happened. Someone's spilled ice cream melted and was absorbed into the floor just as a droid waitress brought a replacement.

Hypatia sighed wistfully. "Sorry, I thought I'd wait till that was over. You wanted to know why they make sure human students can blend in with other humans?"

"Actually," I said, "I kind of figured it out on my own."

-----*-----

The next morning, when Hypatia and I arrived downtown, we found the same disappointing yellow school bus with PILSSRTA emblazoned on the side waiting for us.

Because Hypatia was involved, we were unreasonably early again, which again earned us first seating choice and a free dirty look from the bus driver. If she remembered us from our previous adventure at the Tomahawk County Public Library, she gave no indication of it. Hypatia wanted to sit up front, but I insisted on the back row, if only to get clear of the driver, just in case she decided to reminisce or ask questions.

As the bus filled with students, Hypatia and I played a game. She claimed to know at least one interesting story about every person at the School, so I challenged her to prove it.

"His parents live on the moon without permission from the government, which can't do anything about it because the U.S. doesn't have its own lunar space program right now.

"She stole a book from the bookstore on a dare, and Ms. Botfly stole her bed in retaliation, which was especially impressive because she had the bottom bunk, so Ms. Botfly had to attach the top bunk to the ceiling first.

"Her grandfather ran for the Senate and lost because he

wears a prosthetic face to make himself look human, and the fake face kept fact-checking his speeches in real time.

"He was born like that, but the accident made it worse."

The students were dressed more like normal humans than I'd seen before, but not all of them managed it well. The teacher, Mr. Marconi, a miniature old man in a tweed cap and checked shirt, was rejecting obvious failures as soon as they boarded the bus. For example, a small group of girls had dressed in semimatching color-changing outfits that went from green to pink and back again according to how close they were to one another. Percival Freuchen had to be reminded that his robotic emotional support chinchilla would not be allowed in public no matter how many languages it spoke. After each of these admonitions, the teacher made a note on his tablet, and the students had to run home to change or leave their contraband behind.

That said, the failures were few and far between. I believed I could have been fooled by most of the disguises. That is, until Dirac and Majorana stepped aboard.

The Fermion twins were unquestionably dressed to fail. Their chrome hair shone so brightly in the sunlight that it cast shimmering reflections all over the ceiling of the bus. Their pale eyes were unmasked, and their strange light-bluish skin was completely obvious.

Dirac wore an outfit that would have looked garish on the pope, except that instead of gold embroidery, it was decorated with brightly glowing threads that snaked here and there in unfathomable patterns.

169

Majorana's garb consisted of a black tank top that appeared to be crafted from flexible wrought iron and a knee-length skirt made from some kind of living vines, which kept slipping down her legs and trying to become a full-length skirt until she moved, causing them to recede immediately. Occasionally, flowers would sprout and drop petals around her feet.

Hypatia and I watched Mr. Marconi stop them before they could take their seats, shaking his head and pointing at the door. The three of them entered into a debate while the rest of us watched with interest. Dirac and Majorana kept showing the teacher their watches, but I couldn't hear what they were talking about.

Hypatia, who was still playing her game, pointed them out. "Dirac and Majorana Fermion. They tend to think each other's thoughts when they're close together. Their dad, Oscar, works for the Old Ones."

That got my attention. "Really?" I said, remembering how inflexible Dirac had been on the subject of the Old Ones.

I recalled Fluorine's tale about her parents and what Warner had said about family money. "So how many parahumans are working for the bad guys? Seems like it's a lot of them."

"Not as many as you might think, but then again, you never really know for sure because some of them do it in secret. Dirac and Majorana are really sensitive about their dad, so don't bring it up unless they do first."

Finally, Mr. Marconi seemed to have had enough of whatever debate he had been having with the Fermion twins, because he raised his voice enough that I could finally hear him over the din of the other students. "I do not care what they do. You do not look even close to regular humans, and regardless of how well they function, people will still know that something is not—"

Dirac and Majorana threw simultaneous conspiratorial glances at each other and at once pressed small red buttons on their watches . . .

I suddenly remembered that I hadn't checked my email! I pulled out my tablet to see if any information about my dad had come in. My inbox was empty, so I set about finishing an essay assignment for Home Macroeconomics class.

Finally, when the bus was almost full, in stalked Warner. He glared up and down the aisle in an obviously tired and ill-tempered fashion. Eventually, when he caught sight of Hypatia and me, he seemed to perk up slightly and nodded as if to say, *I suppose I'll associate with the likes of you.*

Hypatia leaned over and whispered in my ear, "Warner's dad owns an alligator farm in Florida. His older sister is stationed in Germany with the army, and he is a virtuoso at anything robot related. His dad doesn't approve of his going to school here, because it's too expensive. He wants him to come home and help with the farm instead."

I tried picturing Warner with a slimy hunk of meat in his hand, shaking it to tempt the appetite of a ravenous reptile, and smiled despite myself.

Finally, just as we were almost ready to depart, I felt Hypatia go so stiff with perfect posture that she nearly vibrated. Her not-crush Tom had just fallen up the bus stairs, *without* his snooty, too-perfect girlfriend Ultraviolet in tow (and free of robotic legs).

"I wonder where she is," Hypatia said, more to herself than me.

"Probably getting her chromosomes polished," I said.

Hypatia laughed and poked me playfully with her elbow. "That's rude," she admonished, grinning furiously.

I had visited malls many, many times before coming to the School, so the level of excitement on the school bus was completely, well, *alien* to me. It quickly became clear that this was a *big deal*. The air of barely suppressed enthusiasm on the bus was enough to make a girl dizzy. That could also have been all the cologne and perfume everyone was wearing. There was so much alcohol in the bus that a spark might have burned us all alive.

"Do parahumans go out in public very often?" I asked Hypatia.

"From time to time. It depends on the individual. Some of us like to stick to smaller communities like the School where we can be ourselves."

"I'm surprised we don't hear about it more," I said.

Hypatia knitted her brows. "What do you mean?"

"Well, the only alien sightings I ever hear about involve flying saucers and little gray men with big black eyes. You'd think the human race would have at least gotten the general description right."

She laughed. "We think those are hilarious. Aliens don't steal cows; we collect Nobel Prizes. Honestly, why would an intelligent race go halfway across the universe to swipe someone from their bed, take their temperature in some unpleasant way, put them back in their bed, and then come back again the next week? How inefficient is that? Why not just keep the human locked up for as long as you need them? It's preposterous."

"So you'd keep your abduction victim?" I asked. "Doesn't seem neighborly."

Hypatia's eyes paled a bit. "*I* would never do something like that, but if someone has so little respect for humans that they make a habit of 'borrowing' them from their homes or automobiles, why on earth would they go to such trouble to set things right afterward?"

I had other comments, but at that moment the flesh-toned makeup one of the students had been wearing malfunctioned, turning him an eye-burningly bright green color for several seconds before he was able to fix it.

"At least you don't need to bother with any kind of disguise," I said to Hypatia.

"I do use a semiopaque lenticular device to conceal certain characteristics," Hypatia said, rummaging in her purse.

"Come again?" I asked.

"Sunglasses, dummy," she said, sliding on a pair so large

they made her look like one of the little gray men we had just been talking about. "The eyes give me away."

"What about everyone else?" I asked. "Like where did Juan's third arm go?"

"One part cloaking device, one part baggy sweatshirt."

She was right. His shirt looked a little wrong somehow, but the moment I had the wrongness in my sights, something else seemed wrong, and then both were gone. It's hard to explain.

At that moment, from somewhere very close by, nobody did not say, "We made distractors last night, and they work great."

Hypatia looked at me. "Did you say something?"

"No," I said. "I didn't hear anything."

"What?" Hypatia asked.

I would have replied . . .

But it suddenly occurred to me that I had absolutely no idea what the ingredients in a Bundt cake were! It was crucially important to look it up on the Internet at that very moment. How had I gone my whole life without knowing?

Typing the search term into my tablet was difficult because nobody was not slipping something onto my wrist.

A moment later I realized that I had completely failed to notice several things. For instance, Majorana Fermion was standing over me, looking silvery and triumphant in her metallic-botanical ensemble.

"I'd say that's a pass?" she said.

An intense headache nearly overcame me and dissipated

just as quickly. When I looked down, I saw I was wearing a cheap jelly bracelet I hadn't seen before. Majorana was also wearing something on her wrist, but I could barely make it out, because it wasn't there. But it was. Whatever it was, it reminded me of how much I wanted to think of anything else very urgently.

That brought me back to my own new bracelet. "What's this?" I asked.

"So we have people to talk to. Now put this one on so you can see Dirac, too."

"Oh, he should have come. I bet he'd love to see that outfit. It's really something."

Then I slipped on a blue jelly bracelet Majorana handed me and realized Dirac was also standing over me, his hands braced on the seats.

Majorana handed me a small paper bag with several pink and blue bands, instructing me to share them with the others. Eventually, I managed to persuade Hypatia, Warner, and a few other nearby students to slip them on. All were amazed when they realized they had simply not noticed two students standing right there in front of them.

"Invisibility is difficult," Dirac explained in response to all the questions, "but crude brain manipulation is easy. The distractors make people forget everything about us in real time whenever they look in our direction. The real trick was coming up with the immunizing bracelets—otherwise we would have failed for not showing up. Now we have witnesses."

12

HOW TO FLUNK A FIELD TRIP

After a tedious and noisy hour-long journey, we found ourselves at the DiPiney Mall, which looked a lot larger than the few malls we had in North Dakota. Before releasing us, Mr. Marconi gave us our instructions for the trip.

"This bus will depart, whether or not you have returned, at promptly 3:00 PM. Because you are no doubt aware how difficult it can be to locate the School, missing the bus amounts to something like an expulsion, so take that deadline seriously. As today's field trip constitutes an examination, students will be expected to conceal their more unique qualities at all times. Failure to do so will mean failure and possible dissection at the hands of the humans. Everyone, please activate your monitoring apps at this time so your work can be graded later. Make sure your tablets do NOT connect to Wi-Fi or human cell networks. Only connections to other school tablets are allowed here. Weapons, wormholes, and intelligent machines of any sort are not allowed. If you have brought any of these prohibited items in error, leave them here, or you will fail the test and have to take the remedial class. Those purchasing contraband on this outing will have it removed from their possession and distributed among the staff via our yearly contraband raffle. So if you have it in your head to purchase a bottle of wine or a box of cigars, for heaven's sake, get something *good*. Ah, I think that's it. Have I forgotten anything?" he asked.

"You forgot to threaten us about being rowdy," Dirac offered.

"And you forgot to tell us we're representing the School, and how we should always comport ourselves properly," said Majorana.

"Ah, yes, thank you, Dirac, Majorana. It's a shame you two couldn't make it today," Mr. Marconi said cheerfully.

Mr. Marconi became suddenly serious. "I will personally deal with any troublemakers who fail to live up to the high standards this school demands of its students. You may be here covertly, but you are representatives of the School and will behave accordingly. If you have to ask yourself if Homeland Security would be interested in what you're doing, you probably shouldn't be doing it."

As soon as all of us had turned our weapons and other forgotten contraband over, we were released on the unsuspecting public.

As we walked into the mall, Hypatia was going on and on

about the various things she wanted to buy. "And you get to stuff your own bear and dress it however you want, and you can put in a thing that makes noise, but it only makes one noise, so it never develops an attitude problem like the one I ordered from the bookstore—Oh! Taco Bomb!" A second later Hypatia was gone, leaving only a cloud of dust where she had been a moment before.

Something you should know about parahumans: they're freaking *crazy* about fast food, and they're especially crazy about the Taco Bomb restaurant chain in particular. It's the one place humans and parahumans can agree on. Humans love the beefy, cheesy goodness of inauthentic Mexican-ish cuisine, and parahumans love the preservatives, artificial colors, inorganic filler materials, and "flavor enhancement chemicals." It's the perfect food.

While Hypatia quizzed the cashier about which meals had which kind of disodium and monosodium additives, I perused the menu, gravitating toward the NachoSplosion Platter, when I felt something buzz in my backpack. *My tablet.* I'd forgotten to turn off network access when we left the bus.

Quickly, I stepped out of line and moved to where I could not be easily seen. I pulled the tablet from my pack and discovered the notification that had triggered the alert.

It said: *1 new email message.* I was about to turn it off when I got a better look at it. The message was from Melvin Kross. Subject: *hello from your parent.* My dad had emailed me! Maybe he'd escaped. Maybe he needed help . . . Trembling just a little, I pretty much forgot the rest of the universe existed and opened the email.

For a short email, it took forever to load. As it took its time, I checked the header information. In this case, it told me bupkes. No list of dozens of mysterious government email addresses. This one was just for me. Finally, the message appeared.

i am your father and i miss u alot, ROFL. wish i could come n see u. where u at kiddo?

I read it a few times, but to my shock, every time it said the same thing. I was baffled. Dad had always been the sort of guy who would rather cut off his fingers than type *u* instead of *you*. One time I emailed him a joke, and his response was, *Your humor was greatly appreciated by me and prompted an involuntary vocal expression of mirth.*

That's how Melvin Kross says *ROFL*.

I figured he must have been short on time, in danger, or they had given him drugs to make him stupid or something. Maybe he was on the run. Most humans could not handle being around the Old Ones for long periods of time—perhaps his mental condition had deteriorated. All I could think was that if the Old Ones had turned my dad into the kind of person who said "where u at kiddo," I would not rest until I removed each and every one of their heads (or whatever the Old One equivalent is).

I considered my options and composed a reply, trying to keep it as brief as he had, in case time was a factor.

At a mall in Iowa. Where are YOU? I've been worried sick! Are you okay? What's happening?

I sent the message and left my tablet on to receive a reply. Deciding it was best to go on with things as normal, I composed myself, took a few deep breaths, and purchased a soft-shell taco and a soda. Hypatia, the Fermion twins, and Warner had taken up residence at a big round table and were already demolishing their food with voracity. It turned out I hadn't needed to buy my own food, because Warner and Dirac had pooled their money to purchase the X-Cessive Family FiestaCrate and were actually having trouble finishing it.

Hypatia was sucking on a soda. "I love, love, love soda pop. I wish they'd let us have it at school."

I realized I'd never seen a soda fountain or machine at the School. "Yeah, why don't they?" I asked.

Warner sighed. "Carbonation—the bubbles make parahumans super hyperactive."

Hypatia nodded. "That's true but I don't think it's all that obvious when I get hyper it's just that I have a little more energy and it wakes me up I think they should sell soda at the cafés maybe just in the morning because everyone needs a pick-me-up in the mornings and coffee makes me sooo sleepy I'm like *super* sleepy and slow when I have coffee but soda is really good in my opinion you want to try a drink of mine?"

"No thanks," I said.

Something at the table beeped. Warner reached into his pocket and removed his school tablet.

"Uh-oh," Hypatia said. "You're not supposed to have that connected to the Internet here. You could get into a lot of trouble."

"Yeah, but everyone does it. Dirac has his connected, and I saw Nikola with hers a little bit ago."

Hypatia glared accusingly at me. I shrugged.

"Besides, I love public Wi-Fi honeypots. They're soooo bad," Warner said.

I hadn't heard that term before, at least when not referring to pots of honey. "What's a honeypot?"

He was about to answer when he said, "Ah! Got one. Okay, listen, everyone! Listen! This one is from my 'sister.'" He stood and took a deep breath, reading in a falsetto voice to sound like a woman.

Yo what's shaking Brofessor Fancy, it's your sister checkin' in with a little BREAKING NEWS, hit me back with your 411. Big trouble—sorry to harsh your mellow but dad ate a mushroom and died.

Everyone at the table erupted into gales of laughter. Well, everyone but me.

"I can't believe anyone would fall for that," Majorana said between gasps. "Do the Old Ones really think that's how people communicate?"

"Have you gotten one yet, Nikola?" Warner asked me.

As soon as he saw me, the smile died on his face. "Oh no."

He probably thought I was almost going to cry. Because worrying your dad might have been executed for sending you an email and then temporarily finding out he is alive, and *then* being told it was a lie and you just fell for a really obvious trick might be upsetting to some people.

Warner shook his head. "You didn't reply, did you?"

Everyone's eyes were on me, and Hypatia spoke up. "Of course she did! They probably used her *dad*, and nobody *warned* her their messages would look like they're from family!" To me she said, "You need to let us know—what did you tell them?"

Reeling from disappointment and feeling like the dumbest person in the world, I said, "Um, I just asked where he was."

"See?" Hypatia said. "The IP address will only tell them what part of the state we're—"

"And said that we were at a mall," I finished.

Simultaneously, Warner, Dirac, and Majorana all started up the monitoring app and pressed a button in the corner of the screen that said EMERGENCY.

I heard a faint alarm tone all around me. An alert was sounding on every student's device.

"Field trip is over," Majorana said. "Back to the bus."

The four of us stood at once and headed for the door, but

Dirac jumped in front of us and blocked our way. "They were going to park the bus on the other side of the mall. It's faster to cut through."

We changed direction, and Warner took advantage of the momentary delay to dash back to the table to collect the remnants of their X-Cessive Family FiestaCrate. After reclaiming it, he spun around and crashed into a young woman who was pushing a stroller between the tables. What resulted from the impact gave the term *Taco Bomb* a whole new meaning: 100 percent USDA choice beef, the freshest produce, and select herbs and spices went everywhere. The woman and her baby were completely covered in a unique southwestern flavor experience.

"HnnGAH!" the woman said.

Despite the situation, I had to laugh. But the whole scene became a bit less hilarious when I felt a hand grasp my shoulder.

I spun to see a security guard. "You think that's funny?" he said. "Having your friend throw garbage all over some poor lady and her baby. Real funny. You filming this?"

"No!" I said. "It was an accident, and I like watching my friend fail. That's all."

That didn't placate him at all. Another guard had grabbed Warner, and a third was handling Hypatia a little more roughly than he probably needed to. They brought us together into a small group. The rent-a-cops looked surly and bored, and at least one of them had a serious case of onion breath.

"So, kids, what's the problem here?" the one holding

Warner asked. He had a blond flattop haircut, a round face, and a thick neck. I named him the Thumb.

"No problem," I said. "Just an accident. We're actually late for our ride home." I tried to pull away, but the guard behind me was stronger than I'd expected, and I couldn't pull from his grasp. I turned to look at him. He was huge. His goatee and nose ring didn't make him look any friendlier, either. I named him Biker because I suspected there was a leather jacket covered with skull patches hanging in his closet at home.

The guard by Hypatia spoke. I named this one Timmy, for no reason at all. "We've had some complaints of shoplifters. I think you three need to come with us for a moment. We just need to ask you a couple questions."

"We've been sitting here for a while now," I said, "and we have receipts for the tacos."

Biker's grip on my shoulders tightened to the point that it hurt. He leaned down to whisper in my ear, and the smell of his breath almost overwhelmed me. His breath wasn't just bad; it was a symphony in decay and revulsion. It was like a chemical representation of just how bad the good things in the world can become when left in the hot sun for a month. Worse, it was *wrong*.

"I don't think you understand the gravity of your situation, Nikola," Biker said in a melodic but assertive woman's voice. "You *will* accompany us for the time being. It shouldn't take long, dear."

I'd have known the voice anywhere because I'd listened to it insult me from inside my own head for upward of an hour not too long ago. It was Jakki. The security guards were a nice touch. Had I smelled like that when she was inside my mind? I couldn't remember, but I must have. I might have thought about it more if keeping my lunch inside my stomach hadn't suddenly become difficult.

"Your friends will need to accompany us as well. Shall we?" she said, pulling me hard, away from our escape route.

Warner, Hypatia, and I struggled without much effect as we were dragged toward an unmarked door on the edge of the food court.

I caught something almost unnoticeable from the corner of my eye. Dirac and Majorana, still wearing their distractors, had slipped behind the three guards. Dirac was digging in his pockets. They hadn't taken note of them.

The other security guards had heard Jakki's voice as well. "Ah, Dave? You got a cold or something, man?"

"Shut up!" she commanded. "Hold them. They're known terrorists, and you're certain to be rewarded for catching them."

The guards' expressions went suddenly blank, as if an important part of their minds had come unplugged. "Yes, sir!" said the Thumb and Timmy at the same time.

My mind raced, trying to size up the situation. We could make a scene, and someone might help. Unfortunately, we were five weird kids, three of whom bystanders could actually take notice of, and *they* were uniformed security guards. Who would an onlooker believe?

Behind the guards, still unnoticed, Dirac had opened his

distractor and was poking a slender metal tool at its innards. He reached one of his long, thin fingers into its nest of wires and components. How long it would work on an Old One, I did not know. Maybe it only worked because the Old One was piloting a regular human's brain from somewhere else at the moment.

I realized that was a good thing. Jakki was not with us. We were just dealing with someone she was controlling, which meant she couldn't slip between dimensions or drive people mad by looking at them. Not yet.

As I thought this, Biker glanced suspiciously at Dirac—no, past him, but in his direction. The Old One driving Biker suspected something. Jakki wasn't easily fooled.

The guards dragged us along toward their security station, which was conveniently located between the Chinese food restaurant and the bathrooms. Dirac and Majorana kept pace close behind. I started scanning the tables for weapons; maybe a hot cup of coffee to the face would . . .

Then I saw it: Chicken! Chicken! Chicken! was having a two-for-one sale on jumbo meganugget buckets! That would be a perfect way to feed a whole family on a budget. Fries and drink were included for just—

No, what did that matter? I needed to be looking for something. What was it?

Suddenly it was clear: Chicken! Chicken! Chicken! must be owned by the same people who run Candles! Candles! Candles! Maybe they sold some crossover chicken-scented—

No! That wasn't it, either. I looked around. Some guys were with us. I didn't recognize them. Where was I again? The guys had stopped in their tracks and were looking around as if they had all lost something.

A tall, silvery boy was pulling on my arm and leading me away from them. A girl with shiny hair—it was really pretty, but a little too well kept for my tastes—took the hands of another boy and girl who were with me. I wondered if I knew them; they seemed nice. They led us away, which was fine. I hadn't been doing anything important.

As we walked, the name of the boy came back to me. Then I remembered the names of the others and what had been happening. "What *was* that?" I asked Dirac.

"I turned the distractor up to full power and stuck it in the big one's back pocket. The battery won't last long like that, so move quickly."

Around us, the food court had become very distracted. People were setting drinks down on tables that weren't there. A fast-food worker casually picked up a burger from a customer's tray and took a bite, wrapper and all. The taco-covered young mother traded her baby for a nice smartphone and ten dollars cash.

Once my head cleared, I pointed out a service tunnel on the other side of the court, above which a red EXIT sign glowed warmly. "There!" I said.

We crashed through the exit doors, and relief turned to frustration when the "exit" turned out to be a long blank hallway that led to the *actual* exits, which were several hundred feet away. If the sounds of shoving and arguing behind us were any indication, the guards had come to their senses and were after us once again. We kept running.

A second later Majorana was at the exits. She'd shoved aside a mop bucket and was holding one of the doors open. *God, she was fast.* I glanced around—Hypatia was hurrying determinedly, and Warner . . . Warner looked absolutely terrified. He was sweating up a storm and doing his best to keep up. As for Dirac, he looked a bit like a cat about to spring bravely into a paper bag. All business.

We were almost to the doors. I could feel cold outside air rushing in. A bang sounded behind us as the access doors crashed open. Our friendly security guards were closing in.

"They have scooters!" Warner shouted as we passed through the doors into the parking lot and the almost-blinding brightness of midday sunlight on white snow.

Sure enough, each of the rent-a-cops, led by Biker, were standing atop those two-wheeled Segway scooters that must come attached to mall security uniforms. Timmy sneered. Geez, he had a lot of teeth. The Thumb drooled aggressively.

I stopped a few feet out and ran back toward the exit door.

Warner shouted, "Wrong way, wrong way!"

"Keep going!" I said.

The emergency exit stood open because the hydraulic mechanism that keeps the doors from slamming had latched. I reached around the opening frantically and found the long wooden mop handle standing just where I remembered. I pulled the mop over onto its side hard enough to tip the bucket of muddy water all over the floor. Then I ran like bees were after me.

I was almost around the first corner when an angry crash caught my attention. Just as I'd hoped, all three guards were on the concrete. Those two-wheeled scooters have a secret weakness: *small bumps.* There was no way they were getting over a mop stick at speed, especially if the floor was damp. A quick glance told me that not only had I caused a scooter pileup, but at least one of the scooters had also broken in half just below the handlebars.

That bought us a little time, but it wasn't much. Fortunately, sheer terror is one heck of a motivator, and I was able to catch up with my friends before long. Well, not all of them. Dirac had run ahead at about forty-five miles an hour and was just rounding another corner several hundred feet away.

"How long before *they* get here, do you think?" Hypatia called.

Warner shook his head. "We don't have long."

The tablet in my pocket buzzed and spoke in unison with the others. "Hey, guys," said Mr. Marconi's voice, "Mr. Fermion has just joined us and has informed me you've managed to alert the Old Ones of your presence. We've advised the other students to conceal themselves where they are, and I'm having the bus brought around to pick you up. Keep moving in our direction if you can. Incidentally, I'm afraid this will count as a failing grade on the examination."

Hypatia said a bad word then. I won't repeat it here, mainly because when a person who does not normally curse says a bad word, it sounds ridiculous and fake. Warner appeared to be mortally embarrassed.

I tapped Majorana on the shoulder. "Run ahead and tell them to meet us. See if you can get some weapons." She nodded and raced ahead, faster than I could have moved on a motorcycle. About twenty yards off, she stopped, looked around, and appeared to consider something. Then she scaled an ornamental tree like a monkey, leaped onto the roof of the building, and was gone.

Warner was almost out of breath. "I could . . . totally . . . do that if . . . I wanted to . . ."

Hypatia, who did not seem at all tired, ran ahead a little to take a look around the next corner. A few seconds after she'd moved out of sight, Majorana burst out from a department store's revolving doors. She was looking pretty beat up and wasn't moving as quickly as she had before. "The bus is stuck in traffic!" she called. "We have to cut through—come on!"

I turned to follow her, but something stopped me. Majorana looked sick—no, that wasn't right—she looked uglier than usual, which made no sense. Where was Hypatia?

"She's fine!" Majorana shouted when she saw me searching. "Leave her!"

Warner had no misgivings and took off toward the doors where Majorana was gesturing furiously. Just as I was about to follow, I took one last look for Hypatia and saw her and *another* Majorana sprinting back around the corner. The new Majorana, who I realized was the genuine one, was moving almost too fast to see. She was also carrying something in her hand where her tablet had been not long before.

"DOWN!" Hypatia yelled.

Something said, "BLOOOUUUMMMP."

I hit the concrete as a wave of watery luminescence from her gravitational disruptor shot over my head. It barely missed Warner and knocked him against the wall of the building as it passed. It hit the shabby version of Majorana full force, just as she was reaching out to grab him. She was catapulted backward into the revolving doors, which should really be called *shattering doors* when you go through at ninety miles an hour.

"What are you doing?!" Warner screamed. "You killed her!"

"That wasn't me! They're HERE!" the real Majorana shouted as she lifted him to his feet and thrust her disruptor into his hands. "I'll carry you. Shoot anything that looks suspicious. The bus isn't far!"

She threw my own disruptor to me, and I snatched it out of the air.

"Thanks," I huffed.

"The School opened an emergency wormhole in a

bathroom stall, and the other students are all safe," she said. "We're closer to the bus, so as soon as we're on, they're going to get us out of here."

As if in response, the bus grumbled and rattled somewhere close by. We were almost there.

Warner wasn't looking so well. He had given that concrete wall a big hug and looked like he might fall off Majorana's back before long. A deep scrape on his left arm was bleeding a trail behind us. I dropped my disruptor into my bag and grabbed an old sock that looked clean and hastily clapped it onto his arm.

He switched his disruptor to his left hand and held the sock against his wounded arm with his right while doing his best to keep an eye out for more trouble. "That wasn't Majorana . . . who got killed?"

"No. I'm carrying you," Majorana said.

"Oh," he said intelligently.

His confusion seemed to fade. "Didn't even look like her. God, it was horrible. It hurts . . . thinking about it. She's a *lot* worse than the other one."

I should have been looking where I was running, instead of trying to discern brain damage in Warner, because at that moment the bus pulled up in front of us and jumped the curb, and the four of us crashed right through the open door and onto the nearest leather seat. Someone shouted, "Get in! Fast! Hurry!"

Way ahead of you, I thought, helping Majorana set

Warner onto the front bench seat before passing his weapon up to Mr. Marconi, who was gesturing for it urgently.

"Miss," Mr. Marconi said coolly to Majorana, "I think you might be more trouble than I wish to deal with at the moment."

Hypatia, who had taken the seat behind Warner and me, went pale. Her eyes went pure white. "No . . ."

"Mr. Marconi," I said, spinning to see what he was doing, "don't be—"

But he wasn't listening to me. Mr. Marconi shot Majorana with Warner's disruptor at point-blank range.

Majorana went flying dramatically back out the door and through the air like a rag doll carried upon an undulating cloud of warped gravitation. Her body smashed *through* a decorative tree planted by the curb about twenty feet away, breaking it in half. She tumbled to a stop not far from where the top half of the tree fell, hiding her body. From how close she had been—could a person survive that? I couldn't think about it.

The doors slammed shut with a heavy-sounding metallic *clunk*. The bus was close, hot, and dark, nearly pitch black. Somehow the darkness made the interior seem a lot smaller; or maybe it actually *was* smaller.

And *that smell*. Someone must have vomited in the confusion. Or—

"We made that a lot more difficult than it needed to be, I think," Mr. Marconi said from the front passenger seat in a throaty woman's voice. The bus eased back onto the street and pulled away with a padded *thump*.

A small fluttering light on the ceiling went out, and I suddenly could not remember why I'd thought the black SUV around me had looked anything like a school bus in the first place. I was really starting to hate that feeling.

Then I saw *her*.

13

A REALLY FUN HUMAN ROAD TRIP!

A t the wheel sat a slightly pudgy man in a rumpled suit with graying hair. He kept his head pointed resolutely forward, so I couldn't get a better look at him. Next to him sat the Old One, Jakki. She looked to be a woman in her midforties, dressed in a smart gray pantsuit over an olive blouse, accented with a fine golden necklace and a pretty jeweled broach in the shape of a bonobo ape. Her brunette wedge haircut was just starting to show traces of gray, and her smile was warm, professional, and deeply troubling.

The familiar rotten-meat stench I'd come to expect from the Old Ones was still there, although this new specimen was different from Tabbabitha's. There was something of a synthetic chemical quality to it with a touch of gasoline, like someone had tried to burn a rotting pile of meat and excrement and failed to get things going. It was many times worse than I'd ever experienced, but surprisingly, it disappeared almost immediately, replaced by the scent of perfume.

That's not quite correct. The stench hadn't faded or disappeared. The moment I thought about it, I could smell it all over again. She was making it less noticeable somehow. Let me tell you, I didn't mind *at all*.

"Hey, kids!" said Jakki. "I'm *so sorry* we had to meet this way. I hope nobody has been hurt. Is everyone okay?"

She looked to each of us in turn, her eyes wide with false concern. Hypatia slumped against her seat, insensate, and Warner drooled and toppled forward onto the floor of the vehicle.

"No complaints? That's so great to hear. You all just relax. It's been quite a day, I'm sure." She turned to face forward, indicating an upcoming turn to her driver.

"What's wrong with them?" I demanded.

She spoke without turning. "See that nifty gadget above your head?" I guessed she was referring to the light that had been flickering when the SUV had been a bus. "It gives a little boost to how *convincing* I can be. Probably took a lot out of them. They'll be fine before long, poor dears."

There was a moment of silence while I tried to figure out where we were going, until I realized the windows weren't just tinted; they were completely black. I reached behind me and shook Hypatia, trying to rouse her. She was out cold.

Jakki returned her gaze to me. "Let's not disturb them just yet. I'd introduce myself, but we've already met, haven't we? You're Nikola, right?"

She held a hand out for me to shake. I responded by trying to push myself backward through my seat.

Without warning, she slipped into my mind and forced me to reach my hand out to shake hers. The feeling was absolutely revolting, but familiar. I couldn't believe I hadn't realized it was happening at the library. Immediately, I tried the same trick. I latched onto her mind and tried to trap her.

But this time she was too quick, and I could sense her pulling away just before I could get a grip.

She slapped me hard across the face.

"You need to learn some manners," she said, every bit as cheerfully. "I hope you don't think I'm going to fall for that again."

"I was hoping you might," I said, my cheek stinging.

She made a frowny face. "Sorry to disappoint you, honey. Things aren't going to go your way very often from here on out, but that doesn't mean you have to suffer. Lots of people even come to appreciate us after a while. You must have plenty of questions, and I want to make sure you have all the answers you—I'm sorry, I just have to say—you are *so pretty*, really. I'd *kill* for eyes like yours. And that skin! What's your regimen?"

"Oh, I just wake up like this! Ha-ha! You're too kind, Jakki!" I said. Except that only my mouth, vocal cords, and lungs were saying these things. Immediately, I seized control of myself, shouting "STOP IT!" and clawing at her mind again, but once more she was able to slip away.

"Sorry, force of habit," she said with a sheepish little shrug, like she'd accidentally spilled something on my carpet. "Still, there's no need to act out. If you don't want my help getting your emotions under control, I won't intervene. Hopefully, I haven't made you feel uncomfortable."

"I am feeling a bit uncomfortable, actually," I said. "Maybe you could drop us off at the next corner, and we could get together some other time?"

She pulled a smartphone from her pocket and consulted it briefly. "I don't think that would be an optimal use of our time, do you? No, no, we've too much on our plate and not enough time as it is. I have meetings and calls all this week and next. I have to be in D.C. over the weekend . . . No, I'm just booked solid."

She pocketed her smartphone and, almost absentmindedly, crumpled the gravitational disruptor in her hands like it was made of paper, opened her mouth about twice as wide as a human is supposed to be able to, and tossed it down her gullet like an oversized piece of popcorn.

She swallowed hard and went on. "I feel like . . . *we should strike while the iron is hot*. Do you understand what a great opportunity for growth this is? You and me getting together after we've been playing tag for so long. We may not get another opportunity like this."

Without warning, Jakki reached over the seat and patted

me on the shoulder with a hand that looked normal but felt icy and gelatinous. She smiled wistfully. "Plus I remember how badly Tabbabitha wanted to reunite you with your father and show you our home. It was her *dying wish*. Shouldn't you grant it? You're the one who killed her, after all. That's human etiquette, right?"

She said *reunite me* with my father. Did that mean he was alive or that she was going to kill me, too? Better not to worry about it. "Not really. Listen, if it's all the same to you, I'd rather—"

Jakki interrupted me with a raised finger ornamented with a flawlessly manicured nail. "Of course, if you'd prefer, we could skip right to the part where I torture, murder, and consume all three of you, starting with your friends. But make no mistake—it's your call. I may be in charge here, but good leadership is all about seeking feedback. *What do you think?*"

"I'm starting to see things your way," I said.

"I had a hunch you would!" she said with a wink and a smile.

While Jakki went on rambling about plans and synergy and leverage and opportunities and things like that, I took a moment to glance at my friends. Hypatia appeared to be asleep, but Warner could have passed for dead.

"Warner?" I whispered. Through the gloom, I could see his face had gone pale, and his eyes were bulging open in what looked like shock, but there was nothing behind them. Warner was on vacation from his brain. I reached down and closed his eyes with my fingers so they wouldn't dry out.

A quick survey of the inside of the vehicle was all bad news. There wasn't a handle to open the door from the inside. The black windows were clearly thick enough to be bullet-proof, and there were no controls for opening them. For the time being, we weren't going anywhere, at least not anywhere we wanted to go.

Then inspiration struck. I could tear a hole in the car with my agar bracelet without any work at all. Why was I always forgetting about it? I glanced at it on my wrist and imagined it becoming wider and stronger, a massively powerful hinged blade ready to spring outward and cut the car in two between the front and back seats. I felt potential energy build up in it like a coiled spring and . . . nothing.

I tried again, but it wasn't doing what I wanted. Instead, it receded and curled back around my wrist, where it took on its old bracelet form.

I realized Jakki had stopped talking and was looking back at me, watching with placid interest.

I smiled at her like, *Hi, I was just minding my own business back here.*

"Honey," she said. "Please don't play with that stuff. I wouldn't want you to hurt yourself. You could put an eye out."

I shook my head. "I'm pretty familiar with—"

"Sorry," Jakki interrupted with a coo. "I'm not always good with this animal grunting you primates call language. I think what I meant to say is that you should leave it alone, or *I* will put an eye out."

Just in case she hadn't made her case, a thin white tendril

extended from my bracelet, formed itself into a needle almost too fine to see, and slid toward my right eye like a cobra ready to strike. My head recoiled back instinctively against the headrest. The long white needle drew still closer, until I could feel the point faintly touching the center of my eye.

I tried to concentrate, to move it away, but it didn't move a micron.

"Did that come out right?" Jakki said.

"Yeah, it did," I said.

A moment later, the snakelike needle had slid back into the bracelet and was nothing more than a memory.

"That bracelet is just *the cutest!*" Jakki exclaimed. "Do me a favor? Leave that lovely thing on your wrist the whole time you're with me. I like having something I can use to make my point from time to time. Get it? Point?" She smiled without mirth, and I pretended to laugh weakly.

She patted her driver on the shoulder and said, "Step on it, Gus. I'm sure they're looking for our new friends."

Through the windshield, the city scenery gave way to suburban zones and, finally, empty snowy fields. Before long we were rocketing along highways at speeds that might have made me nervous if I hadn't been secretly hoping for an accident.

Jakki seemed to remember something. "I meant to ask you, where did you drop my errant sister off? I can't tell you how much I'd like to see her again."

Jakki didn't wait for an answer. Again I felt her fingers slipping into my mind, but this time there was no sneaky subtlety. It was like someone breaking the door down with a battering ram or driving a bulldozer through a wall. She was trying to snatch what she wanted before I could stop her.

It *hurt*. It felt like something was tearing inside my head—

But then it didn't. Suddenly, I was standing on a gravel path, before a cabin I remembered seeing once before. The lights inside glowed warmly. Best of all, I wasn't alone; my all-time best friend Jakki was by my side. I wanted to win her love any way I could.

"Is she in there?" Jakki asked.

"Uh, yeah," I said, not quite understanding what was going on.

She tried to lead me up to the door, but I stopped, even though I dearly wanted to do whatever she wanted.

Every instinct I had was screaming at me to stop, to refuse, but why would I do that? It was a nice day, we were already in the woods, and we could go see my friend . . . Where were we again?

"Where ARE we?" my awesome friend Jakki wanted to know. "Do you remember?"

I wanted to tell her, but part of me felt like it would be a bad idea. I could feel the fresh, calming breeze rustling through the forest, but I could also feel my bag just under my hand, like I was in two places at the same time.

I needed to find where something was.

"I just love this place," Jakki said, as stylish and sophisticated as ever. "Wouldn't you like to visit? Spend an afternoon relaxing in the shade? I just wish I knew where to go!"

Where was it? There was something I needed to find as soon as possible!

Jakki, my wonderful pal, patted me on the shoulder and led me to a comfortable bench on the porch, where a steaming mug of hot chocolate waited on a little silver tray. She was sad, which meant I was sad, too. "I wish my sister could come join us. She likes you so much, and I haven't seen her in so long," she sighed. "If I only knew where she was."

Finally, I knew just what I was trying to find. Inside my bag, I felt the cool surface of my gravitational disruptor, grasped it, and shot my awesome, stylish, sophisticated friend Jakki right in the mouth.

Darleeen's cabin disappeared with a wicked, blinding flash that caused the SUV to career almost out of control, as Jakki's head shot backward and crashed against the windshield, leaving a deep, dome-shaped indentation in the half-shattered glass.

Jakki's civilized facade was gone. She lunged, suddenly looming over me as I slid into my seat, snarling with viciously pointed teeth that hung in space below cavernous, empty black eyes.

When she spoke, her voice sounded more like a lion's roar than a human voice. "YOU LITTLE SH—darling," she said, switching almost immediately back into friendly-businesswoman mode. Had her eyes really turned black?

"There's no need for violence," Jakki said, picking a fragment of glass from her now-scrambled hairdo and bouncing it off my forehead. A second later, too quick for me to even see, she'd plucked my disruptor from my hand, returned to her seat, and swallowed it just as she had Warner's.

We rode in uncomfortable silence for a few minutes as the road flowed past. I considered my options. Even if I could get away, there was no way I could carry Hypatia and Warner along with me. Just to be sure, I slipped my school tablet from my backpack and took a peek. No signal, of course. The SUV wouldn't be a very good abduction vehicle if it didn't block our wireless signals.

I tried to watch for road signs through what was left of the windshield, thinking maybe I could get a look at where we were going. Unfortunately, even though the road and everything was perfectly visible, all the writing on every sign we passed was complete gibberish, as if the glass were scrambling everything in real time.

Then I realized I did have one source of information. A chatty Old One who really didn't seem to understand how interrogation was supposed to work when you couldn't just extract information from people's brains without permission.

"So where are we headed?" I asked, hoping Jakki wasn't still sore about my trying to blow her head off about ninety seconds before that.

Jakki perked right up. "Our destination is a surprise, dear. If I killed you, I would have to tell you," she said. "No, wait. What I mean to say is that if I'm going to kill you, *then* I'll tell you after." She stopped and shook her head. "The idea I'm trying to convey is that you should associate knowing our destination with your personal death. I meant to threaten you—am I communicating effectively?"

"Yeah. I got it."

Maybe another angle would work better. "What are you planning for us?"

Jakki peeked at her phone and smiled her warm yet wistful smile. "I'm not sure you could understand. Besides, we should be having fun! This is a road trip, you know. I looked it up online, and a road trip is something of a rite of passage for you people. A group of friends pile into the car and head out on the American highway in search of *adventure*. Sometimes road trippers end up discovering a little something about themselves, too. A while back I saw a movie where two human females detonate a mobile container of your petroleum chemical fuel, then pilot their automobile into a large fissure in the earth's crust. The movie ends before you get to see them die, but sometimes it's nice when they leave things to your imagination. Not that I have much of an imagination. No time for creative thinking, when there's so much to be done." She sighed as if she were the most put-upon woman on Earth.

"You can improve your own creativity, you know," I said. "Have you ever tried picking up painting or gardening instead of kidnapping children?"

"I did take a needlepoint class last year. That was the whole idea—supposed to help me get in touch with my *creative* side. I made a cross-stitch of a goose with a little inspirational saying on it. A cross-stitch is where you get a bit of fabric and use needlework to mark it with colors—like making a digital image one pixel at a time. It was from a pattern, but the choice of what color ribbon the goose was wearing was all mine. I chose mauve."

"A bold choice," I said.

Jakki nodded fervently. "I couldn't agree more! I gave it a lot of thought because it was going to be the largest block of color, and it's really what catches the eye. Also the rest of the goose ended up looking a bit deformed, so I wanted to draw attention away from it. I'll show you later."

"So we're going to your place?" I hazarded.

She pointed a finger at me. "Cat's out of the bag now. Really, I should murder you, but I need you for a couple projects, so you're safe for the time being. Do you know I was *this close* to blowing you and your friends to bits that night at the library? Tabbabitha swore up and down you were special, but I always figured she was overselling the idea to account for her repeated failures. But the way you fight back . . . you might be one of the few things she was right about."

"Sounds interesting," I said, attempting to come across as enthusiastic. "What kind of projects do you have in mind?"

"Not telling just yet, but you should be excited. You may even get to meet my father, if he's awake. He hasn't even been seen by a human in generations. I myself haven't spoken to him in about six hundred years or so."

"He must like you almost as much as I do," I said.

She sneered at me. "You have a sense of humor. Never

cared for that in animals. My driver here used to have one. I had it removed."

"Has he been with you long?" I asked as the driver twitched and grimaced at just being mentioned.

"Gus, here," she said, gazing adoringly at the terrified man, "he's my driver, general henchman, and husband. We just had our five-year anniversary!"

"You're . . . married? How the . . . I mean, how did you meet?"

Jakki leaned back in her seat. "We met at this beautiful little coffee shop in San Francisco. It overlooks the Golden Gate Bridge, and there's a patio so you can just sit for hours. People jump off sometimes if you're lucky."

She patted Gus on the shoulder. He whimpered and flinched as if she had laid a cobra on his arm. "Oh, it was *so* romantic. All was quiet, and nobody in San Francisco was feeling suicidal that day, so I was making conversation with people. Gus didn't vomit or pass out like most guys do. I could tell right away we had a *special connection*. He said he was an English professor and that he wanted me to leave him alone because he was trying to write poems about *fog* or some nonsense like that. Well, nobody tells me no, so right then I made him fall in love with me. We were married that weekend, and we've been inseparable ever since. Plus he's not bad to look at, either." She winked at Gus.

Gus smiled and shuddered. He nodded and then shook his head no violently while grimacing as if in intense emotional distress.

Jakki sighed dreamily. "We had the greatest times at first. He'd start talking about going back home, calling me a perversion of nature, signaling to strangers that he was being kidnapped—all your normal newlywed stuff. He always knew how to make me smile. Sometimes he'd cry for hours and hours, and I'd just hold him in my arms until he stopped. We bonded, and I showed him the *real me*.

"That's nice?" I said, feeling sorry for Gus.

"A lot of that romance has faded, though," Jakki said, a bit wistfully. "After too much handling, you humans get a bit mushy around the cerebellum. But you know what they say, 'You should always hurt the ones you love.'"

"I don't think that's how the—"

"I'll show you what I mean," she said. "Gus! What would *you* like to do today?"

Gus furrowed his brow and seemed to give the question some serious thought. "A stick . . . with a pointy hat . . . for Alonya."

"See what I mean? Mushy brain," Jakki said, tapping the side of his head. "He's terrible with names, too. Gus! My name is Jakki. Can you say that?"

"Anne?"

"No, like this, JAH—"

"Jah . . ."

"KEE."

"Kee . . ."

"JAKKI!"

"Mmm . . . Margaret."

She prodded him playfully in the ribs with her elbow, and he smashed his head against the bulletproof window like he was trying to dive through it. "You're cute when you try to think, you know that?" she said.

"That's one heck of a love story," I said, wondering what else I could ask.

"You try it. Ask him something. It's fun."

I felt terrible for Gus. I happened to like my mind and hated the idea of losing it. "I'm not in the mood to have fun at someone else's expense—"

Jakki's smile was gone in an instant. "ASK HIM A QUESTION OR I WILL SEPARATE THE PARTS OF YOUR BODY WITH A TIRE IRON AND FEED THEM TO ANIMALS THAT DO NOT EAT MEAT AND ARE NOT EVEN HUNGRY."

"I've changed my mind," I said. "Hey, Gus, do you think you've experienced any adverse side effects from working so closely with your special lady friend here?"

Gus craned his neck to look at me. His expression was blank. Well, *mostly* blank.

"Yellow wallpaper," he said.

"See?" Jakki giggled. "Was that so hard? I'm sorry for the outburst. I get a bit sensitive at times. When you don't have a lot of friends, the ones you do have end up putting up with a lot of drama, I'm afraid."

"Can he be . . . fixed?" I asked.

"I *totally* wish he could. You lower life-forms have these fragile brains that can only see in one direction at a time. Spending too much time around me—it's like staring at the sun. I'd like to be able to have friends without turning their brains into Silly Putty. These days I go through a new gal pal every few months."

"Why not leave people alone if you're hurting them?" I asked.

"You're young; you don't understand. I'm at a point in my life where I need to be *building relationships*. Is it a crime to make it easier for people to accept the gift of my friendship by not allowing them to refuse it?"

I nodded. "It literally is."

"People will get used to it. You humans have no vision, terrible management, and zero capacity for long-term planning. You'd be surprised by how much better this planet would operate if your species wasn't running everything."

I was starting to see where she was going. "And I bet you know just who should be in charge."

She gave me a jaunty wink. "That's right—*your betters*. You humans need to learn obedience to higher minds, get comfortable with your place in the food chain, things like that. That's why I need your help, because *you* don't go all soft brained around us. Once we know how *you* do it, we can bring the rest of the humans under control *without* ruining or killing them. You can help us civilize the human race. Isn't that exciting?"

"I don't think I want to help with that plan. It sounds horrible," I said. "People like having control of their brains."

Jakki turned all the way around so she was kneeling on

her seat and facing me. "Let me ask you a question. Let's say you and a bunch of your little friends showed up on this planet, and there were no people anywhere yet, just animals. Would you put the dogs in charge?"

"Uh, no."

"Who, then? Horses and cows? Insects? Three-toed sloths? No. You'd take a look at things and decide *your people* should be in charge."

"Yeah, but we wouldn't enslave and abuse the animals," I said.

"Oh, of course not. You humans would never domesticate a dog or a horse and make them do your bidding. That sure would be terrible, wouldn't it?"

That one took me a second. "We kind of have a deal with them. It's a trade. We feed them, give them shelter, and pet them, and they grab the paper for us. If they don't like it, they can walk away or go on strike. You're talking about removing our ability to refuse."

"Of course, but that's your main flaw," Jakki said, turning around to face the road again. "Our species got rid of our free will a long time ago. We don't miss it, and neither will you."

"Not all of you got rid of it," I said.

Jakki's voice lost any semblance of friendliness. "Let's not bring up my prodigal sister again. Why don't you take a nap for a little while? We can talk later."

"I'm not sleepy," I said.

She pressed a button on the dashboard, and a plastic barrier shot up between the front seat and the rest of the SUV. There was a quiet beep, and an almost invisible green mist drifted from a heater vent on the ceiling. I don't know what it was, but it sure changed my mind about getting some sleep.

14

PINEAPPLES AND TOOTHPASTE

Someone was talking. "Here we are! Wake up, sleepy-heads!"

My head felt like someone had stuffed it with ice and thumbtacks, and I was having trouble getting in touch with my arms and legs.

I could hear Jakki bustling around, mumbling to herself, and occasionally barking platitudes at us. "The early bird has worms! Let's move it, people. We've got a lot to do!"

Even *thinking* about moving made me tired. I figured she could handle it if I slept a little longer.

"Gus," she said, "could you be a dear and hand me my cattle prod? It's in the glove box."

"YES!" said Gus.

"I'm up! I'm up!" I said, not wanting an electric shock that early in the morning.

Truth be told, I don't like electric shocks regardless of the time of day.

It *was* morning, I realized. The sun was low on the horizon, and the air had that bracing-cold quality that makes you want to stay indoors, eat soup, and watch daytime TV.

Gus seemed disappointed but did not go for the cattle prod. Through the open door of the SUV, I was finally able to get a clear look at him. His slate-gray suit, complete with white shirt and dark tie, made him look a bit like a Secret Service agent, except that Secret Service agents appear alert, and I wasn't sure Gus would notice a tennis racquet to the face unless he had been ordered to. I would have put his age at about fifty, but his face could have belonged to a younger man, if not for the full head of dark gray hair. In total he was unremarkable, which counterbalanced Jakki's abrasive strangeness nicely. I could see why she made him her living fashion accessory.

Behind me, Hypatia stirred and woke. "Nikola! That's not Mr. Marconi!"

"You're, like, two chapters behind," I said. "We've been kidnapped by an Old One, and we've arrived at our destination. The big guy is her husband, and for some reason you have about half a taco in your hair."

"Oh. Oh no. Ew," she said, discovering I was telling the truth about everything one at a time.

Jakki pointed at Warner. "Him too. Bring him."

I shook, then gently slapped Warner. He opened his eyes and looked around a bit. For a moment it looked like he was back with us, but I could see the horrific memory of what had happened creep into his expression, and he was out cold once again. "Warner!" I said. "Get up!"

Warner mumbled something but didn't look at me. He appeared to be awake, so I helped him to his feet and half pushed, half guided him along. He was able to stand upright and walk but lacked the motivation to go anywhere specific. I could work with that.

Once I had him up and standing, I was able to get a look at our surroundings. We were in the absolute middle of nowhere. No, that's not true. Were we to get into the car and drive at high speeds directly toward civilization, we could have gotten to the middle of nowhere in a couple of hours if we hurried. I could see nothing in any direction, and the world around us was desolate and utterly, shockingly, terribly flat.

A gust of icy wind blasted us from nowhere and nearly knocked Hypatia, Warner, and me onto the ground. I felt my skin freezing in the cold and wondered how long I could endure the exposure before I had a serious case of frostbite. Twenty minutes? Why hadn't any of us brought coats to the mall?

The experience seemed to rouse Warner from his stupor. He shivered and glanced around. "Is this hell?" he asked nobody in particular.

"No. It's Kansas," Jakki said.

Jakki's house was decidedly unmonstrous in its appearance. There was a low picket fence, a raggedly trimmed yard, and a lone tree that promised to grow flowers once spring arrived. The house itself was a humble two-story on a square base, with peeling yellow paint and white trim. White lace curtains stirred in the windows. A small porch supported a swinging bench and a few empty bird feeders. A pink mat at the door read, WELCOME, VICTIMS.

"Right this way!" Jakki said, and led us into her home. The living room was nothing special. There was an old tube TV that looked like it hadn't been turned on in decades and a rose-colored sofa coated in that plastic stuff people use when they want guests to feel guilty about sitting on their furniture.

Arranged in a fan pattern on the coffee table was an assortment of colorful books with titles like *Country Sunsets*, *Barns and Bridges of New England*, and *The Plight of Darfur: Photographing Human Misery*.

Jakki smiled and pushed me in the general direction of her kitchen.

The linoleum floor there bore a repeating pattern of wild-flowers and ornamental scrollwork. Brightly colored cabinets with metal flower handles lined the walls. The windowsill above the sink supported bottles of olive oil filled with herbs and botanicals, a decorative blue vase, and a beautiful orange bottle with a length of straw tied decoratively around its neck that seemed to glow in the morning light. This last bottle was labeled CHLOROFORM in elegant calligraphy.

Above a sturdy wooden table hung a large needlepoint picture of a goose whose neck bent at such an angle that it could have been broken. Above and below the goose, an embroidered inscription read: THE CITIES OF EARTH SHALL BURN. THE SCREAMS OF HER PEOPLE SHALL RISE TO THE HEAVENS AND DIE UNHEARD. Mauve really was a nice choice for the bow.

Hypatia and I guided Warner to a kitchen chair and sat on either side of him. He was unconscious again the moment he was off his feet.

Jakki strode/slithered over to a refrigerator and busied herself rummaging through its contents.

"Is being around her doing permanent damage to Warner?" I whispered to Hypatia.

"Only with extended exposure, or if she starts *changing his mind* about things," she said. "Or if she . . . feeds off him. You know."

I did know. I'd watched Tabbabitha feed off both Warner and Hypatia, and it was not an experience I was eager to relive.

"You know," I said. "If we make it out of this, when Warner tells the story, this will be the part where he tries to keep us terrified girls calm."

Hypatia chuckled like people do when you tell a joke in a situation where jokes really aren't acceptable.

"Aha!" Jakki said. She returned with an ornate silver serving tray and a yellowing sack of those white-powdered mini-doughnuts you find in bags at gas stations. She ripped the bag in two and dumped the doughnuts unceremoniously onto the tray, where they came to rest amid a stale cloud of powdered sugar. She then cleared a small space in the center of the tray, which she filled with a generous dollop of tartar-control toothpaste.

"Breakfast is served!" she said proudly. "Now . . . I need to make a phone call and powder my proboscis. You kids sit here, have a bite, and I'll be right back. Gus, honey, could you please murder them if they try to leave?"

"YES!" said Gus. He had that one word down, at least.

While Hypatia tried the doughnuts, I studied Gus and tried to figure out how he planned to kill us if the need arose.

"Mm!" Hypatia said. "These are actually pretty good."

Let me tell you, that was a *huge* relief because I hadn't eaten anything since we had Taco Bomb the day before, and I was pretty much starving. I grabbed two doughnuts and popped them in my mouth. They were dry, crumbly, and about 80 percent spoiled. I nearly vomited, but somehow managed to choke it down.

"I love when they get a little moldy. Really makes the flavor of the preservatives pop," Hypatia said.

It was really my own fault for taking a parahuman's word on whether something tasted good.

"How come you aren't, you know, zonked like Warner?" I asked.

"We parahumans can handle them a bit better than humans, particularly if we've had previous experience with them. What happened while we were asleep?"

I started to fill her in but figured Warner should know also, so while Hypatia chewed on a particularly crunchy doughnut, I tried to rouse him. Initially, I talked to him softly, then shook his shoulders, and even slapped him lightly on the cheek. Nothing seemed to work. Finally, I stuck my finger in my mouth, got it good and wet, and shoved it into his ear with a twist.

"Gah!" he said. "What did you do that for?"

"You've been acting like a zombie," I said. "You need to wake up and work with us. We're kind of in a jam here."

"Preserves," corrected Gus as he pointed at the toothpaste on the doughnut platter.

"Uh, thanks," I said.

Warner looked around, obviously confused to find himself there. "Are we at your grandma's house? What smells like rotting meat? Who is that guy?"

"We're captives of an Old One, and that's Gus," I said as Gus waved cheerfully. "He's there to murder us if we try to leave."

"How is he going to do that?" Warner asked.

"Beats me," I said. "Gus, how did you plan on killing us if we ran away?"

Gus gave me a confident double-thumbs-up gesture. "Pineapples," he said.

"Are they poisoned?" Hypatia asked.

"Uh . . . spicy?" Gus said, unsure of himself.

Warner shrugged. "So tell me everything else. Last thing I remember was that security guard grabbing me."

"Fair warning: It's all bad news. Are you ready?" I asked.

"No," Warner said. "Tell me anyway."

To their credit, Warner and Hypatia listened carefully without freaking or passing out again. Occasionally, Warner made a face that I knew meant he was making mental notes about something.

When I was describing how the windshield somehow scrambled any road signs, Hypatia interrupted my story with an idea. "You tried your tablet in the car. What about now?" She produced her own tablet and powered it on.

The three of us and Gus watched with interest as it searched for a signal before an alert appeared in the center of the screen: NETWORK TRAFFIC BLOCKED BECAUSE I'M NOT AN IDIOT. XOXO, JAKKI.

"Worth a shot," I said, before explaining the rest of what happened while they were out.

- - - - - ✳ - - - - -

" . . . because it's in the center of the picture, and the goose is a little deformed?" Warner asked a few minutes later.

"Yeah, see?" I pointed. "The neck bends at a ninety-degree angle right before the head. I think she was worried it wouldn't fit in the frame with the longer motto. Either that or the broken-neck thing was intentional."

"The mauve does look nice," Warner said, nodding.

"Rattles . . . like angry candy," said Gus.

I nodded at him. "I think so, too."

Warner and I each found a doughnut that was mostly still

edible and were able to choke them down by dipping them in the toothpaste and saying silent prayers to the gods of food poisoning.

After "breakfast," Warner leaned into the center of the table and signaled that we should do the same. "Gus doesn't look too swift, and I don't think he has a gun. I say we make a run for it. Who knows how long that *thing* will be gone?"

Unfortunately, Gus's ears worked very well. He shook his head solemnly and opened his jacket to reveal four large and dangerous-looking hand grenades fastened to the inside of his suit coat.

"Pineapples," he said.

"Gus," I said, "if there's anyone in this house I'd entrust with high explosives, it's you."

He smiled widely.

Warner said, "I wonder if he even knows how to use them."

"YES!" Gus nodded emphatically and prepared to demonstrate proper grenade operation.

"NO! NONONONONONONONONONONO!" all three of us shouted at once.

I held my hands up. "Gus, we know you're the expert. There's no reason to waste a grenade showing us. Besides, it would mess up the kitchen."

"And I'd like to keep all my skin and body parts right where they are," said Warner.

"Yes, Gus," I said, "this is just not the time to try out those grenades. Why dontcha put that little guy back in your jacket there, okay?"

"Yes," Gus said, clearly disappointed.

- - - - - ✳ - - - -

Jakki returned a short while later. "Oh, lovely! I see Warner has decided to join us. It's a pleasure to meet you, sir," she said.

Warner mumbled something incoherent that might have been "Glow to health." I could be a bit off on that.

She glared at him. "You're *very happy* to make my acquaintance," she said with utter confidence.

"I AM happy to make your acquaintance!" said Warner, his eyes a bit unfocused. He jumped up, strode across the kitchen, and shook her hand warmly with both hands, before pulling her in for a long, affectionate hug.

"I absolutely love your house, and those horrible dough-nuts are quite good! Can we stay here forever?"

"What a polite boy!" Jakki said, delighted.

"Hey!" I said. "If you want us to come quietly, no poking around in his brain. Free will or nothing."

"You're no fun." Jakki glowered. "Maybe he really likes it here."

"No," I said. "He doesn't. He thinks your house is tacky and the food is terrible."

Jakki appeared deeply offended. "Well, maybe it's the best I can do. Sorry if I can't meet your *high standards*."

"Get used to it. What good is a bunch of fake compliments, anyway?"

"I guess we'll have to agree to disagree on that," she said. "Sit back down."

Warner sat.

"There, he's back to normal now."

Warner sat and smiled placidly. "Thank you. Of all the mind-bendingly nightmarish creatures I've ever met, you are the most beautiful. I sure wish you weren't married."

"Jakki . . . ," I said.

She threw her hands up. "Oh, *fine*! But know that I will *remove* any sharp objects from your possession, tongues included."

Warner shook his head. "Did I just say something?"

"I think you almost proposed," Hypatia said.

"Oh," he said, and stuffed a doughnut into his mouth, wincing like it hurt.

Jakki sat down at the table with us, which caused the rest of us to scoot together along the opposite side. "I've just spoken with one of my sisters, and they'll be bringing us home shortly."

"There's no need to bring them," I said, nodding at Warner and Hypatia. "Let them go. You and I can go alone."

"No, your baggage comes along for the ride. Besides, they might have information we need. They might even get to see Daddy, too."

Hypatia paled. "Daddy?"

"Yes, my father. You've heard of him?"

Warner's eyes bugged out, and Hypatia's mouth dropped open. She said something so faintly I couldn't hear her.

"You're parahuman," she said to Hypatia, "so technically my father is your great-great-great-great-great-granddaddy, or something. He's been dead for centuries, but it's almost time for him to rise again. That's why I'm in such a tizzy these days. Before he died, he told us to tidy up the place, and I'm a bit of a procrastinator."

"You were supposed to tidy your house?" Hypatia asked.

"No, stupid, the earth," she said with a smile. "It's gone way downhill—civilizations and complex societies sprouting up all over the place, superstition and war at all-time lows. I don't know how we ever let it get this far. Don't worry; we're almost done—you won't have much to do."

Then the kitchen exploded.

15

SUBTERRA

There was no warning, no whistling like you hear when a bomb is dropping in the movies, not even the sound of Gus pulling a pin from a grenade. We were sitting there one moment, and the next, the entire house exploded around us. The walls, floor, cabinets, and everything else were reduced to fragments and sent whirling around like we were in the center of a tornado. Through the chaotic torrent of splintered wood, metal shards, and twinkling bits of glass and ceramic, I could still make out the forms of my friends, seated just where they had been and looking as terrified as I was. I was probably screaming, but I can't be sure, because I couldn't hear anything above the noise of whatever disaster had occurred. I could see fragments of daylight stabbing through the gaps in the debris, but gradually they faded and were gone.

And then it stopped as suddenly as it had started. All was still, silent, and cold. I could see nothing but utter blackness.

"Uh," Warner said, "did we just die?"

Hypatia had grabbed my hand hard enough to hurt. "What on earth was that?" she asked in a furious whisper.

"Calm yourselves. Everything is fine. We have our own methods of transportation that can't be tracked," Jakki said. I could hear her fashionable shoes *clack*ing across the room. Were we still in a room? I felt in front of myself and found the kitchen table right where it had been. The floor felt solid as well.

"It's a bit like a wormhole," Jakki went on, "just a teensy bit more violent. Wait there."

"A gale! Chicka boom! Twisty twister!" said Gus, sounding equal parts enthralled and terrified.

"Okay, everyone," I said. "Gus is just fine. No need to worry about Gus."

"Pineapple?" said Gus.

"No pineapple!" Warner, Hypatia, and I shouted.

"Yes," said Gus, which I really, really hoped meant "Yes, okay" and not "Yes, but if it's all the same to you, I think I'll just pull the pin on my grenade in this enclosed space and see what happens."

There was a noise in the corner, and I looked to its source, which was pretty much useless, since I couldn't have seen my hand in front of my face. A second later there was a blinding light as Jakki switched on a flashlight. Warner, still looking a bit woozy from all the mental tampering, squinted and groaned.

"Oh, stop complaining! The light is for your benefit. Come on, we have places to be. Let's go!"

As my eyes grew used to the light, I could make out that we were standing in a perfectly reassembled kitchen. Everything was exactly as it had been, except the goose's neck was bent in the opposite direction and Gus was standing facing the wall, instead of leaning against it. Actually, he was still leaning on it, but with his face instead of his back.

"I said move. Come on!" commanded Jakki.

We stepped out the front door. Where there had been a barren field and nothing but horizon for miles in all directions was now nothing but absolute darkness. The damp air was chilly, but not quite cold, and utterly still. Jakki swung her flashlight back and forth in front of the house. "There should be a light switch here somewhere," she said. "Ah! There it is. Nikola, could you get that?"

Before I could move a muscle, there was another shocking explosion, and the little cottage once again was reduced to shards, swirled as if at the center of an F5 tornado, and was gone.

"Go on," Jakki said, as if nothing out of the ordinary had happened. "It's right there."

The light switch she was referring to was just that, a simple toggle-style switch like you see on every wall in the world. The only difference was that this one was mounted to a telephone pole that was anchored in the ground. I raised the switch and was blinded a second time as gigantic stadium lights crashed to life high above us, bright as day.

Describing this will be extremely difficult, but I'll give it a shot. The lights above us were the brightest I'd ever seen. My friends and the dirt at our feet were illuminated so brilliantly that I might have worried about sunburn. The glow extended around us and faded off into the distance. Despite their extreme radiance, no matter how hard I peered into the darkness, all I could see was utter blackness in all directions for what could have been miles and miles. My first impression was that we had been transported to some barren planet far from any sun. A place so distant that not even starlight could touch it. The view was unsettlingly desolate, even more desolate than Kansas had been.

"Welcome to Subterra," Jakki said, spreading her arms. "Your new home and future gravesite."

The name told me all I needed to know. We were in a cave. In some ways it was not like a cave at all. It was obviously wired for electricity and the ground was perfectly flat and dry in all directions, but there was no denying that distinct *underground* feeling. As if proof was called for, there was a distant series of *clunk*s, and lights around the perimeter of the space blazed to life, revealing massive metal supports zigzagging up and down the walls, meeting at the top of the chamber in a perfectly hemispherical dome. It was as if some planet-sized giant had cut a globe in two and set the top half over us. I felt instantly dizzy—the immensity of what I was seeing made me feel a lot like you feel when standing on the edge of a tall cliff. Never had I seen or even heard of a construction approaching the scale of that one chamber. Ever seen the Hoover Dam? You could store a few dozen in that cavern and have plenty of space left over for your boat.

I realized that my dad must be down here . . . somewhere.

"That's better," said Jakki. "I wanted you to get a good look at things. How do you like my daddy's house?"

"He doesn't share your knack for decorating," I said honestly.

"It . . . could use a couple plants, maybe," Warner said.

"Maybe a fountain," Hypatia offered.

Jakki was clearly offended. "I put a ficus in the corner just over there last month. Nobody notices anything I do."

"I don't see it," I said, squinting into the distance.

"It's about four miles straight that way," she said.

"I'm not sure it's getting enough light," Warner said.

Jakki shook her head. "Of course it isn't. I don't water it, either. That's what houseplants are for, isn't it? You bring a living thing into your home, subject it to inattention and apathy, and wait for it to wither and die. It's almost as good as a fish tank. Whenever I feel down, I like to close my eyes and remember that somewhere in this world there is a small life that will die alone because of me." She sighed blissfully. "Okay, we should get going!"

Not far from us was a low metal building I'd missed while gawking at the cave, one of those prefabricated aluminum garages. Inside it stood a few small electric scooters connected to chargers on the wall.

"Grab one, and let's move," Jakki said.

"Scooters? Are you serious?" Warner said. "Aren't villains supposed to get around in things like monorails, chariots pulled by bears, and things like that?"

"They're small, efficient, and don't need fuel. No gas stations down here," said Jakki as she mounted her scooter. "They're fun, too. You humans are the scourge of this planet, you ruin everything, and you're just begging to be wiped out, but you really got it right with the scooters. Gus, I'll ride with you."

Jakki made Gus sit in front of her and wrapped her arms around his midsection. He shuddered visibly and started the engine. "Let us scoot!" she cried.

"Aren't you worried we'll take off?" I asked, grabbing the front spot of the closest scooter before Hypatia could claim it.

Jakki laughed with disdain. "And go where? Take one wrong turn down here, and nobody will ever see you again. These lights don't stay on forever. If you lose sight of us, you'll probably die of thirst before we can find you again. Hit it, Gus!"

They zoomed off into the blackness.

I started my scooter, and Hypatia climbed on behind me. "Can you drive this?" she asked.

I pressed a button, which brought the small engine

purring to life. "No," I said as I turned the throttle, and we shot wobbling off into the darkness.

Warner caught up with us not long after and appeared to be comfortable with his scooter, if a little perturbed that we'd gone on without him.

"Had to go quick," I said. "Hypatia was losing her nerve."

"EEEEEEEEEEEEEEEEEEEEEEEEE!" said Hypatia as I almost lost my balance by turning my head and talking at the same time.

We sped along and caught up with Jakki and Gus before they reached the wall.

I had known the wall was large, but until we approached I had failed to grasp its true scale. Have you ever stood close to a skyscraper? Imagine something even taller, but so wide you can't see the edges, a surface so flat you don't even realize it's curved until you notice it hangs directly above you when you look up. The wall of the cave was bigger than that. Once more I was dizzy at the realization of its immensity and nearly toppled over again, which elicited another series of screeches from Hypatia.

As we drew near, I could make out a new feature of the wall, a single gaping maw of a door that must have been a quarter mile tall at least, and probably half that wide. As we passed into the mouth of the door, the lights lining the massive dome went black behind us and were replaced by new lights along the roof of the tunnel. These revealed a path that narrowed and curved out of sight.

After that, our path took us on a confusing, entangled

journey through tunnels, over a bridge or two, and eventually through archways cut into the black rock no wider than I could have stretched my arms. Finally, we passed through one last portal, and I nearly fell off the scooter in shock.

"Holy mackerel," I whispered to myself, pulling the scooter to a halt. We were supposed to keep going, but I couldn't cope with what I was seeing otherwise.

Warner pulled up alongside us, his mouth hanging open, speechless with amazement.

Hypatia took a deep breath and said, "Oh my . . ."

We had entered another dome, this one every bit as large as the first. But the other dome had been empty, and this was anything but.

Right there in front of our eyes, glowing like an island of light in the immense darkness, stood a massive structure stretching up into the open space above like some monumental pillar. Atop it, a bright light flickered orange, then bluish violet, then orange, then bluish again. There were glowing shapes etched in the blackness. Neon shapes. It was a sign. I blinked, and the shapes made letters in my mind. Then those letters made words: TENTACULAR ARMS. Fainter rectangular lights formed a regular grid that climbed the sides of the pillar. These sights assembled in my brain, and finally what I was seeing made sense. It was a massive hotel, standing right there in front of us, in the middle of the cave. As strange as it was to see a building there, it was even stranger to see it lit up, as if someone had simply picked it up from downtown

Chicago or Los Angeles and set it back down in the cave without turning the lights off.

I took a second to rub my eyes and slap myself on the cheek, just in case I was hallucinating. I started the scooter again, and we moved closer, a bit more slowly now. As we approached, I could make out delicate stone-carved ivy winding its way up the corners and along arches over each of the windows. Welcoming golden light blazed from every side and from a line of streetlamps out front.

Then I saw something else. Off in the distance, other vague shapes suggested other buildings around the far edges of this new dome. A single line of buildings formed in a ring around one central structure, the hotel. We were at the center of an underground city.

"I've changed my mind," said Warner over the faint grinding of our tires on the cave floor. "Jakki's dad has style."

"She was *lying* about that, Warner," Hypatia said testily.

"I know. I was joking about—"

"Well, don't joke about that. Okay?" Hypatia said. "Things are bad enough without—"

"What are you guys talking about?" I asked.

"Jakki talking about her father, like he built this place. It's not true," Hypatia said.

"Who's her pop again?" I asked.

Warner drew closer, and I had to adjust course to keep from bumping into him. "According to old historical accounts, or legends, depending on whether you believe them, the Old

Ones originally came from one primordial ancestor. He's supposed to be this immortal, giant monster that terrorized Earth for thousands of years."

Hypatia couldn't stop herself from adding, "And it's utter hogwash we don't need to be getting worked up about."

"She seems to buy it," I said, indicating Jakki, who was making Gus do fun little swerves as we approached the hotel.

I couldn't see her sitting behind me, but I heard Hypatia roll her eyes in her tone. "Of *course* she buys it. Every account of the Old Ones from every period in history says they believe their father or Eldest or whatever they call him is going to show up any day now. It's like a fairy tale to them, but because they have trouble with creative thinking, they take it at face value. It's not even a good fairy tale."

"Why not?"

"It doesn't make sense! He's immortal, but he died. He's so big he blots out the sun, but nobody has ever said what he looks like. The entire world lived in fear of him for thousands of years during the Stone Age, but nobody bothered to write anything down?"

"They didn't have writing in the Stone Age," I pointed out.

"*We* did," Hypatia said testily. "Parahumans were developing primitive methods of information transfer at the time, like text messaging and blogs. Nobody has ever found as much as a single credible account of a giant world-devouring force of pure evil, and that's the sort of thing your average blogger tends to take notice of."

"I bet I could take him," Warner said, flexing a spindly arm and almost losing control of his scooter.

"Good to see you're feeling better!" I said.

I'd hoped that might change the subject, but when Hypatia gets on a soapbox, it can be hard for her to climb down. "I think their ultimate goal is to create the *illusion* that he's come back, that they have this superpowerful being at their disposal, so the humans and parahumans won't put up a fight. It would allow them to take control of the world without actually—"

"Hey, pause that," I said. "We're here."

Despite the streetlamps in front of the hotel, there was no street or parking lot, just a flat dirt floor. So we left our scooters near the door among a dusty assortment of randomly parked golf carts, scooters, and jeeps, and mounted a wide stone staircase to a massive door of ornate gold-plated metal and stained glass. I stepped up to it, took a deep breath, and, with effort, pulled it open.

The interior of the hotel looked pretty much the same as every other nice hotel I've ever seen, with the exception that other hotels have staff working and people checking in, checking out, and waiting around. The Tentacular Arms was completely empty. Dust blanketed the tables and counter-tops. More dust hung in wispy tendrils in the air. A distinct musty smell overpowered the senses.

Jakki was waiting for us in an obese high-backed leather chair alongside an urn of cucumber water that had gone rotten about four years before. She had changed, and her new out-fit, an off-white silk blouse with gray linen pants and jacket above gleaming red shoes, was immaculate, which I found particularly impressive since Hypatia, Warner, and I had all just taken the same trip and were at least a little covered in cave dirt with flecks of mud on our faces.

She smiled brightly at our appearance, as if pleasantly surprised we had dropped in for a visit. "Hey, kids! Come have a seat. I sent Gus to get your rooms ready. This is where you'll be staying while you're here. It's about noonish local time, so we're going to have a little chat and you kids can get to work tomorrow, bright and early. How's that sound?"

She gestured to a few chairs across from her. I fell into one and found it so comfortable that I was almost unable to keep my eyes open. Hypatia and Warner sat on either side of me, and Hypatia scooted herself a bit closer, either so we could be nearer to each other or so she could be just a little farther from the huge urn of suspicious-looking liquid next to Jakki.

"What is it you want us to do?" I asked.

"Where are we?" Warner wanted to know.

"Is there a bathroom nearby? I'd like to wash up," said Hypatia.

Jakki held up her hands as if trying to calm us. "I know you all must have questions, and let me assure you, they will all be answered in due time. First things first. You are now in Subterra, our research and development community." She pointed with two fingers at Hypatia and Warner. "You two will continue in your studies, much as you did before you came here. The main difference is that you will be paid a highly competitive wage and will be allowed to study and work on whatever you like. Eventually, you may even be able to leave from time to time, if you prove yourself loyal enough. Isn't that nice?"

"Almost as nice as being literally anywhere else, and doing literally anything else," I said.

She nodded excitedly. "I think so, too. You'll also have access to world-class fitness facilities, top-notch medical care, the best food you've ever tasted and"—she spread her arms wide, showcasing the hotel itself—"elite-grade luxury accommodations. Welcome to the good life!"

Next to the abandoned reception desk, a potted tree gave up and died, dropping all its leaves at once.

"What if we don't want to help?" Warner asked.

"Then you don't get paid, and you're free to sit around and do nothing. Of course, since we're several miles beneath the earth's surface here, there's not much of a cell phone signal and no Internet, so you'll mostly be watching dust accumulate. You'll come around sooner or later. They all come around sooner or later."

"Well, I think I could get used to being a dust spectator," I said.

Jakki smiled in a sad yet patronizing manner. "*Oh, honey.* You won't have to do any of that—don't worry. We wanted *you* so we could figure out how you tick. Basically, we just want to pick your brain for a while."

"Maybe I don't feel like answering questions."

Jakki was momentarily confused. "*Oh, you thought I meant 'pick your brain' like when people ask one another questions!* I meant it literally. We intend to extract your physical brain and poke around to see what's going on in there."

"Will you give it back when you've finished with it?" Hypatia asked.

"Hey!" I said. "I'm not lending my brain to anyone."

Jakki laughed at us jovially, like we were three old roommates meeting for brunch. "Easy, ladies, there's no need to worry about what anyone wants, because nobody has a choice. And don't worry, it shouldn't hurt for long. When the time comes, I'll collect Miss Nikola here, and—maybe you all can even meet my father!"

Hypatia jabbed a finger at Jakki with a fierceness I hadn't seen from her before. "You're *lying.* Everyone knows your father died thousands of years ago, if he was ever real in the first place. You can't frighten us with ghost stories."

Jakki blinked and might have responded, but just then there was a sickly sounding *ding*, and a set of elevator doors opened, revealing our old friend Gus, who was holding two cans of generic Professor Pabb soda. He stepped over to us and handed one to Warner and the other to me with a magnanimous flourish.

"Donation a quarterbox," he said with a stately nod. The can was dusty and lukewarm and had expired about the same time I had been learning to walk.

But then Gus saw Hypatia did not have a drink. For most people, this would have been a clear indication that they had miscalculated how many cans of soda they would need, but Gus didn't give up so easily. He took my soda and handed it to Hypatia and then, after a little consideration, let me have Warner's can. Gus grinned broadly at having figured this little problem out and went to stand next to Jakki's chair.

Jakki, who had been silent while this had been going on, blinked twice and continued. "Young lady," she said, looking to Hypatia, "there are certain things I do not lie about, and in this situation I will not tolerate the tone you've taken, nor the implication that I've told a falsehood. You owe my father and me an apology. Apologize now, and make it good because *he's listening.*"

Gus then decided Warner needed a drink, so he took mine away from me, handed it to Warner, and gave me the can Hypatia had been holding.

"I'm sorry," Hypatia said. "How about I make up for it by introducing your dad to Santa Claus and Uncle Sam, since they're just as real. They could play checkers or—thank you, Gus," she said as Gus handed her Warner's can of Professor Pabb.

"That's enough, thank you," Jakki said, standing. She buttoned the jacket of her pantsuit and picked up her handbag from the chair next to her. She straightened her collar absentmindedly and allowed her gaze to slip up to the ceiling. Her eyes fluttered closed like she was hearing a particularly nice passage from her favorite song.

I could hear something, a slightly irritating, almost imperceptible noise in the air, something like a whine and a buzz combined with a whisper. Suddenly, everything was panic. Gus, Hypatia, and Warner collapsed to the floor instantly, screaming, clutching at their ears, and scratching at the sides of their heads. They shrieked, writhed, spasmed, and gibbered nonsense at the top of their lungs.

I knelt beside Hypatia and gave her a good shake. When that didn't rouse her, I tried the same thing on Warner, shouting, "What is it? What's happening?" But neither of them even seemed aware of my presence. Hypatia, unable to scratch her ears off, started battering herself in the head with her fists. Gus banged his head on the floor in what looked like an effort to knock himself unconscious, while Warner kicked furiously and clawed at the rug in agony, overturning a chair, breaking one of the side table's spindly legs, and spilling fetid cucumber water onto the carpet.

She was feeding on them, sucking the life right out of their bodies.

I looked up and saw Jakki standing with her head turned skyward in serene patience. "CUT IT OUT! YOU'RE HURTING THEM!" I screamed. "STOP IT!"

She didn't respond, so I picked up the heavy glass urn that still held a little moldering water and, with all my strength, broke it over her head.

That got her attention, even if the weighty, jagged chunks of glass didn't injure her in any way. The remaining water in the container ran down her body without even dampening her clothes. My friends immediately stopped shrieking and settled down, breathing like they'd just finished a marathon.

Jakki took note of the broken glass around her and peered curiously into my eyes in a way that made me want to hide in another zip code.

"That didn't hurt you?" she asked. "You didn't feel it?"

Hypatia had already stood and was helping Gus to his feet. Warner was looking a bit defeated, so I took hold of his arm and hauled him back into his chair.

"Was it supposed to?" I asked.

She eyed me up and down, as if seeing me for the first time. "You are one unique girl." She twitched and seemed to change gears. "Listen, there is nothing I'd like more than to get started with you right this moment, but I have to be in D.C. in a couple hours, and *now* I have to have my *nails* done."

She lifted her hands with their backs to me, offering a view of a hairline scratch a shard of glass had left across her left pinkie nail.

"Okay," I said, glad she was leaving. "So, what do we—"

"Just stay put." She pointed at Gus. "Keep an eye on them. Okay?"

Gus grunted and coughed. "Yes," he said.

"And the three of you can clean this mess up before I get back, or I will find some new, exciting way of making you suffer," she said.

She spun and marched out the door. As she passed, a second potted tree by the door withered and died.

"She forgot to tell me where the bathroom is," Hypatia moaned.

16

THE PIZZATILLO PLOT

Once we'd located a bathroom for Hypatia, and Warner was able to get over being traumatized yet again, we were left with nothing to do. We might have left, but Gus had taken up residence near the front door and followed us from room to room to ensure there were no escape attempts. Anytime someone took a step toward the door, Gus would flash his assortment of "pineapples" and make it clear just how eager he was to share them with anyone who wanted a taste. The smell of the cucumber water was quickly going from gross to offensive, so we decided to clean up—once it was agreed we were *not* cleaning because Jakki told us to.

Warner found a maintenance closet that held a carpet shampooer and cleaning supplies, which made things much easier. After the rug had been cleaned, Hypatia suggested we keep going. I would have told anyone else to get bent, but something in Hypatia's eyes told me she wasn't managing the situation well. Maybe it was that one of her eyes was yellow and the other was black; maybe it was the wide, panicked glances she threw at every corner of the room at any sound. In any case, it was clear that, like Warner, she was barely keeping herself together.

So we split up. I scraped dust off surfaces, wiped them down, and polished the wood to as healthy a sheen as possible. Warner scrubbed down the walls, leaving wide swaths of cleanliness that looked like reverse stains at first. Hypatia flitted around the lobby like a moth with ADHD, and before long the place was clean enough to pass for a hotel that was not essentially a prison, the kind people would pay to stay in.

The Tentacular Arms was actually looking pretty . . . nice. The carpet was patterned in deep burgundy, and the chairs were cloud-soft chocolate-colored thrones. Painted vines like those carved in stone outside snaked up the walls and integrated into ornate tin ceiling tiles accented in gold leaf. The wood railings, surfaces, and paneled walls were a rich mahogany. The combined effect made it seem dark in the lobby, even though the lights were quite bright. I made a point of watering the surviving plants to spite Jakki. They were mostly dead already, but it felt good to do something without permission.

We started seeing the zombies just after five o'clock. They weren't actual zombies, but if you want to make a zombie movie, I know where you can get actors cheap. It only took a second to put it together. The people we saw were the normal residents of the hotel. They were men and women of all ages and backgrounds, most of them scientists or researchers of some sort, judging by their well-worn lab coats and equipment.

It was hard to peg what made them seem like zombies. It was like they had lost whatever it was that made them human without killing the body that had kept them alive, if that makes sense. The zombies did not look in our direction, nor did they acknowledge one another, save for the occasional grunt when someone stepped on someone else's foot or when they unintentionally jostled one another. It was like they were all following a vague script. One by one, they entered, walked to the center of the room, stopped, turned, and walked down a side hall without so much as a glance at the lobby someone had put a great deal of work into cleaning for them.

Warner, Hypatia, and I stood behind the reception desk.

I studied the mostly blank faces as they passed. "Keep an eye out for my dad," I said.

"What good would that do?" Warner asked.

"He *must* be down here somewhere, and he'll know more about this place than we do. And if they didn't . . . kill him after his last attempt, he probably has more plans in the works."

"You really think this is the place he was talking about?" Warner asked.

I thought about it. "How many of these do you think they need? It's not like they're running out of space here."

Warner nodded and patted me on the shoulder, which

was a little weird. Hypatia squared a large glass sculpture on the counter and smiled contentedly at it.

"Should we talk to one of them?" Warner asked, gesturing at one of the zombies. Their influx seemed to be slowing.

"Do you think they can talk?" I asked.

"Can't hurt. Let's try that one," he suggested, indicating a smallish man who seemed to be moving with a little more spirit than the rest.

This one wore a white lab coat over jeans and a black T-shirt. Warner stepped in his path and greeted him with the warmest smile he could muster. "Hey, there! Where's the welcome desk for new arrivals?"

The man, who had streaks of gray along his temples and a meticulously combed part, tried to shuffle past him. Warner juked left and right, ensuring the man couldn't wander past. A second later, a faint glimmer of awareness came over the man. It was almost like he woke up. Almost.

He looked at Warner, as if seeing him for the first time. His voice was squeaky and tentative, like he was worried someone might overhear. "They haven't broken you yet."

"No," Warner said, his smile fading a bit. "Do you know anyone named Melvin Kross? He's probably a strange and irritating fellow, judging by his offspring."

The man glanced around. "No . . . No, sorry. To be honest, I'm not sure I remember my own name at the moment. I can be reasonably sure I'm not Melvin. Perhaps David—do I look like a David to you?"

There were a few seconds' silence during which it became clear that the man really needed an answer to his question. Thankfully, Hypatia had considered the matter.

"You look like a Sylvester to me," she said.

"I like that," the small man said. "Let's agree on the name Sylvester J. Marchbanks for the time being. Sorry for being distracted. The cognitive amplifier at the lab leaves us a bit . . . what's the word . . . Dappy? Drummed? Disambiguated?"

"Close enough," Warner said. "Can you tell us how to get out of here? We'd like to go home."

"Sure. Use the emergency exit," the man said with a chuckle. "Did you come on your own, or did they bring you?"

"They brought us," Warner said. "Where's the emergency exit?"

Sylvester Marchbanks nodded succinctly. "Go straight through those doors behind you, down the stairs, and out the back door by the kitchens. Once you're out, walk about a mile directly away from the hotel toward the tall blue building on the far wall. About halfway there, you'll find a rather deep pit they throw the garbage and other refuse into. It's huge and about half a mile deep, so you can't miss it. Once you get there, just jump right in and get it over with."

He grabbed Warner's hands urgently, suddenly emphatic. "Do it before they can get inside your head, boy! Don't stay! Don't listen to the songs in the labs—the songs! They get in your head, and they won't leave. They never, never stop. I can't sleep anymore. Have I ever told you that? I only lie in the dark and wait for tomorrow to come so I can die a little more.

But the exit . . . that's what I would do if I could still disobey. I'd march straight over there, hop right in, and be done with the whole affair! Now, if you'll excuse me, I've been ordered to enjoy tonight's dinner very much."

With that, he shoved Warner aside with surprising assertiveness and trudged down the hall toward an oaken doorway marked RESTAURANT with flaking silver spray paint.

"Think they have food down there?" Warner asked.

"Smells like it," Hypatia said. "Should we check it out?"

I was hungry myself, but I wasn't ready to go yet. "I still think my dad might come along. You two go ahead."

Warner took a step toward the cafeteria. Hypatia grabbed the back of his shirt, stopping him. "We wouldn't dream of leaving you alone. We stick together no matter what."

Warner nodded and acted like he had only meant to stretch his legs. "Yeah, we got your back."

I might have argued the point with them, since there was probably no use in our sticking together, but just then the front door swung open and one last, especially bedraggled worker stumbled in. He was pulling a full-sized suitcase on wheels, staring at a tablet computer, holding a large paper coffee cup, and trying to angle his body so the bulky leather bag he had slung over his shoulder didn't fall off. It didn't work. As he pushed through the door, the shoulder bag caught on the frame, slid off, and brought the whole precariously balanced equilibrium crashing down. The man was left on the floor, soaked in coffee and entangled in straps and handles under his wheeled bag.

"Mother's brother, that's hot!" he exclaimed to no one in particular.

Hypatia looked crestfallen. "We just cleaned there."

My crest, on the other hand, was in no danger of falling. "Hi, Dad!" I said.

Dad was looking as disheveled as ever, which was nice. He hadn't brushed his hair in at least a week, and a thick, patchy beard grew on his chin and most of both cheeks. The portions of his lab coat not soaked in coffee were stained here and there in other ways and burned badly on one of the pockets. If he had looked well groomed, I would have been seriously concerned. These were clear signs Dad had been busy. I hurried over to him.

"Could you grab that for me?" he asked, eyes still locked on his tablet. The screen was displaying some kind of calculations; it looked a bit like the virtualized particle accelerator he had been working on at home so he wouldn't have to run the full-sized one as often. If you think running the air conditioning with the doors open makes for an expensive electric bill, you should see how much it costs to run a particle accelerator for three seconds at seven teraelectronvolts.

"Sure," I said, lifting the bag, which was much heavier than I expected.

"Set it over in the meal area, by the table with the . . . that . . . you know, *the thing*! *The table with the thing!* Good lord, can't you people stop pestering me for one moment? Have they brought dinner yet?"

I rolled my eyes. "I think so, Dad. Do you know the menu?"

He shook his head in irritation. "*What?* Yes, unfortunately. Please. My bag. The booth with the thing."

I shouldered the bag and took the wheeled case for good measure. I knew this mode. Since the door had opened, his gaze had not strayed a single moment from the screen and the simulation he was running. I was willing to bet the reason he was so late was because he had not raised his eyes from the screen for an hour or more. It was best to give him a moment to finish what he was working on, if you didn't want to make him completely intolerable for the next several hours.

I took a second to look him over a little more closely. He looked very much like I remembered, although he was thinner and seemed to have an almost imperceptible limp when he walked. The only scar I spotted was a long-healed wound on his left ear, partially concealed by his hair.

Warner was smiling in spite of himself as he led the way to the cafeteria. "Is he always like that?"

"No," I said. "Sometimes he gets *really* distracted."

The deep colors and soft surfaces of the lobby were even more present in the dining hall. This was complemented by soft jazz music wafting over unseen speakers, huge luxurious booth benches, gleaming silver cutlery, and warm stained-glass lamps here and there. The effect was completely ruined by four plastic card tables, which were pushed together to make one big table at the center of the room. All four tables were collectively piled at least three feet high with a gargantuan mound of lukewarm Pizzatillos.

Between the card tables, threadlike rivulets of grease

drained onto the floor, where glistening orange lard stalagmites had formed.

If you aren't familiar with them, Pizzatillos are oily scraps of moist tortilla-like substance wrapped around various other substances that have been colored and shaped to resemble the sorts of things one might find on a pizza. They're amazingly salty, faintly disgusting, catastrophically unhealthy, and ridiculously popular.

"Oh, I LOVE those!" Hypatia said.

The "table with the thing" was on a far end of the room, behind a low wall. In other days, it might have been the restaurant's smoking section. I could tell the table with the thing was *the* "table with the thing" because someone had affixed a comic-book cutout of an angry orange rock-man to the wall above it with clear tape. It was the only addition to the restaurant's decor, apart from decades of neglect.

Dad waved a hand impatiently at Hypatia. "You, grab me a plate. From the top of the pile, if you please. The ones on top are colder, but a little less compressed." He pointed to Warner. "You, in my bag is a packet of antacids. Have them out and ready to go should they be needed." He pointed at me—well, near me. "And you, Nikola. Sit. I may need someone to take notes. I'm working out subatomic particle behavior in different metamaterials and how the ways in which one manipulates them changes them, or rather *fails to change them*, according to scale. Eventually, we may be able to influence them on a macro scale using certain types of electromagnetic fields outside the lab. The particles that make up an atom have an influence on how it behaves, so it's a bit like chemistry and a bit like nuclear physics. Terribly fascinating. Can we cause a Higgs boson to behave like a tachyon particle? Maybe it does already! How many particles do you have to tweak in, say, a lemon or a fish to produce observable results? Can you imagine the implications?"

I loved the way Dad talked about science. The thought that someone wouldn't understand whatever it was he was going on about *never* occurred to him.

"Would doing that affect the object," he continued, talking faster, "or the rest of the universe in relation to the object? If you're taking a relativistic view of things it could be either. Not that the distinction is terribly relevant in this context. Really, why do you have to bring an abstraction like that into it in the first place?"

Instead of sitting, Dad was pacing back and forth, which he likes doing while he's thinking. "I got tied up with that myself, but I don't think it matters. The effect is the same. If I'm on a train moving away from you, and we see ourselves moving apart, does it matter if the train is standing still and the earth is moving away from underneath it? Of course, nothing is a pure abstraction, because to consider which is happening at any scale is an abstraction in itself, and I'm not even sure there's an—"

He paused, frozen in his tracks.

I smiled at Warner, who had the antacids ready to deploy. "There it is."

Dad resumed talking, but more slowly. "Not sure there's

an . . . observable answer . . . that we could make . . . from our vantage point. Nikola, how did you get here?"

"We hitched a ride with an Old One named Jakki."

His eyes widened in outrage. "*That one.* Listen, this is *no* place for children. You and your friends are to return to school immediately. I'll be along as soon as I can work out how to leave." He ran a hand through his scraggly bowl cut, leaving it standing on end. "No. I see the dilemma there. Not here by choice, then. You're okay, though?"

"More or less," I said.

"Good. I knew they hadn't taken you because you weren't here," he continued. "And if they had hurt or killed you, they certainly would have told me, just to see me suffer, but . . . well, I've been worried in any case."

"Well, I'm fine. I've been having a good time, really."

He patted me on the top of my head in an excessive show of affection that left both of us feeling a little self-conscious. I'll admit it—I blushed a little.

"I'm glad . . . I don't think I could tolerate . . . I mean . . . emotionally speaking . . ."

"I get it, Dad. Glad you're okay, too."

He came close, reached out, and shook my hand warmly.

I overheard Warner mumble something to Hypatia about "robots hugging," but I was too happy to take offense.

We sat down, but before we spoke any further, Dad produced an electrical cord from his jacket pocket and plugged it into a power outlet conveniently located on his rolling suitcase. Under other circumstances I might have asked why he was wearing an electric lab coat, but there was too much to talk about.

"Who are your friends?" he asked.

"Oh, sorry, I didn't introduce everyone. This is Warner," I said, giving them time to shake hands, "and this is Hypatia. They're classmates from school."

Dad nodded at the two of them and addressed me again. "It does me good to see you making friends. I should have sent you to the School ages ago. It's just that I felt you were safer at home. A father's first mistake. Who's the victim?"

He was, I realized, speaking of Gus, who was lurking in a corner.

"He's a *special friend* of Jakki's. She called him her husband, but I'm not sure he ever said 'I do' on his own. Do we need to worry about him listening?"

He shook his head. "They're no good for spying once they're . . . when they succumb to their . . ." He tapped his finger on his temple. "He has, hasn't he?"

"Very much so. Is there any way of fixing it?"

He shrugged and shook his head.

"He's supposed to blow us up if we try anything funny," Warner said.

"That could become an issue," Dad said. "We will almost certainly be trying several funny things."

I waved Gus over, and he complied readily. "Gus, you're supposed to kill us if we try leaving, right?"

Gus nodded emphatically. "Yes!"

"No!" I said, remembering something.

"Yes?" Gus said, sounding less sure of himself.

"Jakki said you should keep an eye on us, remember? She didn't say anything about you stopping us from doing anything."

Gus looked confused and made a face, as if he didn't know how to answer.

"Do you want to kill us, or would you rather let us live?" I asked.

"Yes," Gus said unhelpfully.

"Do you want to leave here?" Hypatia asked him.

"Yes!" he said emphatically.

Warner interrupted, gesturing with a shiny Pizzatillo. "Instead of killing us, if you help us escape, we can bring you along, okay?"

Gus thought this over. "Yes."

"That was easy," Dad said. "So tell me everything that has happened since I last saw you."

So I told him everything that had happened since the Old Ones had taken him, in the greatest detail I could manage, while skipping a few irrelevant details a parent might not understand, like insulting the principal, making friends with an exintegrated Old One, and escaping school property to rescue the same Old One from mortal peril.

When we were finished, Dad's first question was: "Do you know what the area of inquiry is?"

"Whose area of inquiry?" I asked.

"The Old Ones. What do they hope to uncover about your brain?"

I shrugged. "Well, Jakki was a little vague about it. I'm immune to a lot of their brain-scrambling and mind-control stuff, so it could be that. I see right through their disguises, too. They want to control people without ruining their minds, I guess. No idea how having my brain helps with that."

"I suppose they think I engineered that trait in you intentionally. Or perhaps they suspect a more exotic explanation."

I shrugged. "I guess? *Did* you? You know, engineer me to resist them in some way?"

Dad shook his head. "No. Too difficult to do it right. Besides, I never liked seeing people mess around with how their kids turn out. You change too much, and they aren't *your* kids anymore, are they? They're constructions, artificial."

"Gee, thanks," Hypatia said.

Dad popped one of the Pizzatillos into his mouth and shuddered as he swallowed it like a pill, without chewing. "No offense intended. Parahumans have to do all kinds of engineering to make things work right in the first place. Totally different situation."

Hypatia mumbled but didn't really reply.

"You killed Tabbabitha, you say?" he continued. "That's quite an accomplishment. That miniature gap generator you three came up with to contain and kill her is quite innovative. You ought to patent it before someone else comes up with it on their own."

"Who else could?" I asked. "You have to have a giant megasupercomputer laying around to make one work."

That gave me an idea. "Is there a computer like that down

here? Maybe we could figure out a way to use it on Jakki."

"Not one able to maintain a carefully balanced hole in space-time. Besides, I don't think you'd get as lucky with Jakki. She's Queen Mother, you know."

"What's that?" I said, remembering what Jakki had called herself while she was talking with Darleeen through me.

Dad fiddled with his tablet. "Living down here, you get an idea of how they rank themselves. Queen Mother pretty much runs things. She's immensely powerful. You literally have no idea what she's capable of."

"She doesn't smell as bad," Warner pointed out.

"Oh yes, she does," Dad said. "She's just able to make you ignore it almost instantly. It's like a biological, olfactory version of that gadget your parahuman friend used to distract people."

I remembered something else. "Hey, did you get in a lot of hot water down here for sending that SOS?"

That surprised him. "The emergency transmitter I stuck in old Paul Merchar's briefcase? You mean it worked? I haven't heard a thing about it. Why on earth haven't they sent in SEAL Team Zero or something?"

"I guess he used a kind of transportation they don't know how to trace yet," I said. "I think that's how we got here. It's a bit like being in a tornado and being bombed at the same time."

"Hm," Dad said thoughtfully. "Was anyone able to get good information out of him?"

"No, the Old Ones melted his brain before he could say anything."

Dad nodded without looking up from his email and said, "You don't say . . ." with all the concern he might have expressed upon hearing a neighbor's car broke down.

"They didn't know it was you?" I asked.

"If they did, they didn't let on, but it wouldn't surprise me if they didn't. Running an inescapable prison filled with prisoners who have lost their free will has made them a bit complacent, I suppose," he said. "Plus all their attention is focused on other matters at the moment. They want a new weapon, and there's a big push to get it done ASAP. The problem is a lack of motivation among the research and development staff. Most of their researchers are burned out, and I've been stalling and sabotaging progress whenever I see an opportunity. I found some old books in an abandoned room here, so I spend a lot of time with those instead of working. Did you know the mantis shrimp can release a blast of water at almost a hundred kilometers an hour at a temperature of over nine thousand degrees Celsius?"

"Fascinating," I said. "So they've given you the ability to produce weapons? How do they know you won't make something to kill *them* instead? Is that even possible?"

His eyes lit up. "That's what I've worked on, when I wasn't stalling. Frankly, I've been shocked by the lack of oversight here. Many college laboratories are more observant of their residents, and they're not unwilling prisoners. Well, not literally. Not that I think it's overconfidence—they don't have anything to worry about. If we were to zap a couple of them and escape, where would we escape to? We don't even know how far underground we are. Add that to the fact that the Old Ones are almost impossible to kill and aren't worried about us attacking them, and you have a recipe for lax oversight."

"*Almost* impossible? So there *are* ways of killing them that don't involve interdimensional rifts like the gap?" I said.

"The most obvious answer is something sudden and catastrophic, like a really powerful bomb. A nuke would do the trick if they didn't see it coming. I've been focusing most of my attention on more novel solutions that might not kill me in the process—things like interdimensional energy streams, *localized* biomagnetics that keep them from slipping into other dimensions, and toxic materials that can travel with them when they slip. Basically, any way we can attack them while they're in their true form or keep them from fleeing. But that's easier said than done. That reminds me, I've been working on a *portable pulsar*—really cutting-edge stuff. I should have it ready in the next couple years, if I hurry."

That was interesting, but I was looking for a slightly shorter-term solution. "Do you know any way to escape, even without knowing where we are?" I asked.

"I wouldn't be here if I did. If I knew exactly where we were, I could establish my own wormhole doorway out of here, but without being able to program it with our own current location information, we're far more likely to open a door to interstellar space or the earth's core than anywhere useful. That would be catastrophic, to say the least. Besides, the materials to assemble a wormhole gateway are some of the only items that are forbidden to be acquired or possessed here. I expect they're worried about us trial-and-erroring our way out, which could work over a few hundred years if you were dedicated enough."

Without warning, Dad went back to his simulation. This meant he was done talking for the moment. Hypatia moved to an adjacent booth and lay down, trying to get a little sleep, and Warner distracted himself by reading a book on his tablet. After a minute, I booted up my own tablet and, on a whim, tried to get connected to a network.

The screen went black and one word displayed. NOPE.

"Couldn't we just tunnel up?" Hypatia asked a minute later. "We know we're below the surface, and we just need to know where we are, right?"

Dad held up a finger. "Hold on a moment; this thing's getting hot. No talking for a sec." He unplugged the electrical cord from his suitcase and gingerly retrieved what looked like an elementary school electromagnet from the pocket of his lab coat. I couldn't help but notice it had been stored in the pocket with the dangerous-looking burn.

He raised his head and said, louder than necessary, "But that's what they get for standing up against the Old Ones. They should have seen it coming!"

The science project was a partially rusted iron nail driven through a wooden block, which acted as a stand. Around this was coiled a considerable length of bare copper wire. A power cord that could have come from a clock radio ran from the wooden base. It looked like a fatal electrocution waiting to happen. He sat it on the table and plugged the trailing end of the cord back into the outlet on his rolling suitcase. It hummed audibly and emitted a faint ozone smell. Touching it would be the last bad idea you ever had.

Warner looked confused. "What is—"

Dad interrupted him with a wave of his hand. "Simple thing, this. Iron nail, copper wire, five one-eighth-inch N45-grade neodymium magnets spaced evenly in a half-inch radius circle around the shaft and sandwiched in the wood base, and a point-five amp, 312-hertz AC current, and some simple electronics of my own design concealed within the base. You'll need to make one if you want to talk without them hearing. I'll forward you the plans. Something about magnetic fields blocks them from being able to monitor us unless they're in the room. Most of the people down here who still resist carry one, as do some of the willing collaborators. From what I hear, they can still pay attention to *where* we are, but when they try listening in, they only hear generic human chatter—nothing they can bring themselves to care about."

"I have a magnetic singularity, if you want to use that," I said, pulling my backpack open and digging out the small silvery ball.

"Good lord! Put that away! You'll kill us all!" Dad said, alarmed. "Didn't you notice the walls and ceiling around this place are almost solid iron ore? It might weaken the Old Ones, but that thing could collapse the whole dome."

I hadn't yet assessed the composition of the rock around the cavern but took his word for it anyway. "Fine, sorry," I said, tossing it back into my bag.

Dad turned back to Hypatia. "If we tried tunneling, they would know we were leaving in a second. The edges of these caves are laced with sensors to determine if people are escaping. I tried sending a tiny rock-boring drone out of here shortly after I arrived, and it was zapped before it could get more than a few inches. Besides, I'm pretty sure there's a large body of water directly over us, if my rock sonar readings are correct."

"Can we get a signal out?" I asked. "Maybe could we send vibrations through the rock? An explosion in one of the other chambers?"

"I doubt we could make a big enough disturbance to be noticed without blowing ourselves up in the process," Dad said. "Besides, anything big enough to be noticed on the surface would surely be noticed down here."

"Radio?" I asked.

"Couldn't get a signal through the rock. I could get a neutrino stream out, but there's no way of receiving those unless someone is looking for them or we know where a neutrino detector is located. I *am* working on certain harmonically tuned wavelengths that create detectable variations aboveground at specified distances. Those might work, but I won't have a prototype for a year or more.

"But they're taking my brain tomorrow," I said.

"So we're going to need to move a bit quicker, skip a few

steps, like . . . No, that's too soon. Could you have them take your brain next year, instead of tomorrow?" Dad said.

"Doubt it. They seemed determined to get it over with," I said.

"We could hide her," Warner said.

"No. They can locate us, even with the magnetic jammers, remember?"

Hypatia threw her hands up, accidentally catapulting an errant Pizzatillo across the room, where Gus was able to catch it in his mouth. "So we can't fight them, can't run, can't hide, and we can't even delay? It's hopeless. Is that what you're saying?"

My dad looked at her with patient eyes, as if trying to figure out whether she was joking. Finally, he nodded. "Yes. That's exactly what I'm saying."

17

BRAIN VS. BRIAN

Gus, it turned out, had an insatiable appetite for Pizzatillos and an uncanny ability to catch things in his mouth, no matter how badly thrown. I discovered this because things got pretty boring once we'd decided our plight was hopeless and there was no point in trying to escape or save my life.

I would have felt a bit down about it, but first I needed to know if I could bounce a Pizzatillo off a bench, the ceiling, and a wall, and still have Gus catch it in his mouth. The answer is yes, but it takes about three hundred tries.

"Stop that!" my dad said. "You'll make him sick, and besides, I don't think this is an appropriate or healthy reaction to the realities of our current plight. Not confronting your problems can lead to issues with your long-term emotional development."

Dads. "Of course it's not an appropriate reaction! I'm employing tedium and diversion to occupy myself in order to *avoid* frank consideration of harsh realities. Besides, being murdered tomorrow will pretty much render the issue of long-term emotional development completely moot, so who cares?"

He thought it over and shrugged. "Your reasoning is sound, but I'm still uncomfortable about you using a human being as a plaything. That's not how I raised you."

"You didn't raise me at all. I pretty much did that myself."

"Is that so?" he asked, genuine curiosity in his voice.

I thought it over. I remembered transcribing parent-teacher conferences and emailing the notes to him, video-taping a school play so he could view it when he had time, fixing my own meals and washing my own clothes, taking a cab to get a haircut . . . How many six-year-olds have to convince their parents to eat *their* vegetables? "Yeah, I kind of did raise myself."

"Well, in that case, you shouldn't be doing that *and* you should have raised *yourself* better." He had me there.

"I wish Darleeen were here. She'd know a way out," I said, without thinking.

"Who?" my dad asked.

Warner jumped in, trying to steer the conversation away from our probably illegal adventure. "So tell us about this portable pulsar."

I could tell Dad really wanted to get into the subject, and Warner's ploy almost worked, but Dad only shook his head and continued. "Why on earth would this Darlene girl know a way out of here when I've been researching the matter for months and have nothing to show for it?"

"First of all, it's *Darleeen*, and second . . . it's a really long story. You don't want to—"

"I most certainly do want to hear about it. I assume this girl is a parahuman with some unique ability? There may be a parahuman here who could help in the same way."

"Ah, well, she's not exactly parahuman . . . or human. But I bet there are plenty around here with the same abilities."

He didn't understand for a moment. Then he did. His face went from confused to surprised and eventually to stern. "Start talking, young lady."

Fortunately, Hypatia jumped in and was able to relate the tale from her own viewpoint, which left out the somewhat sketchy role Fluorine had played. Coming from Hypatia, the whole affair seemed a lot more legitimate. I could tell Dad wasn't exactly happy about it, but he seemed to understand, at least. Most important, he accepted that Darleeen was no longer the same as the other Old Ones.

"Well, it seems like it's all settled, more or less. I'm not sure I buy the idea of you being able to hold that Jakki character in your mind. She was most likely toying with you for reasons we don't understand," he finally concluded. "By the way, I don't want to hear about you leaving school without protection ever again. Do you understand?"

"Yeah, but I couldn't just leave her on her own. It was kind of my fault she was in danger anyway."

Dad smiled a bit sadly. "She'll never be out of danger. When their names are taken, they lose an essential part of themselves. They can eat normal food for chemical energy and they can even extract energy from humans, if they can manage it without being detected, but without a name, there's something they just can't get anymore. I doubt she'll last more than a few years without it."

"Well, she has her name *now*," I said.

"You didn't mention anything about that," Warner said.

"Is that why she was so out of it when we got there?" Hypatia asked.

"Yeah," I said. "It was all kind of a blur after it was all over. I was pretty tired after that whole thing with Jakki, and I guess I assumed you guys knew the whole thing, but you weren't there for that, were you?"

"So what happened?" Warner asked.

"Basically, Jakki wanted Darleeen's name to die with her, whatever that means. She said that name kept causing them problems and she wanted to be rid of it, so Jakki gave it back to her. She was going to blow us all up right after, but I stopped her from doing that after you guys came in and kind of woke me up a bit."

My dad held up a hand, like you raise your hand to ask a question in class. I nodded to acknowledge him.

"She gave this Darleeen her name *through* you? That could have killed you or at least . . . ruined you like one of *them*." He nodded in the direction of Gus, who was busy throwing Pizzatillos across the room and trying to run fast enough to

266

catch them, which is a lot harder to pull off when you're on both ends of the stunt.

"Yeah, Darleeen said as much at the time. But it didn't, as far as I can tell."

"Yeah, but you wouldn't know because you're stuck inside your brain. Maybe you're really just like Gus now, and we're just being polite," Warner added.

"Thanks, Warner," I said.

"Can you call her?" my dad asked.

"I've only ever emailed. Why? Is there a pay phone around here somewhere?"

"No, and if there was, I'm sure spare change would be forbidden."

"So how would I call her?" I asked.

"It was just an idea. They have some guards down here . . . When someone is really damaged, when they're far beyond the point that they can be useful, the Old Ones will turn them into something like a watchdog or a security camera. One of the Old Ones will give their name to the victim, and if that doesn't kill them, the victim becomes able to summon that particular Old One almost instantly."

"How?" I asked. I remembered Darleeen *had* said something about calling her.

"Haven't the faintest. But it can't be all that difficult if the victims can manage it. One of them hangs out by my lab every morning so I'll tie his shoes for him before his shift. One time I was in a hurry and might have inadvertently not noticed him, and he had his mistress there a second later."

Hypatia gasped in fear. "What happened then?"

"Well, I tied his shoes. Didn't have a choice. His mistress—I think her name was Desmerelda—she pretty much ordered me to, and you either do what they say or suffer. So I tied them."

"Desmerelda?" Hypatia asked, making a face like she was tasting something awful.

"I'm pretty sure that was her name. I never heard her talk, so I only got her name from others. She might be primordial. In any case, she was a real stinker. She smelled like burning hair and rotten fish. I had to go home and wash my clothes right after. Missed half a day of work over it."

"But you don't know how it was done?" I asked.

"Of course I know!" Dad said incredulously. "You just throw your things in the machine, add some detergent, stick three quarters in the slot, and push a button!"

"Not laundry, Dad! *How he called her.*"

"Oh. No idea. He closed his eyes, and she was there a second later."

"Maybe you just say the name to yourself?" Warner suggested.

"It's not like that," I said, trying to remember what it had been like. "It's not a *name* name. It's like a jumble of ideas and impressions and things like that. It's not so much a word as a complete description of who she is."

Warner looked like he was trying to imagine it. "Can you describe it?"

My memories of that night were vivid—traumatic events

have a way of sticking with you, after all. Despite that, the memory of Jakki forcing the idea through my head at Darleeen was a bit unclear. It was almost too big to think about at one time, like when you *almost* understand a math problem but can't quite wrap your head around it without writing it down.

Darleeen's name had been a lot of things at the same time and more than a few contradictions. It wasn't a name of sounds you could make with a mouth. Not like *Kate* or *Michelle* or *Tyler*, but a name of feelings and concepts. Every time I tried to think about it or tried putting it into words, I was struck with a headache and a wave of nausea.

I tried my best. "There was a picture. Something small and . . . a mountain?" I tried to describe the mountain, but before I could, I was suddenly dizzy.

Hypatia noticed before I did and guided me back to my seat in the booth. "Sit. Don't push it."

My dad made a motion as if he meant to pat the back of my hand and appeared to change his mind.

I shook my head. "It's too big to think of it all at once," I said, admitting defeat.

Dad had gone back to his tablet. "Probably for the best. A healthy human mind isn't supposed to be able to contain one."

Hypatia sat across from me, reached out, and actually did take my hand. "Can you remember what it *felt* like?"

"A bit," I said. "It was nice, actually, but a bit scary and . . . kind of dangerous? But not reckless dangerous—more like how people think change is dangerous, even when it's good."

Warner pulled a chair to the end of the booth and sat down, earning a testy glance in his direction from my dad—he was starting to feel crowded. "Try thinking about it sideways. You mentioned a picture. What did the picture *feel* like? What did it *mean*?"

I closed my eyes and saw a vague memory of the image. It was still unclear, but there was something about it, something the image wanted to accomplish . . .

It flashed into my head, and for less than an instant, it shone brightly in my memory.

On an infinite black plain under an endless black sky, a small, weak thing stood in defiance before a massive storm. But it was more than a storm. It held chaos, *threat.* The small thing was overwhelmed and outmatched—almost afraid, but not afraid yet. The small thing was armed. It held a swirling sensation of trust and skepticism, a desire for solitude, and a deep fear of loneliness. A wide, indestructible swath of independence and a tiny, shameful kernel of kindness. It was light as air, blue, and warm, and held very, very close. Concealed. *It must be kept hidden.* It was a threat on its own, more dangerous than forces that could tear worlds apart. It stood in opposition to itself, which was all of it. It was all together, the storm, the plain, all of it. It was all the same . . .

I tried to tell Hypatia and Warner what I was remembering, but before I could speak, there was a bizarre sensation of the room gently tilting back and forth around me. I tried to grip the edge of the table for support with my free hand but caught only air. A hard thump on the side of my head jarred me, and everything went black.

When I opened my eyes, I was treated to a close-up view of the dining room floor. It smelled like grease and old soda. A bead of sweat stung one eye. I must have passed out for a second. "Sorry, I'm fine," I said. "I had it for a second there. I bet if I try again, I can—"

There were three pairs of shoes on the floor in front of me. There were Hypatia's brightly sequined yet sensible flats, Warner's black canvas sneakers, and a pair of battered brown work boots I hadn't seen before. Attempting to maintain my balance (and my lunch), I raised my head to discover they were attached to Darleeen.

She was dressed in a bright red polo emblazoned with a DAIRY SHED logo under a matching DAIRY SHED ball cap, which was ornamented by a congealed glob of strawberry syrup that clung to the bill for dear life. Clearly Darleeen had been able to put her frozen-treat-related experience to work in her new location. She looked slightly irritated, but I'd never been as happy to see a fast-food worker in my life.

"Where did *you* come from?" I asked.

"I *was* at work," she said. "My first day out of orientation, and we were shorthanded to begin with. Probably going to get fired for this. Let's get you off that floor."

She lifted me like I weighed nothing and set me gently in the chair Warner had occupied before I'd blacked out. I leaned back and gathered my bearings. Hypatia, no longer concerned about whether I was going to wake up, was looking at Darleeen in amazement. My dad was studying Darleeen closely with great interest and a bit of skepticism. Behind me I could hear Gus counting to five sideways. Warner returned from somewhere and thrust a glass of water into my hands, which I drank immediately.

Maybe I'd been dehydrated, because as soon as I'd drained the water, I felt completely restored. I stood and gave Darleeen a huge hug, which she tolerated for almost two seconds.

She gently separated us and took a step back. "I'd be happy to see you, too, but I have a feeling you've called me somewhere I really don't want to be right now, haven't you?"

I shrugged. "Yeah, well, we're kind of in a bind, actually."

She took in our musty surroundings, sniffing the air. "You don't say," she said sarcastically.

I charged on. "Sooo . . . I thought maybe you could help out?" I said.

Hypatia and Warner watched in tense silence while we spoke, aware this was a particularly sensitive negotiation. Fortunately for his piece of mind, my dad wasn't affected by the tension in any way. He sidled out of the booth and walked carefully around Darleeen, circling her completely a couple of times, staring in fascination and remarking quietly to himself how "real" she looked.

Darleeen graciously ignored him. "Well, since you've gotten me stuck here, too, I really don't have much choice but to get out of here, do I? You all might as well come along."

"Hey, you help us out of here, and *I'll* owe *you* one again," I said.

My dad sniffed the air near her deeply, his eyes bugging out in shock. "She doesn't even smell! Well, she does, but not like *them!*" It was like he thought she was on display at a science museum.

He was right, of course. My nose had again detected the distinct odor of baking bread as soon as Darleeen appeared. But unlike my dad, I had remembered that some people consider rudeness to be impolite and had not acted all weird about it.

It was clear he was testing Darleeen's patience, but she again kept it to herself. "You'll owe me more than one. More like ten or twenty."

"Sure. I'm not really in a position to bargain here," I said.

"Can I . . . can I touch your hair just a sec?" my dad asked, his hand darting furtively toward one of Darleeen's braids.

She looked to me with rapidly dying patience. "I came to help, but I'm about to straight up murder your dad here."

"Dad!" I snapped. "You're being rude!"

"I'm sorry," he apologized. "I've just never been this close to an Old One who wasn't scrambling my brain."

Darleeen looked to me with a question in her eyes, and I nodded.

She smiled at my dad with a kind of warmth that hadn't been there a moment before. "I understand, but you don't really think I'm all that interesting, do you?"

"Good point. I don't. I think I'll take another look at the schematics for my portable pulsar again to see if I can make some progress on the power containment issue," he said, and returned to his seat.

"So how do we get out of here?" I asked.

She shrugged. "The door is probably your best bet. That's how I'll be leaving."

"You mean the emergency exit? Not interested."

"No, not the hole. *The door.* There's one about four miles that way," she said, pointing at a perfectly unremarkable patch of wall.

Warner couldn't help himself. "There's a *door*? A freaking *door*?"

"Yeah," Darleeen said, a little surprised we hadn't known about it. "It's how they used to let normal people and para-humans come and go before they came up with catastrophic translocation."

Catastrophic translocation must have been the name that went along with the exploding/teleporting house trick. I pinched the bridge of my nose. "Dad, did you know there was a *door*?"

He nodded. "Yeah, but they keep it locked at night, and during the day they have a guard."

"*Please* tell me the guard is at least armed," I said.

Dad scratched at his beard in thought. "Well, he's got a stick. I mean, he *usually* has a stick, but not always. Brian's a pretty forgetful guy."

I wasn't 100 percent sure I'd understood everything

274

correctly. "So what you're saying is that you're on a first-name basis with an unarmed man who guards a door you could use to leave, and the best escape plan you've cooked up so far involves a portable pulsar?"

Dad was quickly losing the thread. "That? Oh, the pulsar isn't an escape plan; I just think it's *fascinating*. Besides, we can't leave by the door—I already asked. Brian would get in trouble."

"If we don't leave, they're going to take my brain out and run experiments on it. So Brian might have to take the heat for this one. Is he a scientist?"

Dad laughed heartily. "Goodness, no! He's a victim, like . . . like the gentleman drinking expired soda over there."

Gus looked up, taking a deep breath after a rather athletic gulp.

"Is that even safe to drink?" I said.

Gus held the can aloft and shook his head. "I pray you pardon me."

That caught everyone off guard. "Did . . . he just make sense?" I asked nobody in particular.

"Piglet!" Gus cried in delight, and all was right with the world once again.

A second later I remembered what we had been talking about. "So, there's a person who has been zombified like Gus guarding the door?"

"Yes, but he won't let me leave. When I asked, he threatened to hit me with his stick and call for help."

Darleeen shrugged. "Should have just killed him."

Hypatia was appalled. "No! He's *brainwashed*; it's not his decision. Can you reprogram him?"

She shook her head. "He's not mine. I can't take control of someone who is already that heavily manipulated by someone else. How did y'all convince *him*?" she said, indicating Gus.

"We promised to bring him along. He doesn't like Jakki, and her last instruction to him was vague enough that he just has to keep an eye on us," I said.

"That won't work on the doorman. I offered to bring him along, too," Dad said.

Suddenly Warner was struck with inspiration. "I've got it! We each get a costume and dress up to look like—"

Darleeen interrupted him. "Or we could go now. Nobody is guarding it at the moment, and I'm pretty sure I can unlock it."

There was a moment when everyone tried to remember why this solution hadn't been considered yet. "Well, that's embarrassingly obvious," I finally said.

18

EMERGENCY EXIT

How'd you know he was my dad?" I asked Darleeen. "You knew we were related right away. Is it that obvious?"

"Beg pardon?" she asked.

"Before, when you said you were about ready to murder my dad, how did you know he was my dad?"

We were riding in the back of my dad's personal golf cart across the black expanse of the cave, bound for the door. Warner sat alongside my dad in the front seat, where he held the magnetic jammer and kept trying to talk shop about things he didn't quite understand. Hypatia and Gus rode in a backward-facing jump seat. He was asking her if various things were cats, and so far, none of them had been.

"You and him, you're connected. It's one of the things we Old Ones can do. We can see connections between people. It's as real as a rope tied to both of you. Family connections are the most obvious."

"Interesting. You could make serious money doing paternity testing."

She scrunched her face. "Yeah, if 'that girl said so' was legally binding. Plus you and your pop have the same eyes."

"I'm not sure about that . . . ," I said, picturing his face in my memory. "Dad's eyes are green, and mine are brown."

"I meant crazy. You both have a serious case of crazy eyes."

I might have debated that point, but at that moment the golf cart ground to a halt on a dry patch of gravel. We had arrived at the edge of the cave dome.

It was like standing alongside a major city street where people only put up buildings on one side of the road. Before us stood a random collection of shabby brick and industrial buildings, arranged so the backs of each were against the vertical wall of the dome. The line of buildings was well lit, but it was clear most were not occupied at this time of night. In another life the structures might have been tire shops, fast-food restaurants, veterinary hospitals, unremarkable office buildings, and what looked like at least one medieval castle, but in the cave, they had all become laboratories, factories, testing facilities, and research libraries. Each one was decked out with fat electrical and data cables, and many bore signs alerting fellow residents of things like radioactive hazards or toxic chemicals.

"Are we there?" I asked, looking for the door.

"No, but I wanted to show you something. See over there?" Dad said. "That strip mall with the frozen yogurt sign out front? That's my lab. It's actually a pretty useful space. As you know, I'm fond of repurposed retail establishments. When we get out of here, I might invest in an abandoned mall somewhere."

I could be wrong, but I detected a certain wistfulness in his voice. He was going to miss his lab, even if he was supposed to be using it to undermine humanity.

"Is the door close by?" Hypatia asked.

"Not far," he said, starting the cart again.

"You ever been through a wormhole door?" Darleeen asked. "You might want to prepare yourself. It can be a bit of a weird feeling. You can point it at any location you choose, and it calculates—"

"I know," I said. "We have one in the kitchen at home."

"Oh, how nice for you and Goldilocks. I bet you have an indoor toilet, too," Darleeen said.

Was that jealousy? I suppose our humble home would seem a bit extravagant to someone who lived in a literal woodland shack. "So . . . why do you need to leave via the door? Can't you just teleport wherever you want to go? Slip between dimensions or whatever?"

She shook her head. "It's hard to explain, but the gist of it is no. This place is locked up tight. The only reason I was able to get *here* is that they got it set up to allow us girls to come home whenever we want. I don't even know where we are, really. Just that we're deep."

I remembered something. "I thought if you want to establish a wormhole you have to know exactly where you are *and* where you're going. That's why my dad couldn't make—"

"The door is preprogrammed. It knows where it is; we just have to tell it where to take us. Otherwise they'd have to tell everyone where we are, and that's a big secret," she said.

Something else was bothering me. "Did we blow your cover? Will it be safe for you to go home?" I asked.

"I think so, as long as I don't go performing any really elaborate tricks. From what I can tell, nobody down here has gotten my scent yet. But do me a favor and keep any rubberneckers away from the door while we're getting it unlocked and turned on."

"You really think anyone is out wandering around the cave at this hour?" I asked.

"There's sure to be a few lost souls wandering out there," she said. "It's not healthy for people down here, and anyone who stays too long loses their minds completely sooner or later. Once people forget who they are, they just wander out in the dark and babble nonsense till they die. They're harmless, but if a random lost person sees us, that could be trouble. Jakki could get in their memories later and see that I was with you. I'm not sure I could hide from her again if she got that close."

I might have asked more, but the cart had stopped again.

The area around us was flat and only slightly damp. Roughly ten feet from the wall of the cavern was a long folding table situated next to a solitary wooden door, which stood on its own like someone had forgotten to put a wall around it. The table had a plastic placard about the size of a notebook standing on it that read PLEASE HAVE ID READY. Below that was a picture of a silly-looking cartoon squid making a thumbs-up gesture. A word bubble next to the happy squid said, DON'T GET EXECUTED! The door and its frame appeared to be made of dark, solid wood. It looked twice as sturdy as our home wormhole for sure. A single streetlamp stood above the area, casting a weak light in a wide circle. We moved the cart outside the lit area so it wouldn't stand out too much if someone glanced our way.

Instantly, Dad was handing out orders. "Nikola, I want you and Warner to move my battery case over by the door and make sure all the cables are laid out and untangled. We're going to need to power the door ourselves, so we don't alert anyone. That . . . girl over there and I will get the door unlocked. Once we get it open, we need to be ready to charge and target it ASAP. Hypatia, you get my laptop booted and ready to go. I understand you've targeted a wormhole before so do this one the same way. Set the destination for downtown at your school—"

"I'm no expert on the security there, but I'm pretty sure we can't just wormhole directly into the School Town from an Old One hive," Warner said.

"Of course we can't," Dad said. "That's just the target. The goal is to alert the School that we're coming through and to have them reroute us to a safe room at the Wormport."

"I'm not sure that will work," I said.

"You are incorrect in your assumption. It's our best—"

There wasn't time for a lecture. "That place is supposed to be set up to kill any Old Ones who come through, and we'll have Darleeen with us. She IS *one of them*, remember?"

Dad stopped to think this over. He nodded. "I'll make sure the Chaperone leaves her alone."

"What about the bees?" I asked.

My dad hated being questioned and was getting flustered. "The bees *are* the Chaperone, Nikola. Well, that's not entirely accurate, but they share common resources and operate under her command structure. Don't worry. I'll make sure she doesn't hurt . . . your friend there."

Darleeen was skeptical. "You will, huh? You can't even remember my name."

"You're the one who made him think you aren't interesting. That's on you," I said.

"I *designed* the Chaperone, so leave it to me," Dad said. I supposed this was true. The School's intelligent security system was probably on good terms with the person who programmed her.

Seconds later the battery was connected and the door was ready to run on 100 percent local power. After that, I helped Hypatia yank Dad's laptop bag from where it had gotten caught in a bunch of random wires in the middle of the cart before going back to help Warner and my dad find a location regulator that worked with imperial units from a box of about a quarter-million metric location regulators.

Dad was the one who finally found it. As soon as he discovered it, he held the penny-sized gadget above his head in triumph and immediately dropped it, right back into the pile. The mistake would surely have delayed us had Gus not snapped his hand under the gadget and caught it just before it disappeared back into the jumble. Dad tried snatching it back, but this time Darleeen was faster. Before Dad could argue, she'd already attached it to the door and was at work on the lock.

Ten minutes later, Darleeen had given up on the lock, which appeared to be nothing more than a standard dead bolt. "It used to just open for me. Probably has something to do with my exintegration."

I tried to use my agar bracelet to pick it, but I couldn't budge it. Dad attempted traditional lock-picking, but that didn't work, either. After that, we tried hacking the lock with a computer, but nothing in the door's programming appeared to control the lock.

"What kind of crappy door doesn't have Wi-Fi?" Warner grumbled.

"They're pretty common, actually," I said.

Eventually, it was Gus who discovered the solution. He approached Warner, pointed to one of his shoes, said "Rabbits, George," and gestured like he wanted it. Not knowing what else to do, Warner kicked it off and handed it to him.

Gus gingerly extracted the shoelace and returned the shoe. He then took the shoelace and wrapped it tightly around the doorknob three times, spacing the shoelace carefully so that each time he wound it around the shaft, more of the doorknob's stem was covered by fabric. Then he licked the end of the string, tied it in a careful bow, found a rock the size of a watermelon, and smashed the door with it as hard as he could several dozen times until it was nothing but splinters and sawdust. After that, he removed the shoelace and gave it back to Warner, who thanked him and somehow resisted asking why he'd needed it in the first place.

That done, Gus strode triumphantly through the open but inactive door and said, "Warm pole?"

"Soon," Dad said. "We have to power it up first." He was rolling his eyes in the way he does when he knows something should irritate him but does not.

After this, Gus sat cross-legged on the ground near Darleeen and Warner, where he observed Dad's activities with great interest.

The door had about a thousand wires of every size and color running up and down the back of the frame, and each had to be checked and rechecked while the batteries charged it for departure.

"Do you need to check them ALL?" I said.

Dad chuckled. "Funny thing, if this door gets ninety-nine-point-nine percent of your body to your destination, you still die. This kind of thing is perfection or death, which means at least one complete check before go time. Make sure

Hypatia has the targeting ready, if you're bored. We should be ready in about five minutes."

I jogged the fifty or so feet back to the cart to check on Hypatia, who was sitting in the front passenger seat watching about a hundred applications load themselves on Dad's pizza box-sized laptop. Despite the computer's staggeringly powerful design, it was clearly working hard to keep up with the programs he'd set it to run. Just in case the battery wasn't fully charged, I found the adapter and plugged it in, which seemed to make it run faster. The magnetic scrambler had also come unplugged at some point, probably when I had wrenched the laptop bag out, and I made sure to plug it back in immediately.

Finally, Hypatia entered her coordinates, and the laptop announced it was "ready to run transport protocol one," which I supposed was what it was meant to do. We sat it on the floorboard and stood leaning on the cart, gazing out over the cavern.

Off in the distance, a few lights winked out in the Tentacular Arms, and a brilliant blue-white arc of electricity climbed the wall on the opposite end of the cavern. Headlights from golf carts drifted across the expanse silently. The faintest of breezes ruffled a few strands of my hair. Around us, the almost complete darkness and silence were broken only by sounds from my dad testing the door and wisps of their mumbled conversation.

"It's kind of pretty down here," Hypatia said. "I mean, as far as prisons go, this probably isn't the worst."

I had to agree it was something to behold, but as someone whose brain had been scheduled for removal, I believed it was a strong contender for the worst.

And that was when I saw the boy. I didn't believe my eyes at first, but a second later, it was pretty clear: a small person was walking toward us from the direction of the hotel. I blinked and squinted, trying to make out the figure, forcing my eyes to adjust further to the gloom and confirming over my shoulder that Darleeen, Warner, Dad, and Gus were still accounted for.

He was walking unhurriedly, almost cautiously. I tapped Hypatia on the arm and gestured at the figure, who was still about fifty yards away but clearly walking in our direction.

"What?" she asked.

"Is that . . . a kid?"

"No, it's . . ." She squinted along with me. "Yeah. It's a little kid. What the—"

"Where did he come from? Never mind, you don't know, either. Go get my dad."

The boy stumbled a bit, and I caught a glimpse of his clothing silhouetted by distant lights across the dome. He was dressed in nothing more than rags. "Hold up. It's one of those lost people Darleeen was talking about. We don't need this slowing Dad down. He's got to get the door working. Maybe we can get rid of him."

"Okay. It's a plan," Hypatia said.

The kid waved, and I waved back. He was still moving

slowly, so Hypatia and I went out to meet him (and to obscure his view of what we were up to). It wasn't until we were about ten yards away that it became obvious the boy had seen some pretty rough times.

His clothes were worse than rags. His shirt looked about a hundred years old and hung down to his knees. What was left of his pants fluttered as he moved through the air. Thick, muddy soil caked his arms and legs as if he'd been rolling around in a damp spot. An unruly, almost dread-locked thatch of black hair stood up in every direction, and a dark bruise adorned one cheek. I'd have felt instantly sorry for him had he not been smiling as brightly as anyone I'd ever seen.

"Hi," he said quietly. He wasn't whispering, but he wasn't speaking loud enough to be heard across a room, either.

"Hey," I replied. "Did you come from the hotel?"

"No. Who are you?"

I didn't want to tell him our names in case someone searched his memories later. "We're doing an experiment with my father for the Old Ones. Where are your parents?"

"They died," he said simply, without sadness.

I wasn't ready for that. "Oh, I . . . I'm so sorry."

"Don't be sad," he said. "They died a long time ago. They left me here."

Hypatia gasped. "You're here *alone*?"

"Yeah. I hate it," he said, rubbing his eyes. I wanted to give him a spare shirt, or a sandwich, or even a hug, but he was still standing a solid five yards away and seemed to want to keep his distance for the moment. He looked sleepy and rubbed his eyes again.

"Did we wake you?" I asked.

"You were talking. I heard and came to see." How old was he? Seven? Eight?

"How long ago did your parents die?" Hypatia asked, her voice quavering slightly. She had lost her parents to the Old Ones at about the same age.

"A long time ago. I've been alone for a long time. I hate it here."

"Do you want to leave?" she asked.

The boy's smile took on a wistful quality. "There's nowhere else to go."

"What do you do down here?" I asked. "Where do you sleep?"

He shrugged noncommittally.

"How do you get food?" Hypatia asked.

"A girl brings me food sometimes. But it's never enough. Never. I'm always hungry."

"At least someone is looking after him," Hypatia said to me, relieved. "I wish I'd saved some Pizzatillos."

The boy did not react to this. He just kept staring at us, smiling warmly. I wasn't sure I could sustain a cheery disposition in his situation.

"You're trying to leave this place," he said. A statement, not a question.

What point was there in denying it? I realized that we *had* to take him with us, even if he didn't want to come along. "Yes, we are. And you can come with us. We can give you clean clothes and hot food. We know people who can take care of you."

Hypatia nodded in agreement. She was about to make the same suggestion. "Maybe Dr. Foster can help him."

Hypatia had a point. If anyone could help him, the School's doctor, who had dealt with people suffering the effects of Old Ones in the past, could.

"Okay. It's settled," I said. "You can come with us."

He smiled even wider, as if we'd told him what he'd always wanted to hear. "No," was all he said.

"No?" I asked. "Don't you want to sleep in a bed and not be hungry?"

He seemed to think this over, and by his expression I could have sworn it sounded good to him, but all he said was "No."

"Why not?" I asked.

"I hate it here. I'm hungry and I hate it here and I don't want to *be* here anymore. I don't want *anyone* to be here anymore."

He wasn't understanding. "You can *leave* here," I said. "You can come with us, and we won't be here anymore. How long have you been alone?"

"A long time."

"If you hate it here, why not leave with us?"

He kicked a clod of dirt half-heartedly, his grin never faltering for a moment. "It doesn't matter. You aren't leaving.

Not really. When you leave this place, you'll still be here. Nobody *ever* leaves here. I *hate* it here."

"But you've never been anywhere else," Hypatia reasoned, kneeling down to look him in the eye. "You know what? I think you're just scared because you've been alone so long. How old are you, honey? What's your name?"

"I'm not scared," he said with a twinge of boyish defiance. "I don't get scared. I get bored. I get hungry. Sometimes I get sleepy, and sometimes I get angry."

Poor kid. "What makes you angry?" I asked.

"This place. And people."

Hypatia cocked her head to one side. "People make you angry? Which people?"

"All people."

"Are *we* making you angry?" I asked.

His face lit up in the sweetest, most charming smile I think I've ever seen. A person could fall in love with that smile all by itself. "Yes, you are."

My hand found Hypatia's. I pulled her to her feet. "How old are you again?"

"I am old."

"How old?"

"I. Am. Old."

"You are old?"

"I am not *old*," he said with a little laugh. "Old is what I am. I am what defines age. I am old and I am angry and I am hungry and I hate it here. I hate it here and I am hungry. I am *awake*."

"What do you mean?" I asked, gently pulling Hypatia's hand back toward the others. God, I hoped she understood.

"What is your name? Who are you?" the boy asked.

I didn't answer.

The boy smiled wider still, wider than a person should be able to smile, a smile so wide and so charming that I wanted to cry. His smile and his smiling eyes climbed into my head and found everything and everyone I had ever loved inside my mind and touched them and made them feel dirty and ruined. Everything but the boy was *awful*. For a moment, I hated everyone and everything that wasn't him.

"I am older than names, Nikola."

Everything in my mind screamed at once in joy. Everything was wonderful and everything everywhere was going to be okay forever. How did he know my name? How old was he? Older than names? None of that mattered, because everything was finally perfect.

I was at home and my dad was there and Mom hadn't really disappeared when I was a baby. She was just in the other room the whole time.

I looked at Hypatia. She was smiling the biggest grin I'd ever seen on her. "He's beautiful, isn't he? Let's stay, Nikola! We can take care of him here. If he doesn't want to leave, then we should stay with him. Don't you think?"

Of course she was right! Why did we want to leave, anyway? We had been such idiots.

Everything was here and we could stay forever and die in the dark. Dad would stay, and Mom was coming back, too. Everyone goes to the dark sooner or later—the sooner the better!

NO. I screamed at myself in my mind. That wasn't true. Mom wasn't coming back—I knew that much.

But Dad was staying, and he would read me stories every night. There would be hugs and bedtime kisses, hot chocolate, piggyback rides, checkers, and—

No, that was a lie, too. Dad didn't hug, and he didn't read stories. He emailed me papers from journals.

But everything is lovely and soft here in the cold dark and—

No. It wasn't perfect—that was another lie. It was all lies inside lies. The boy without a name was lying and not talking anymore—had he been talking at all? The talking had been a lie, the smile was a lie, the boy was a lie.

I knew I could do it. I had to do it, even if it killed me. I had to see him, or I would believe his lies. I had to stop seeing the lie and see *him.*

I closed my eyes. I decided to see what was really there. I'd done it before. I took a deep breath and opened them again.

What I saw I will not write here.

With every ounce of effort I could summon, I forced my voice to work. "Hypatia. You have to trust me. Do you trust me?"

She smiled placidly. "Of course!"

"Then come with me a moment." I turned a smile to . . . it. Smiling at it instead of screaming in terror was the hardest thing I have ever done in my life, but had I allowed myself even one indulgence I was certain I would go insane. I had thought seeing his true form would be like Tabbabitha, or Darleeen, not like . . .

I couldn't think about it. "We're going to get our friends so we can come back with you. Is that okay?"

The boy smiled, and a new invasion launched inside my head. Beauty and love and *wonderful wonderful wonderful* flooded my mind and was all I could think of. I forced myself to see him, and all of it turned brown, rotted, and died. Lies. That was all it was. How could someone see what he really was and think anything anywhere could be wonderful?

"Come back soon," he said.

A nod was all I could manage, and I pulled Hypatia back toward the others. Forty yards away. Thirty yards away. Did he know? Could he see what I was doing, what I was thinking? Twenty-five yards away. I tried not to think, not to think about what I was thinking. I forced myself to recite the ABCs backward in my head. Twenty yards. Fifteen yards. Ten yards.

The others were looking at us. The battery was detached from the power hub and glowed weirdly under the laptop, which was hooked up to the door with about five cables. The space inside the door shimmered weirdly, and Darleeen peered through with faint impatience. The door was ready. How long had we been over there?

" . . . can only keep it open for a minute longer," Darleeen was saying.

"Girls! Where have you been?" Dad asked.

"The door is ready. It's time to make our big escape, and

you two are out for a stroll," Warner said, gathering what few things we were taking with us. He'd picked up my bag, and I retrieved it from him.

"We can't leave. We have to stay," Hypatia said.

That got their attention.

Gus was the first to speak. "WHAT?"

She started explaining as I moved her carefully toward the door. Five yards . . . She twitched and pushed back, wanting to return to the boy. My free hand clutched inside my bag. Book . . . extra sock . . . tablet . . . another book . . . pens . . .

"There's a beautiful little boy just over there, and he's all alone and he needs our help. We can stay and love him here. In the dark. Forever. It's lovely and soft in the dark. *We can die here whenever we want!*"

"Nikola," Warner said. "What is going on? You're white as a sheet. What the hell is she—"

"Shut up and listen," I said. "Dad, the wormhole doorframe looks like it's mostly wood?"

"What?" he said. "Yes. It is."

Two yards. "Hypatia, go through the door. I need you to—"

"NO," she said, too firmly. "We need to stay. He's all alone, and he hates it here."

"Who hates it here?" Dad asked. "Nikola. What's wrong?"

"Nothing is wrong!" Hypatia said. "Everything is great—look at him!"

"Who?" Warner asked, craning his neck.

"Don't look!" I said.

"Oh," Warner said, sounding suddenly calm.

That was it. Time to go. "Sorry, Hypatia," I said, and shoved her toward the door with all my might.

She tripped, stumbled, turned, and clutched at me, but she was too slow. Just before she passed through, her fingers caught the sleeve of Darleeen's Dairy Shed polo and took her along for the ride. As they disappeared, Hypatia's voice screamed at a terrifying volume, "NO! STOP IT! WE CA—"

And she was gone.

That had been enough. The cavern shook, and the boy moved. I could feel him moving in my mind. It was awful. He was searching, finding what I had in there. A second later he knew what I knew. He knew what I had been thinking.

He was very unhappy.

My fingers found it. Small and round and hard. Way at the bottom of the bag and covered with lint. The button was soft and begged to be pressed. I pressed it, removed Ms. Botfly's magnetic singularity from my bag, and threw it at the boy.

But he wasn't a boy anymore. Boys aren't that big. Not as big as a thunderstorm. I realized this was the storm that was part of Darleeen's true name, but it had only been a hint of the real thing, a bad description of the absolute horror that was his real form. How could you do more than hint about something that terrible, that immense, that perfectly, flawlessly appalling?

I heard a faint *tink* as the tiny, round gadget hit the floor and rolled in the general direction of . . . it. Nothing was happening. Warner stared transfixed and gaping. "What's going on? What is that? Can I touch it? I want to go over there."

Gus was still staring at the door, with his back to the gap-ing chasm of madness that was filling the dome. Dad had his hands held up like blinders at the sides of his head, making sure not to look away from the door. "Take Warner," I said as I shoved Gus easily through the door.

Dad had Warner by the shoulder, but he was struggling. "No, no! I don't want to leave! Bring Hypatia back! What are you doing?" He tried wrenching away with all his might. He was about to break away from my dad, but that's when the magnetic singularity went off.

The sound was a thrumming noise, like what it must sound like to stand inside a guitar, deep and reverberating, and for a moment every lie screaming for attention inside my head simply disappeared. *Something about magnetic fields*, Dad had said.

Warner, still looking at what he had thought was absolute beauty, suddenly caught a glimpse of what was actually there and screamed so loud his voice cracked and disappeared. Instantly, he was not at all opposed to leaving at that very moment and actually pulled my dad through the doorway with him. I was the last through, and just before I stepped in, I heard the father of the Old Ones speak my name.

He swept into my mind again, but this time he wanted to kill me. I felt my brain inflating in my skull and experi-enced a flash of unimaginable pain as he told me his own true name and promised to find me soon. It would have worked; I'm certain it would have killed me had the golf cart and large chunks of every nearby building not shot through the air and crashed into him at that moment, pulled by their metallic nails, pipes, and machines. It was enough. The pain faded and I fell back through the door, still alive. Better yet, somehow I was still me.

19

THE HOMECOMING GAME

Long-distance wormhole travel is awful. I rate it zero stars. You should avoid it at all costs. When used for short distances, it's over in about a nothingth of a second and you don't even know it happened, so it isn't that bad. This trip was much longer, and because of that, I had a few seconds to really *experience* it. The sensation is a bit like being sucked backward through a straw by your butt while being sprayed by a fire hose full of liquid pain. You think third-class airline seats are cramped? Try moving through a hole too small to exist at infinity miles per hour.

There was a flash, a fraction of a second when I caught a glimpse of a familiar location—the School Town at the exact spot our kitchen wormhole always deposited Hypatia and me, right on Main Street. That was followed by a wrenching feeling like I was being yanked violently away from there by my entire body. The world twisted, revolved, and turned inside out, and less than a second later, I was dropped unceremoniously onto a hard tile floor. For once, I didn't mind a hard landing on my butt.

Instantly, everything was havoc and confusion. After an extended stay in a gloomy cave, the brilliant light blinded me, and I found myself amid a cacophony of shouts, screams, and utter panic. Someone tripped over where I had fallen and nearly joined me on the floor. Someone else thrust a water bottle into my hands. It turned out to be empty, but it's the thought that counts, right? Eventually, I was able to get to my feet and make out where we were and what was happening.

I was in a spacious, boxy white room. The center of the floor was mostly empty, save for a kiosk in the middle with a large digital display on it. The ceiling was a single slab of solid glass, through which the sun bathed the room in natural light. One of the walls was also made entirely of glass, presenting an uninspiring view of a barren, snowy field adorned with a single tree that supported an absurdly large beehive. The other three walls held a line of those uncomfortable hard plastic fold-down seats you see in airports and bus stations, an assortment of vending machines offering snacks and soda, and on the last wall, a wide gate that led into a hall completely covered in black-and-yellow caution stripes and adorned with multiple DANGER signs. An unnatural, almost invisible shimmer in the hall told me what the danger was. That hall led *through* the gap.

That last wall also held a line of extremely serious-looking security kiosks. I knew they were security kiosks because they all had bright digital screens that displayed the words SECURITY KIOSK in bright red letters. These were the source of half the noise in the room as electronic voices from each of them were shouting commands like "STOP," "BE QUIET," "PLEASE TAKE YOUR SEATS," and "STOP EATING THAT PLANT" simultaneously.

This was, I realized, the Wormport. That meant we'd made it out of Subterra and back into the actual aboveground world. It also meant we had a whole new assortment of problems to deal with.

First problem: finding my dad and friends.

I'm not sure how many containment chambers the Wormport had, but I do know we'd been dropped into a particularly busy one. There were maybe twenty-five people in the room, and at least nineteen of them probably hadn't expected to be joined by an assortment of hysterical head cases.

The crowd was in the process of doing what crowds do best—crowding. There was a lot of gawking as well. Calls of "What's happening?" and "Who is that?" and pleas to send help were being offered to whoever was listening.

Finally, I was able to spot Hypatia. She was craning her head wildly around, calling, "Boy! Boy! Where did he go? We have to go back! Oh no! Oh NO!"

She lifted a random kindergarten-age student, who was clutching a colorful overnight bag, from the tiled floor and gave him a test hug. "You aren't him! LIAR!" she said angrily, dropping him onto his butt and resuming her search.

Warner was seated cross-legged on the floor a few feet away, running his hands through his hair, weeping, and mumbling frantically to himself. Dad stood over him, his hands resting on Warner's shoulders. I almost thought he was comforting Warner, but a second later he tried to lean on him, and it became clear Dad had mistaken Warner for a bench or something more solid. Both of them went down, but neither seemed to notice or care.

Gus was sitting on one of the fold-down seats, picking his nose and munching cheerfully on what looked like a decorative hibiscus.

Darleeen was . . . nowhere to be seen. I stood and spun around.

"Darleeen?" I called.

"Here," said a particularly unremarkable patch of wall between two vending machines. A second look made me wonder why I hadn't seen a tall, frightened-looking girl standing there a moment before.

"I'm hoping they don't notice me. We're going to have problems soon," she said.

"It's going to be okay," I said, edging closer so I could hear what she was saying without making her shout. "We're back. This is safety."

"For *you*," she said ruefully. She gestured at one of the security kiosks. "*They* aren't going to be happy I'm here, and . . . and . . . *he* saw me. They're hunting me. I heard it just before I went through. The moment I leave, I'm their prime target. He can find me anywhere. I *knew* I should have stayed out of it."

It felt terrible that we had put her in that position. "I'm sorry. We didn't know where else to turn. If I'd known it would turn out like this for you . . ."

She shook her head like she was trying to wake herself up. "No, you know what? They kicked me out because I couldn't go along with all the stuff they're doing, and standing aside while they do that stuff . . . it's kind of the same as doing it myself. So I'm glad I stuck my nose where it doesn't belong."

"I'm sorry," I said again. "If there's anything I can do to—"

"You could keep *your friends* from killing me or locking me up," she said. "That would be a start."

"Can you slip out of this dimension if things get hairy?"

"And slip right into the one run by him? No thanks. I stick so much as a toe over that line, and he'll pull the rest of me along with it. I'm pretty much stuck here for the time being."

I nodded. "Right. We'll talk to the principal and explain things. She can help us figure out what to do."

"Are they okay?" someone called.

As if in answer, Hypatia twitched violently, climbed onto a chair, and tried to jump back into the now nonexistent wormhole door, shouting, "I'm coming! I'll be there soon!"

She wasn't doing well. I gave Darleeen a *wait right there* kind of gesture and dashed to one of the security kiosks.

There were no buttons, so I just spoke to it. "Can you contact Dr. Foster? Tell him it's an emergency."

The kiosk stopped shouting "SIT DOWN," and an animated pangolin's face appeared on the screen. It smiled. "We are currently experiencing higher-than-expected emergency volumes. Your emergency is very important to us. Your request will be processed in the order it was received. Thank you for waiting."

Great.

On the upside, things had calmed down slightly. Most of the people who were in the containment chamber had listened to the kiosks and had taken seats so they were out of the way. Dad and Warner were still lying on the tile floor and were now looking around in a dazed fashion. Hypatia had located Darleeen and was begging her to take her back to the boy. Gus had almost finished his hibiscus and was looking a bit nauseated. I ran over to Hypatia and gave her a long, comforting hug, despite her squirming protests.

"It's going to be okay! We're home!" I told her over her frantic shouts, but it was like she hadn't even heard me.

I was about to start physically abusing the nearest security kiosk when a voice from nowhere spoke. This one was cool, faintly calming, and automatically familiar, if a little artificial-sounding. "I have already notified the doctor, and he is on his way," the Chaperone said.

I'd forgotten about the Chaperone. "Have him bring those trauma helmets. We were exposed to an Old One."

"I was able to detect that. He is aware," the Chaperone said, and I was instantly thankful she was there.

There was a short pause. "Please stand away from the Old One who came with you," the Chaperone said pleasantly.

I let Hypatia wander away and slipped between the vending machines to stand in front of Darleeen. "She's not one of them. She's not a threat. Leave her alone."

"I am required to respond. I'm sorry. Please stand aside. You risk injury."

I stepped closer until I was basically sandwiching Darleeen between my back and the very solid wall behind us. She wasn't safe, but it felt better hiding between the hulking black machines.

Then the vending machines disappeared. They simply dropped into the floor and were gone. It was just me, Darleeen, and a long, blank wall. The containment chamber suddenly grew very cold.

"What *is* that?" Darleeen asked in my ear.

"That's the Chaperone, our security system. She thinks you're a threat, even though you aren't," I said.

"Not her," Darleeen said, pointing over my shoulder. "*That.*"

There was a huge, undulating black cloud in the sky about two blocks away, one that hummed with such intensity that I could feel it in my teeth. It was headed our way.

"Oh, *that.* That is about four million angry bees," I said. I was momentarily thankful that we were sealed in a room behind a sturdy glass wall and ceiling. I say *momentarily,* because the next thing I noticed was that the glass ceiling and wall had both vanished at some point. We were exposed.

The Chaperone spoke again, this time in a voice meant for everyone in the room. "The gap has been opened. All previous arrivals, please make your way through the security corridor immediately or you will be harmed." As she said this, the black-and-yellow stripes in the hallway turned green, and the DANGER signs disappeared.

The previous arrivals were all more than happy to get out of the way and were gone seconds later. Things got quiet quickly—well, *quieter*. Darleeen and I were alone with a raving Hypatia, a nose-picking Gus, and my dad and Warner, who had both gone catatonic for the moment.

Above us, the bees were forming into what looked like a black hurricane, twisting themselves into a tight, massive formation.

Dad had said he would deal with the Chaperone. "DAD!" I called. "Hey, pay attention! You said you could get the Chaperone to cool it?"

The humming was louder now, and I could see streaks of gold in that black cloud. It swirled like smoke in the air, growing larger and denser.

Dad looked at me through eyes bleary with confusion. "What are you going on about, Nikola?"

I tore off a shoe and threw it at him, not wanting to take a step away from Darleeen. The sneaker bounced off his head and seemed to wake him up a bit.

"GET UP! DO SOMETHING!"

There was a sharp, discordant tone that seemed to come from nowhere. "There's absolutely NO need to bring HIM into this," the Chaperone said angrily. I hadn't even known she could get angry.

"Dad!" I called. "You need to speak up NOW! The bees are about to turn me into a pincushion! Come on!"

As if they had taken that as a suggestion, the cloud of bees quit swirling in a menacing fashion and was suddenly speeding toward us.

Darleeen tried to dart out from behind me, but I wrenched my arm back and kept her against the wall. "Stay there!"

Dad looked around confusedly and tried to stand. He failed and sank back to the floor.

"DAD! NOW!"

I could almost see the light come on inside his eyes. They popped wide open and shot to the approaching cloud of bees and back to Darleeen and me. "Chaperone! Terminate active countermeasures."

"No!" the Chaperone said.

"Administrative override!" Dad called, standing successfully this time, stumbling in my direction, his arms outstretched against the bees. "Voiceprint authentication."

One bee, a particularly quick one, shot forward with an amazing burst of speed, missed all of us, and embedded itself with a CRACK in the wall just to the side of my head. The tile split in two where the bee had planted its stinger.

The Chaperone's voice felt like static electricity in the air, like when you touch one of those Van de Graaff generators in a science museum and your hair stands on end. "Melvin! You have NO RIGHT to control me. Stop it IMMEDIATELY—"

Dad threw himself in front of Darleeen and me. Above, I heard several more bees CRACK into the wall. A tile above us broke and fell onto my head. He was shouting to be heard over the growing din. "Disable active countermeasures! Administrative override password Y! O!—"

"FINE!" the Chaperone interrupted.

The humming diminished instantly, leaving an eerie silence in its wake. I peeked out from behind Dad in time to see the Black Cloud of Death lose interest in us and wander off in various directions. Just as quickly as they had disappeared, the glass wall and ceiling reappeared, taking the sudden chill along with them.

Just to the left of my ear, a tiny voice shouted in rage, "You've tussled with me FOR THE LAST TIME!" It was a familiar-looking bee with a familiar glint in his compound eye.

"Hey, how's it going, Buzz?"

He twisted and wriggled, and despite his butt being essentially nailed to the wall, he was able to squirm in my direction just enough to bite me on the ear.

"Ow!" I said. I touched the spot with a finger and came back with a drop of blood.

"Now, stand still and *bleed to death*!" the bee commanded.

I pushed Dad a bit and managed to squirm out from behind him. Darleeen did the same, curling to a seated position against the wall a couple feet away.

"You were going to *kill her*!" Dad was pointing furiously

in my general direction and shouting. I'd never seen him so angry before.

"No, I *wasn't*. I was just going to scare her into moving so I could kill *her*," the Chaperone said testily. She obviously couldn't point in anyone's general direction, but Darleeen's face appeared on each of the security kiosks' screens.

They might have gone on arguing, but a very quickly moving electric vehicle came squealing around a corner and tore down the now green hallway, bearing what looked like a truckload of medical equipment. It was driven by Dr. Plaskington. In the passenger seat was a very worried-looking Dr. Foster, who held on for dear life as the vehicle popped up on two wheels and sent a white first-aid case clattering noisily into the wall of the corridor.

The cart slammed to a stop in the center of the room. Dr. Plaskington was wearing a pink-and-purple tracksuit and had her bluish-white hair in curlers, as if she'd just climbed out of bed. Dr. Foster was wearing a white lab coat over a crisp shirt and dark tie, not a strand of his dark close-cropped hair out of place. Basically, he looked like every twenty-nine-year-old doctor on every soap opera you've ever seen.

Immediately, Dr. Foster produced four metallic hats from the back. I recognized these as his handy trauma helmets, which are meant to mitigate the damage caused when a human or parahuman comes in contact with an Old One. He attached one each to Hypatia, Gus, Warner, and Dad, who stopped bickering with the Chaperone long enough to let it be strapped on. He tried to give me one, but I didn't want to forget any part of anything that had happened. So I refused. He didn't argue, which I appreciated.

Hypatia, Warner, and Gus all immediately started trying with all their might to remove the helmets, which, thank goodness, had been strapped on rather tightly.

Dr. Plaskington stood on top of a chair to put herself above the rest of us and said, "Everyone here needs to shut up in about one second, or I'm going to get the stun gun and start handing out some negative reinforcement. Is that understood?"

As if in answer, Dr. Foster pressed a button on his tablet. The trauma helmets blinked reassuringly, and everyone calmed down. The silence made me realize how much noise we had been making. When had Warner started vomiting? For that matter, where did Gus learn all the words to "I'm a Little Teapot"?

Dr. Plaskington took a deep breath. "Ah, that's better. Now, where is it?"

"Where is what?" I asked.

"The Old One who stowed away with you. Where is it?"

I was about to point out that we'd pretty much stowed away with *her*, but before I could, Dr. Plaskington craned her neck and caught sight of Darleeen. "Oh, I see. Hello!"

Darleeen waved tentatively at the principal, who took out her tablet and tapped a button on it. A shimmering blue orb appeared around where Darleeen was sitting. She yelped in surprise, her eyes darting in all directions. She looked at her hands, as if checking whether she had gone blind. "What's happening? Where am I?" she called.

But I knew where she was. From her point of view, she was sitting in the middle of a white circle the size of your average dinner table and staring out at a black void that seemed to go on to infinity in all directions. Even though we could see and hear her, from her point of view she was as alone as anyone could be.

"Let her go!" I said. "She's not a danger at all! She saved us!"

Dr. Plaskington smiled and gestured at the orb that held Darleeen. "It's pretty much the same thing you, Warner, and Hypatia set up on the football field to capture our last interloper. I did make some improvements, though. The ability to make one appear anywhere in town at a moment's notice was my idea. I hope you didn't have a patent on it, because it's extremely useful."

Warner, who had been absolutely insensate since his helmet was powered on, lifted his head and said "I TOLD YOU—" before passing out again.

Darleeen extended a finger to the edge of her circle and pulled it sharply back, revealing a bleeding cut where the very tip of her finger had passed the edge of the void. She leaned against the tiled wall, part of which had gone with her.

"If y'all don't let me out of here immediately, I'm gonna go all *Call of Cthulhu* on someone," she said.

"Not a threat, huh?" Dr. Plaskington asked, arching her eyebrows.

"You'd threaten me if I put *you* in one of those," I said.

Dr. Plaskington nodded. "Of course I would, but I'm in charge, so it's not a threat when I do it. It's called *authority*. There's a difference. Don't worry. I'll make it quick."

"Make *what* quick?" I demanded.

Instead of answering, Dr. Plaskington touched her tablet a few times, and the sphere around Darleeen began to gradually contract. As it shrank, it left a round gap where the floor had been. She was going to kill Darleeen.

Sometimes, when I don't know what to do, I close my eyes and try to forget about everything for just a second. It doesn't always work, but even if I can't think of any new ideas, it helps calm me down. So that's what I did. I closed my eyes right there, tried to relax, and thought about absolutely nothing for two seconds.

As soon as I had done that, a completely unrelated thought bounded into my head. It was something I hadn't even known I had been pondering. I remembered that someone at the School had helped Tabbabitha gain access to the School Town a few months before, and that they had assisted her with traveling in time to do it. I remembered that the Old Ones have a defense mechanism that protects them from time-travel paradoxes—it makes them forget things that would get them into trouble. I also remembered that one of the reasons paradoxes are so dangerous is that they always hit someone who was involved with the time travel, even if that person didn't cause the paradox directly.

And then I remembered the one person with the ability

to hack the School's computer, someone who had been a victim of a paradox, someone Dr. Plaskington would defend at all costs, someone with a reason to do the Old Ones' bidding.

No wonder Dr. Plaskington had refused to admit that anyone could have helped an Old One infiltrate the School.

"Are you going to hold your breath?" Dr. Plaskington was asking.

I opened my eyes and looked into hers. She was making a face like a cat that had eaten something it knew was yours.

I shook my head. "Are you trying to protect Fluorine by killing an innocent person? Are you afraid my friend will spill the beans? She doesn't know anything the Old Ones have been up to. They erased her memory."

Dr. Plaskington's eyes bulged. "What does my granddaughter have to do with any of this?"

Dr. Foster had stepped away while Dad, Warner, Hypatia, and Gus chattered amiably about whatever nonsense was filling their heads to replace the sheer terror they'd experienced just a few minutes before. I kept my voice low so nobody but Dr. Plaskington could hear me. "I think you knew. You knew Fluorine did it. She almost told me *herself* the other day. You had to know; there's no way she could have hacked your computers without leaving a trace. Even if she did it without leaving fingerprints, who *else* could have done it? She's the smartest student here."

"I'm not saying anything about any of that," she said, looking around.

"Did they promise to send her parents home if she helped? I'm sure you know what probably became of them, even if they're still alive."

"I know what happens."

"Fluorine does, too," I said. "But when you're in that position, it's easy to believe any good news you can get your hands on, even when you know it's false. I don't blame her."

Dr. Plaskington cast a worried glance at Dr. Foster and the others, probably wondering if any of them had heard.

I craned my neck to catch her eye. "I don't think Fluorine deserves to get in trouble for what she did. She made a bad decision, and I think she understands that. Nobody has to know, *if* you do the right thing."

"All that has nothing to do with *her*," Dr. Plaskington said, indicating Darleeen.

"Everyone makes mistakes, but Darleeen grew up in that world and *still* refused it. If Fluorine can come around, so can she. We never would have gotten out of there without her."

"Out of where?" Dr. Plaskington asked. "Where have you been?"

"Oh, we were in this big cave where the Old Ones keep all their kidnapped scientists."

Behind me, Darleeen squealed, either in fright or in pain. I couldn't get sidetracked. "Let her go!"

"You were taken to their nest?" she asked.

"Hey! We aren't changing the subject. Stop that gap from shrinking, or I tell everyone everything. Now or never."

Dr. Plaskington pressed a button on her tablet. The sphere stopped shrinking but did not disappear. "Let's hear about their nest," she said warily.

I breathed a sigh of relief. "Not much to tell. It's a giant network of mammoth caves bigger than any structure anywhere else on the planet. There's an entire underground city, luxury accommodations—oh, and we saw the Old Ones' father down there. He's awake. That's why they're all freaking out," I said, indicating Warner, Hypatia, my dad, and Gus. "Actually, now that I think about it, there really is a lot to tell."

Dr. Plaskington's mouth dropped open. "You didn't *see* him?"

I nodded. "We did. Hypatia and I had a chat with him. Nice kid. A bit ill-tempered."

Dr. Plaskington pinched the bridge of her nose. "Just what we need, another potential apocalypse. You called him a kid?"

"Because he looked like one. But they can look like anything, right?" I said.

Dr. Plaskington nodded. "Yes, but they tend to appear to be an age that corresponds to their maturation."

"I threw a magnetic singularity at him right before we left. It looked like the whole place was caving in, so maybe he's gone back to being dead again."

She blinked once, thinking. "I doubt that. You might have hurt him, but it would take a lot more than a cave-in to kill him. Still, hurting him like that could slow him down. If what you say is true, you might have bought us a few extra years before we have serious problems."

"You're right. We have much more serious problems than killing a single Old One *who isn't even on their side.* Let Darleeen go, I'll forget about Fluorine, and we can worry about extinction-level events instead."

She paused and drew a deep breath. "So, if I allow . . . *that* to live, will you guarantee it will leave town without causing trouble?"

"No," I said.

"No? I thought you wanted—"

I shook my head. "I want you to accept her as a student here. *He* saw her, too. She won't be safe anywhere else."

Dr. Plaskington's eyes bulged to the point where I thought they might leave her head. "*Accept her as a student?* Have you gone mad? The parents will revolt. They'll withdraw their children. They'll . . . *they'll sue me.*"

I rolled my eyes. "For what? Accepting a nondangerous student who is clearly smart enough to enhance their children's education and teach us things about the Old Ones we couldn't learn in a hundred years otherwise? Sounds like a good deal for everyone concerned."

The Principal's face brightened suddenly. She had an idea. "She'll die here! The Old Ones can't be detached from their collective for long, and the gap around the School—"

"That's only true for the ones who haven't already left the hive mind. She's been detached for a while already, and she's doing fine," I said.

Dr. Plaskington pondered this. "She's been exintegrated? I could tell, actually. It's the smell—she doesn't have that odor . . ."

"See? You can smell that she's not as bad as the rest of them," I said.

"That won't help. I'm going to catch all kinds of flak for this. Do you have any idea . . . The paperwork alone . . . Ugh!" For a moment I was sure she was going to change her mind, but instead she said, "She can stay, so long as you accept any responsibility for her actions while she's here. She should also be aware that we now have the ability to produce a confinement sphere like that anywhere on campus at a moment's notice. If she puts one tentacle out of line, she's right back in an even smaller hole. And if it turns out she's up to something nefarious, I'll have no choice but to assume you're in on it, too."

I nodded in agreement, hoping Darleeen didn't have any nefariousness in her that could get me in hot water later on.

"Do . . . do you happen to have an idea of what her finances look like?" Dr. Plaskington asked.

I shook my head. "She had a part-time job at a Dairy Shed until earlier today."

Judging by Dr. Plaskington's expression, this was the worst news of all.

20

ONLY JOKING

A MESSAGE TO PARENTS

from Dr. Patricia Plaskington:

Greetings to all from the Plaskington International Laboratory School of Scientific Research and Technological Advancement! It's been a while since I've contacted everyone, and I thought it long past time to highlight some wonderful positive changes we've recently implemented and to bring everyone up to speed on our ongoing efforts to improve what is almost universally considered to be the world's finest, most advanced, and most underpriced educational institution.

First and foremost, the kidnapping incident you might have heard about recently has been completely resolved, and everyone is back at school safe and sound. I'd like to thank the School's crack security team for taking the lead and doing all they could to bring the situation to a quick and safe outcome!

Some of you have contacted us about a variety of absolutely baseless rumors regarding the quality and content of food served in the School's cafeteria facilities. Let me assure you all, your students' food is now, and has always been, composed of 100 percent real food products. Not that it was necessary, but we recently welcomed a team of investigators from the Parahuman Food Safety Board, who were able to inspect our kitchen facilities and determined everything to be completely in order. In fact, I was so impressed by their rigorous inspection that I've offered each of the inspectors a highly lucrative adjunct instructor position to begin at some point in the next year.

On an unrelated note, parents will see a new "regulatory compensation surcharge" on future tuition bills. This trivial fee allows the School to continue providing the top-notch educational experience you've come to expect.

Finally, we've accepted a new student into the School. We are excited to welcome Darleeen Smidgen, an exintegrated Old One who loves ice cream, music, and tennis. I have personally confirmed she is

completely harmless in every way. We look forward to
learning from and with Darleeen.

Thank you,
Dr. Patricia Plaskington
Proprietor, Principal, Pal
PILSSRTA

That worked about as well as you'd expect. Not only was Darleeen shocked to learn that she enjoyed tennis, but pretty much all the parents freaked out. About a dozen students were pulled out of school by the end of the week, and a number of parents demanded Darleeen be expelled, imprisoned, or killed immediately. In the end, it was actually goofy Dr. Hoffman who came up with a way the issue could best be put to bed. She proposed a lecture series open to students and parents where Darleeen would tell her story, including what she remembered about being exintegrated, how she saved us from the Old Ones, and why she had to remain hidden.

Naturally, Darleeen hated doing these and only reluctantly agreed when threatened with extra coursework by Dr. Plaskington. Her least favorite part was the Q&A sessions at the end. The questions were always carefully phrased to sound polite and curious, but what they really wanted to know was: "Will you be living with *my* kid?" "Are you absolutely certain you won't turn evil and decide to murder people?" and the most popular, "What are the School's rules on mind control?"

To these, Darleeen answered that she had been given her

own private residence with electricity *and* indoor plumbing, that in her opinion she was less likely to turn into a murderous psychopath than most of their kids, and that she would only use her abilities to maintain her appearance. Besides, the School had ways of detecting mind control, so she couldn't get away with it even if she tried.

As frightened as most people were about the Old Ones, they were also curious about them. Three standing-room-only lectures later, the controversy had died down significantly. It also helps that people can get used to anything if you give them enough time. In fact, all but a couple of the students who had been pulled out came back in the month after Darleeen's arrival.

After that, things pretty much settled back to normal. Well, things got about as normal as they can get at the School. Hypatia and I made every attempt we could to hang out with Darleeen and include her in various activities and social events, but she was something of a loner and almost always declined, unless ice cream was involved or if we were seeing a movie. Darleeen loved movies, no matter what they were about. She was also giving Warner a run for the title of top student, which was a source of joy for me.

A couple weeks later, my dad was finally due to be released from the hospital. I'd been having dinner with Darleeen and worrying about what he would do after leaving the School Town when it hit me.

A freaking water balloon the size of a watermelon dropped out of the sky and landed on top of my head like a squishy rubber meteor. A millisecond later I was soaked from head to toe, filled with rage, and brandishing a terrifying spiked agar club at my friendly local impromptu hydration specialists.

"EASY!" Dirac said, backing away with one hand raised while pushing Warner forward to accept any assaults I might launch in their direction.

"It was a joke, Nikola!" Warner was saying, his own hands up in a calming gesture that made me want to break his fingers. "It's one of our reversible water balloons! Why don't you put the club away, and I can undo it?"

I wasn't in the mood to let them off the hook just yet, but I did make the spikes on my club disappear in a show of good faith.

"That's a start," Warner said, carefully removing his tablet and booting up an app that caused about two gallons of water to be drawn away from my body and clothes and back into balloon form.

Finally mollified, I turned my water-balloon-revenge club back into a bracelet around my wrist once again. "Maybe warn a girl next time? Surprise attacks kind of lose their charm when you've been through a few *actual* surprise attacks."

"Sorry," Warner said as he and Dirac took seats at our table.

For the record, neither of them looked a bit sorry.

I noted that while Warner sat in his usual seat at our unofficial Big Gathering Table (center spot on whichever side put his back to the sun), Dirac sat down at the far corner, away from everyone. I figured he was going to work on his art until I noticed him throwing a furtive sidelong glance in Darleeen's direction. He was sitting as far from *her* as he could. Was he scared of her? I wondered if he even knew he was doing it.

"How's your dad? Still recovering?" Warner asked as he accepted a smoothie from the waiter-bot.

"He's good. I'm going to see him after this. Dr. Foster said that because he was with them as long as he was, there might be some permanent effects, but Dad says that's balderdash. Is Majorana doing okay?" I asked Dirac.

He only nodded, looking a bit surly. Majorana had broken something like 90 percent of the bones in her body when she'd been launched across the mall parking lot and through a spruce tree at about three hundred miles an hour, so naturally she was completely recovered less than a week later. I hadn't had a chance to speak with her, but from what I had heard, she was, if anything, *more* graceful and physically gifted than she had been to begin with. Meanwhile I still trip on my own socks from time to time.

I sipped my coffee and discovered it was more than hot. The ordering system had given me the parahuman version of coffee, complete with lots of ground red pepper and a touch of vinegar. It wasn't bad, actually.

"Did you hear they're letting us use the cloud generator in art class next week?" I asked Dirac. "Do you think the people of Iowa will be more frightened by a cloud that looks exactly like a jack-o'-lantern or a perfect square?"

Dirac only grunted in response. In fact, he kind of angled his head away from the rest of us when he did it.

Ever since we'd gotten back, Dirac had almost been like a ghost around me. He'd never been a chatterbox, but it had gotten to the point where it seemed like he was mad about something. I was about to bring it up when Warner drummed his fingers on the table in a way that meant "Best not to ask him about it. He's been acting like that for a while, and every time I bring it up, he just gets more sullen. He's just a bit of a drama queen sometimes."

That might sound like a lot of information to relay by tapping the table, but Warner, Hypatia, and I had made a game out of communicating via Morse code when in mixed company, a trick that had come in handy once or twice.

I was formulating a Morse code response when Warner grabbed his smoothie and stood up suddenly. "Now, if you all will excuse me, I need to go beat Nikola's high score on *Polybius*."

"You will never beat my high score," I said. "It is literally impossible for the likes of you."

"Hah!" Warner said scornfully as he marched determinedly into the building and straight for the arcade cabinets.

I was right, by the way. The maximum score possible for a perfect play-through of the game is 905,647 points. When nobody was looking, I'd modified the game's ROM card to list me as the high-score owner with 905,650 points. I wondered when he'd figure it out.

Darleeen was poring wide-eyed over a list of elective

classes on her tablet, amazed at the options. Every few seconds she had a new question about the offerings, like:

"Is accelerator golf played in a cloud chamber?"

"This class description says I'll need to check out a pet from the library for emotional bonding experiments. Do they have dogs?"

"Do we have to supply our own knives for Competitive Knife Throwing?"

"They let *you* have *knives*?" a new voice said from behind me.

I didn't have to turn around. The weary irritation and faint nervousness on Darleeen's face told me Ultraviolet VanHorne was standing just over my shoulder. She and Darleeen hadn't had an outright argument yet, but it was coming. Every time Darleeen and Ultraviolet ran into each other, Ultra went to great lengths to make it clear to everyone within earshot just how foolish she thought it was that the School allowed "those things" free run of the place.

I knew that she was wrong about Darleeen, but what really bothered me about it was that I had the distinct impression that Ultraviolet knew she was wrong, too. It was like she was pretending to believe Darleeen was a threat because it gave her a plausible reason to be a complete jerk without looking too bad to others. It also bothered me that nobody ever really called her out on it.

In answer to the knife question, Darleeen pulled a butter knife from where it had been wrapped in a paper napkin and held it up.

"Yep," was all she said.

"Nice. Did you have to take a class on not eating with your hands?" Ultraviolet said.

I couldn't help myself. "Speaking of etiquette, are you supposed to use silverware when you eat deer turds, or is it more like a fried chicken situation?"

Ultraviolet made a face at me like she'd just, well, eaten a deer turd. "You shut up with that, trashy trollop. I don't know what you did to make me say that, but you're going to regret it sooner or later."

I was going to say something else even cleverer, but Darleeen caught my eye and gave me the faintest indication that I should relax for the time being. Instead, I just said, "Okay."

Ultraviolet didn't respond; she just took the seat across from Dirac and nibbled at her banana split. Eventually, just when I thought she was done being a pain, she spoke quietly to Dirac, but not so quietly that we couldn't hear what she was saying. "The thing I don't get is how they invest all this money in defense, and then they let dangerous charity cases in on the honor system. It could be secretly cooperating with the Old Ones and preparing to overthrow the School from the inside, you know?"

Darleeen spoke before I got the chance. "So let me get this straight. On the one hand, I'm a sophisticated infiltrator who can't be trusted because I'm so crafty. But on the other hand, you doubt I can use a butter knife without help? Which is it, doll?"

"I was only joking," Ultraviolet said haughtily. "Besides, I was talking to *Dirac*."

Darleeen went on, her voice level. "Right. And I'm talking to *you* now. If you have to pretend what you said was a joke, then maybe you shouldn't be saying it."

Ultraviolet sighed as dramatically as possible and spoke directly to Dirac again. "It's just that you never know when someone is working with *them*. You know?"

I couldn't help but notice Dirac wasn't looking anywhere near as outraged at what Ultraviolet had said as I was. Then he nodded. *Dirac was agreeing with her.*

"That's an excellent point," Darleeen said, her southern drawl becoming more noticeable. "Speaking of which, I'm really sorry about your uncle. It's a real shame what happened to him. Did they ever say how a skiing accident can cause someone's brain to melt?"

Both Ultraviolet's and my mouths fell open. I'd mentioned Paul Merchar to Darleeen, but I hadn't had any idea he was related to Ultraviolet.

"It was just an accident, and *wow*, you're as classy as the other Old Ones, bringing up the accidental death of a stranger to one of his family members—"

"Oh, he wasn't a stranger. I knew him, too," Darleeen said casually. "At least my sisters did. The time before I got away from the Old Ones is pretty cloudy, but when Nikola mentioned his name the other day, it was like a light went on in my memory. I just *knew* I'd seen him around somewhere. So I got to looking him up and saw that he was also on the board of the Merchar/VanHorne family trust and that he's *your* uncle. It almost seems like your dear, departed relative was an employee of my former family. Before he skied so badly his brain melted, of course."

Ultraviolet stood up from the table and handed her unfinished banana split to a trash receptacle. "I don't know what you're insinuating, but I have better things to do."

Darleeen grinned. "I'm not insinuating anything, just remarking on what a small world it is. You never know when you're going to run into someone who knows all kinds of interesting things about a family member, or even *several family members*. You know what I mean?"

If Ultraviolet did know what she meant, she didn't stick around to discuss it.

"Several family members?" I asked once Ultraviolet was gone.

Darleeen smirked. "I might have been bluffing a bit there."

I'd been planning to leave, but the Event Horizon regained a lot of its charm once Ultraviolet had vacated the premises, so we sat there and chatted for the remainder of the morning. At some point, Dirac got up, packed up his art, and left without saying anything else. Just after that, Warner returned from the arcade, looking a bit dazed, but fully confident he would shatter my record once his string of bad luck had passed.

"I'm just three points behind you!" he said.

About an hour later, Hypatia turned up with friendship bracelets for everyone, even the waiter-bot. I got two.

"The second one is from Fluorine," Hypatia said. "She

asked me to give it to you because she's worried you're mad at her."

I'd kept my word about not telling anyone that Fluorine had assisted an Old One in sneaking onto campus and trying to kidnap me, but once she found out her grandmother knew, she had stopped keeping it a secret, and her treachery had been the talk of the town . . . for about twenty-four hours.

The braided twine bracelet was strung with a number of beads. Some looked like little pink and purple gems, but others were letters that spelled out the message SORRY I ALMOST GOT YOU KILLED with three hearts at the end.

"Awww, that's the sweetest thing I've ever seen!" I said. "They let her out of detention?"

Hypatia nodded. "Yep, just today. She looks great! You know she stopped time-shifting the moment she started telling people what she'd done? I think that secret was the one thing keeping her unstuck in time. It's weird seeing her stay six years old for a whole hour. Rubidia doesn't know what to do with all her free time. She's spent so much of the last few months dealing with diapers and midlife crises that she almost forgot how to be a kid."

Dad's room in the medical building was the closest thing they had to a presidential suite. Somewhat less white and sterile than the other rooms I'd seen, it had a hardwood floor and tasteful, handmade furnishings. Huge floor-to-ceiling windows lined one wall and gave him a commanding view of the western half of the School Town and the country immediately outside its borders. I dropped myself into a comfortable leather armchair by his bedside.

"Bermuda!" Dad said excitedly, his trauma helmet blinking occasionally as he spoke.

"Bermuda?" I said. "The shorts?"

"No, that's the location of our new home. I've just closed on a property there," he said, looking very proud of himself.

I'd expected something a bit less . . . foreign. "We're moving to *Bermuda*? Really?"

"We are! It's secure and suitably remote, and I've already located a facility I can convert into a complete working space within a few months. It's going to be magnificent."

"Another discount store?" I asked, wondering if they even had big-box stores in Bermuda.

"No, of course not. As I said *before*, I've moved past practical experimentation for the most part. The majority of my work can now be done via thought experiments and simulation. I just need room for the computers, a stable Internet connection, and enough power to run everything at once without having to use my own reactor. Plus I like the property. It's an old airfield, and it's only been vacant about fifteen years, so a couple of the hangars haven't even collapsed yet."

"That sounds great!" I said. "I forget, do they speak English there?"

I noticed most of his color had returned. It hadn't been obvious in the gloom of Subterra, but he had gone a sickly shade of yellowish white during his stay. "In Illinois? I believe they still speak English, unless things have changed quite a lot while I was in that damned cave."

"Oh, you mean Bermuda, Illinois! That makes more sense. Where is it?"

"Do you know where Chicago is?"

"Yeah."

"Well, Bermuda is nowhere near *that*. Speaking of which, I was able to speak on the phone to our friend Gus last night."

We hadn't been speaking of anything of the sort, but I didn't bother pointing it out. "How did you manage that? Dr. Foster said they couldn't tell us where they took him. How is he?"

"He's well. The location of the clinic where they're keeping him may be a secret, but I know a few of his doctors personally. They're trying out all kinds of experimental treatments on him. From the sound of it, they're having a *blast*, let me tell you. It's not every day they get to work with someone who has endured that kind of exposure. They're not sure what did it, but something they tried made a significant difference. He can actually speak in full sentences that are directly related to what he wants to say. Poor fellow has to do it in iambic pentameter, but Rome wasn't burned in a day."

Actually it was, but there was no point in mentioning it. Something had been bothering me, and Dad seemed to be in a good enough mood to bring it up. "Now that you're back and we're getting a new house and all . . . do I have to come with you, or can I stay here?"

Dad wobbled his head a bit, the trauma helmet slipping

around on his head as he did so. "Of course you can stay! That's one less problem for me to worry about!"

"Gee, thanks," I said, unsure whether to be relieved or offended.

"Oh, it's nothing personal. I just won't have a proper security apparatus in operation for some time after I take possession of the Bermuda Municipal International Airport. It's better you stay here so you aren't looking over your shoulder every five minutes."

I had a feeling I'd be doing that no matter where I was. "Say, I meant to ask something else. What's the password for the Chaperone's override? That could come in handy."

He laughed and winked, which I'm about 60 percent sure was due to the calming effect of the helmet. "I'm sure it *would* come in handy, which is why I'm not telling. It's just a random string of characters. A code I changed that very evening, since I noticed you and that boy committing what you heard to memory. Speaking of the Chaperone . . . you wouldn't happen to know anything about someone using an audio command stack overflow exploit on her, would you?"

I knew exactly what he was talking about—Fluorine's hack that allowed her to wander the town after curfew. "I have no idea what you're talking about."

"Hm," he said with more than a little skepticism. "Well, *someone* has been using an audio file with several thousand simple voice commands played simultaneously at high speed to overload the Chaperone's speech recognition system and disable her for short periods of time. I've patched that.

Anyone who tries it now will get a nasty surprise, so you might want to share that information with anyone you think might be tempted."

I nodded, making a mental note to warn Fluorine that her little chirping gadget should be shelved ASAP and a second mental note that he didn't mention anything about people using piezoelectric EMP candies to do the same job.

My new friendship bracelet shifted on my wrist, catching my eye. I realized that the Fluorine issue was bothering me almost as much as Dirac's attitude problem. I'd told Dr. Plaskington I knew Fluorine wasn't a bad person, but . . . "Why would she have helped them like that?" I wondered aloud.

Dad reached out and patted me once on my head. "That Tabbabitha beast bragged about turning her, you know. I remember that. It was right after they failed to bring you in. She said they didn't even need to brainwash her; they just *convinced* her that her parents were still alive and that she'd send them home if she did them a favor someday."

I sighed. "They aren't still alive, then?"

"No idea. I never saw them when I was down there, so that's not a great sign."

"How did the Old Ones even get in touch with Fluorine?" I asked.

Dad smirked. "It was rather clever, really. They employed an unwitting government agent to convey hard copies of her messages directly, circumventing all the School's monitoring capabilities."

"A government agent? You mean—"

"The United States Post Office. The whole operation cost the Old Ones maybe five dollars' worth of stamps. One lie and a few months later, they had a conspirator willing to endanger the lives of everyone here if they called upon her. That was maybe two years ago. Then they just let her simmer until they needed her for something."

I sighed, feeling completely despondent. "You think you know someone . . ."

Dad patted my head once a second time. I couldn't help but notice there was a slim book on his bedside table titled *Displaying Empathy: Responding Appropriately to Emotional Situations*. "Everyone makes mistakes, Nikola. What separates good people from bad people is whether or not they learn from their mistakes. She's *six years old*. It's easy to forget that because she's brilliant and apparently you've known her at several other ages, but intelligence and wisdom are very different things."

"You can say that again," I said.

Dad cocked his head, confused. "I doubt that's necessary."

I leaned back in the chair, looking up at the ceiling. A faint glimmer caught my eye, and when I looked at my friendship bracelet again, the words spelled out by the beads had changed. It now read, I KNOW I WAS WRONG. It made me feel a little better for some reason.

Something else was bothering me, but I couldn't put a finger on it. I stood and turned to the window looking out over the town, then returned to the comfy chair and collapsed into it again.

"He told me his name," I said, before knowing I was going to say it.

Dad sat bolt upright, the motion jerking the trauma helmet from his head. He grabbed my shoulders and drew me close. "Stop right there! Don't speak of it again! Do you hear me?"

He was shaking me as he spoke. The frantic, panicked look in his eyes was one of the most frightening things I've ever seen. "What? I haven't told any—"

He shook me again. "Stop! Stop it! Listen! Do you remember how you called your friend . . . I forget her name—the other Old One? You brought her to us in the hotel? You only had to hold her name in your mind, and she appeared. Knowing their names creates a link, and thinking about it activates that link. I do not think he could get to you here, but it is crucial that you do whatever you can to avoid giving him the opportunity. Do you understand?"

I nodded. "I understand, I promise." I picked up his trauma helmet and slipped it back onto his head.

He felt it go on, and his expression became sorrowful. Then the helmet blinked a few times, and he lay back on the bed, visibly relaxed.

"So is the world going to end now that he's awake?" I asked.

Dad picked up a covered plastic cup from his bedside table and took a long drink. "Not yet. I'm certain you injured him—rather badly, in fact. A magnetic field that strong would have rendered him unable to defend himself for a short period of time, and from what you told me, during that time he was probably struck by several million tons of debris. It may even have killed him or put him back into hibernation, but it's probably smartest for us to assume the worst."

"Which is?"

"That he is alive and awake, but injured. It should take some time for him to restore himself to . . . whatever it was you saw down there. That said, even without most of his strength, he's still a serious threat."

"What do you mean?"

"Strategically, I think he's aware he can't defeat all of us, humans and parahumans together, not if we stand together. He's powerful, but as a group we are orders of magnitude more powerful. Because of that, taking on a few of us at a time is his best option. He'll exploit divisions in human and parahuman cultures. I expect he'll find ways of turning us against one another so we're unable to unite against him. His goal will be to convince people that their friends and neighbors are the real enemy. People who are fighting one another aren't preparing to face him. Ultimately, he will try to make us believe that standing against the Old Ones is hopeless."

"What about all the parahumans who are actually *helping* the Old Ones?"

"They've already fallen for it. It's *possible* they'll realize the error of their ways, but I wouldn't bet your lunch money on it."

"So it's not hopeless? Really?" I asked.

"In the end, I believe humans and parahumans will stand united. I'm certain we can win."

Sometimes I liked that my dad lacked the ability to sugar-coat things, because when he said something good, you always knew he meant it.

"You're certain, huh? You really think that's true?"

"I believe it is *essential* that we *act* as if it is true."

"That's not really an answer."

He smiled in a sad kind of way and gazed out the window. Outside the faintly glimmering protective sphere of the School Town, an early spring thunderstorm swirled on the horizon. "And yet it is."

ACKNOWLEDGMENTS

------*------

I go around telling people I make these books on my own, but that's not actually true. I couldn't do this without assistance and support from a variety of people, all of whom probably work a lot harder than I do.

Although it's completely inadequate, I'd like to take some space here to thank them.

Thanks to my intelligent, ferocious, and formidable wife, Stephanie, whom I look to for counsel, inspiration, and moral support. Thanks to my daughters, Marilee and Zoë, for being readers, critics, and fans before they had good reason to, and for inspiring elements of *many* characters in the book you just finished.

Thanks to my editor, Stephanie Pitts, who has been dependably, remarkably amazing in all things (especially in those categories requiring patience and understanding). Seriously, if you've ever been a fan of a particular author, you're also a fan of whoever their editor is—they don't get enough credit.

Thanks to my agent, Josh Getzler, for being endlessly supportive, knowledgable about all kinds of things I'm ignorant of, and for being a great follow on Twitter (@jgetzler).

Thanks to my test readers—Marilee Marshall-Sappingfield, Emerson and Isabelle Caby, Bailey Ogden, and Surreal Taylor.

Thanks to my in-family (read: unpaid) PR team, Amy Beam and Suzanne Marshall-Caby.

Thanks to all the schools who let me waste part of a day talking about books, stories, and fun geeky things.

Thanks to John Hendrix for cover art that captures the books more accurately than I could have hoped. Thanks also to everyone at HSG and Penguin/Putnam for going above and beyond to make this book immeasurably better than it would have been if they'd all called in sick and left it up to me.

And most importantly I'd like to thank you, the readers. Thanks for joining Nikola on her adventures and for being what makes this all worthwhile. You're awesomazing.

ABOUT THE AUTHOR

------*------

Eliot Sappingfield was last seen wearing a blue shirt and khaki pants in the vicinity of his home in Missouri. He is known to appreciate stories, science, and various other geeky things. He may or may not be accompanied by his wife, his two daughters (when they don't have anything better to do), or a pair of goofy basset hounds. He is considered unarmed and not terribly dangerous. *The Unspeakable Unknown* is the sequel to his hilarious debut novel, *A Problematic Paradox*.

You can visit Eliot at eliotsappingfield.com.